Believe in Me

Believe in Me

JESSICA INCLÁN

ZEBRA BOOKS
KENSINGTON PUBLISHING CORP.
http://www.kensingtonbooks.com

ZEBRA BOOKS are published by

Kensington Publishing Corp.
850 Third Avenue
New York, NY 10022

ISBN-13: 978-0-8217-8084-8
ISBN-10: 0-8217-8084-0

First Zebra Trade Paperback Printing: March 2007
10 9 8 7 6 5 4 3 2 1

Printed in the United States of America

Believe in Me

Chapter One

Sayblee Safipour appeared out of swirling gray matter and blinked into the warm, dark glow of a living room that smelled like coconut, pineapple, and a soft ocean breeze. She breathed in something spicy and sweet, the scent of desire floating in the air. As her eyes adjusted to the light that pulsed with yellow heat, she pushed away her hood and flicked her long blonde hair behind her shoulders. A slight, warm breeze moved in through the open windows, the sounds of night bugs and frogs a buzzing song coming from the wet foliage outside. She unbuttoned her robe and took it off, letting it drop into a pool of blue-velvet softness on the couch, and smoothed out her blouse and skirt, until she realized that neither was at all wrinkled from her journey to Hilo from London; matter was an unbroken flow of energy tonight.

Traveling through matter wasn't usually hard, though sometimes waves of energy made things a bit bumpy, space bunching up in rough, uneven pockets, sometimes due to someone's bad magic or simply mischief, the gray like a roller coaster rather than a brisk walk on a flat escalator. What would have made this journey difficult, though, was her reluctance to arrive in Hawaii at all.

Sayblee rubbed her forehead. She didn't even need to look around the room to know what she would find. But she couldn't resist. She took her hand away from her head and surveyed the scene. Yes, it was predictable. Pathetic, even. Basically male. Basically *him*. *Look at this place!* she thought to herself, gazing first at the creamy beige couch with the pink lace bra dangling on one arm. She scanned the thick white carpet, sure she'd find a tiny matching thong somewhere, but there were no other undergarments to be found. Probably, Sayblee thought, the woman didn't even wear any, knowing what Felix was like and not wanting to impede his progress. And, clearly, Felix had made progress. On the bleached wood coffee table were two crystal glasses, a quarter inch of pale yellow liquid still in each.

His damn concoction, she thought. *Couldn't even wait to finish his drink before pushing the poor woman into the bedroom.*

Soft music that he undoubtedly thought would soothe the jumbled nerves of his date filled the room, a tremble of light guitar riffs, flute solos, and some kind of indigenous instruments. A didgeridoo? A rain stick? Sayblee thought, shutting off the annoying sounds with a flick of her mind. The stereo lights blinked and the room fell silent.

An unbuttoned white linen shirt lay on the floor by the hallway. As she stared at it, she heard a soft giggle float under the bedroom door and then a smooth, seductive laugh followed it, the sound of which somehow reminded her of caramel.

Pig, she thought. *No, that's too harsh. Dog. Goat, maybe. No, a goat is too cute. Skunk then. Or just pig.*

Sayblee walked to the bookcase, picked up photo frames full of happy people she knew well, his brothers and sisters-in-law, his mother Zosime. She stared into their eyes, and soon she felt the impressions of their warm feelings for him as she held the images in her hands. Funny guy, she heard or, really, pulled into her mind, as she moved her fingers over the photos. *Why doesn't he settle down? So handsome. All he needs is a good woman. If he wasn't so adorable, I'd kill him. Can he ever be serious? What a charmer. Those eyes would do anyone in. That smile!*

Sayblee's shoulders dropped. She breathed in and took her hands away from his photos.

When she'd accepted this mission, she'd agreed to work with him, and work with Felix Valasay she would, even if it killed her. But it was hard to deal with someone who could live like this, who probably did a seduction scene like this every night of the week in this so-called post. Who could he possibly find here, that would lead any member of *Les Croy-ant des Trois* to Quain Dalzeil, the *sorcier* who was deter-mined to destroy the *Croyant* way of life? The *sorcier* who had managed in recent years to affect all of Croyant life—creating fear, enchanting the best and brightest, leaving peo-ple to live in fear. Sure, Felix managed to come to the aid of people needing him now and again. He'd been there with her just a year ago when a group of *Croyant* had fought Quain and Kallisto in the English countryside. But the Big Island? This house that smelled like tacky perfume and was filled with enough sexual energy to make the very floor vi-brate?

Sayblee shook her head and turned toward the hallway. Why did Adalbert Baird, the Armiger of the *Croyant* Council, insist that Sayblee was the only sorcière who could go on this mission? So what that she had her particular skill of being able to burn anything she wanted: steel, concrete, quartz, ti-tanium? But from what Adalbert had said, there would be no magic for a while as they blended in with the *Moyenne,* setting up the trap so slowly and ordinarily that they would attract no attention from Quain or his followers. Her spe-cial powers weren't needed at all, or at least until the very end of the mission. So why did she have to end up with this particular *sorcier?*

Another annoying giggle and then a lazy laugh slipped

into the living room. The very air seemed to pulse with gardenia and hyacinth and rum. This was horrible! Intolerable. How was she supposed to interrupt that? She sat down on a beautifully carved wooden chair and sighed, staring at the rows and rows of hardback books, most of them probably uncracked since Felix graduated from the Bampton Academy. What to do? She'd never known how to engage Felix, to move smoothly into conversation with him. Since their days together at Bampton, she'd steered clear of him, even though Sayblee was very fond of his older brothers, Sariel and Rufus, boys who had turned into solid, reliable men. Married men. Committed men. Men!

But there was something about Felix that was just plain dangerous, and Sayblee had recognized that when she was twelve. She'd turned a corner one afternoon after a long class on levitation, and there stood Felix, smiling at her with that smooth, slightly crooked smile, his almost-green eyes full of a fire so unique that Sayblee didn't have a clue how to kindle it. Even then, his black hair was long, held back for classes with a leather string, strands always coming loose and falling in front of his face. Hair she'd wanted to touch, push away, tuck into place.

She'd barely managed to hold on to her textbooks and keep walking, ignoring his taunt of, "Baby, can I light your fire?"

Now, sixteen years later, Felix still had the ability to disarm her. The last time they'd been together had been at Adalbert's house at Rabley Heath, and she'd left one morning early to avoid an awkward good-bye. Her awkwardness. She hadn't wanted to see him smirk, listen to him tease her about her school pranks, rattle on about how she used to set the cafeteria cooks' hats on fire when meatloaf was on the menu. She hadn't wanted to look into his lovely eyes and see, well, so much satisfaction.

And this situation here? Well, it wasn't going to be easy

to pull Felix away from Hilo and his little lifestyle. But Sayblee had no choice. What had Adalbert said to her just before she left? He'd stared at her with his kind eyes, his hand running through his long gray beard as he spoke.

"We have the chance, finally, to end this troublesome situation with Quain once and for all," he said. "I think you'd do just about anything to make that happen, Sayblee. Am I not right?" He'd looked at her from where he sat in his deep upholstered armchair. A fire crackled in the hearth. His dog, a Zeno Hungarian Kuvasz, dozed at his feet, the dog's quick breaths full of rabbit dreams. And Sayblee could see the image of her brother, Rasheed, flicker in Adalbert's mind. The Armiger was right. As always.

More than anything, Sayblee wanted to find Quain. They'd been so close to catching him last year. For a moment, he'd been right in front of her in the cavernous room of the Fortress Kendall as she fought with Felix and the rest, but, as always, he'd gotten away. Oh, how she'd wanted to push her fire at him, subdue him, flatten him to the floor. Sayblee wanted to lean over him and demand he tell her what happened to Rasheed.

She wanted the impossible, to have Quain croak out "Your brother's still alive." She wanted Quain to tell her that Rasheed hadn't left of his own free will, that he'd been enchanted, charmed, drugged, coerced. She wanted to strangle out of him the truth that Rasheed was good, that he'd never turn his back on *Croyant* life or his family. She wanted to have the perfect answer to give to her mother, Roya, so that she would burst into life again and forgive Sayblee for not saving Rasheed in the first place. She needed to obtain all the information she could from Quain, and then . . . and then. . .

Sayblee closed her eyes and sat back hard against the wooden chair, trying to ignore the further giggles that floated toward her. No. She wasn't doing this just for Rasheed and for her mother, who had never recovered from Rasheed's betrayal of all that the Safipour family believed in and his alliance with Quain. Sayblee was on the mission for all *Croyant,* and what she had to do was get Felix Valasay out of his bedroom, preferably dressed, hopefully alone, and she couldn't sit here one moment longer.

She stood up and in her mind she moved down the hallway, into the bedroom, and heard the noise of two people moving together—their bodies warm, their minds full of anticipation—could hear Felix whisper into the woman's ear, "You smell so good. I just can't breathe in enough of you."

Sayblee opened her mind and shot out a thought. *Yeah, she smells like your house. In about a minute, I myself will be smelling like a cheap drink from Chevy's.*

She heard his intake of air, his body moving away slightly from the woman's. *Sayblee?*

Yeah, it's me. I'm in your living room. I managed to figure out you had a special guest when I was in the air. You and I need to talk. It's Council business.

Right now? Couldn't you go hit the bars for a couple of hours and come back later? Maybe take a nice long night walk on the beach?

Sayblee checked her irritation, biting her lip before thinking tersely, *Adalbert sent me.*

She waited for a reply, but there was no thought, no sound but the rustle of bedclothes and then the soft murmur of the woman asking a question. Felix's low voice rumbled an answer. More rustling. Then there was silence. Sayblee sighed and turned her mind away from Felix and what was going on in the bedroom and sat down on the couch. She tried to get comfortable, crossing her legs, uncrossing them, smoothing the sleeves of her blouse, the fabric of her skirt on her thighs. She pushed her hair away from her face and then pulled it forward, finally sighing and tying it back with a band she pulled from her pocket.

She looked toward the bedroom door, leaned forward, sat back. Then she stood up, realizing she didn't want to be lower than Felix when he came into the room, giving him the advantage of looking down at her. She walked to the window, stared out at the ocean which was flat and strangely calm, the moon a pan of white on its surface.

"Could you have knocked?" Felix said, walking into the room shirtless and barely wearing the Levi's he was slowly buttoning up. "I could have arranged a later date with the fair maiden, Roxanne. You know I always say business and *then* pleasure." He paused as he spotted the shirt on the floor, bent down, and picked it up with a crooked finger, smiling to himself.

Sayblee breathed in, kept her mind closed tight because, *God!*— she couldn't let him know how she was seeing him at this very moment in the living room's soft light. Impossibly, he looked even better than he had the year before, his tall, lean body golden tan from all his important *Croyant* visits to the beach and the pool and hot tub. He must also have crucial *Moyenne* contacts at the gym—his shoulders, arms, and abs tight and firm, each muscle clear under the tight gold of his skin. Clearly, he worked out for hours every day. His black hair was lit gold at the ends by days on Hawaiian waves and fell down his back like a silk curtain. He smiled, watching her with his almost-green eyes, his expression full of good humor, even though she'd interrupted him in his pleasure. She swallowed and lifted her chin, her mind clamped so tight that she knew she'd have a throbbing migraine by morning.

"Adalbert wanted me to come right away. I . . . We didn't have a chance to contact you. But, uh, where is your, um, friend?"

Felix finished buttoning his jeans and walked into the kitchen, opening the fridge. "I just took her home, erased this date from her mind, and made sure she'd have a long, lovely night's sleep. And she'll awaken fresh and lively, remembering this great dream about me, the wonderful man she met at the gym the day before. But, dammit, Sayblee, I'll still have to start all over next time."

"Oh, poor, poor baby," Sayblee said. "I'm sure it will be torturous work. All that sweet talk and those longing glances. But your date with her will have to wait."

Felix shrugged and took out a can of pineapple juice from the fridge, setting it on the counter. He opened a cupboard and took down a can of cream of coconut and a bottle of Cruzan Rum.

"What are you doing? You can't be making a drink!" Sayblee said, putting her hands on her hips. "I have some pretty important—I have some Council work . . . There's stuff I have to talk to you about."

"Now, now," Felix said, holding out his hands for a second in a mock defensive pose. "Don't set fire to my blender. I know how you suddenly lose it, lighting fire to whatnot unexpectedly."

He put down his hands, opened the lid of the coconut cream with a can opener, and spooned a bit into the blender. Despite herself, Sayblee found herself staring at his hands, strong and tan, the fingers long and slim.

"Scorched coladas are not my specialty," he said.

"What?" she asked, looking up.

"Fire. Losing it." Felix glanced at her as he worked, smiling again. "You're already scaring me."

"Knock it off. I am not going to lose it," she said. But maybe she was. She could feel it in her palms, the slight itch in the middle of her hand that always warned her to breathe, to close her eyes, to count to ten. Sometimes, though, she didn't pay attention. "Can't you just, well, whip it together without the blender?"

"Some things without magic are just better," he said,

splashing rum, pineapple juice, and ice into the blender and putting on the lid.

"I take it that doesn't include dating. You must need your magic—" Sayblee began, but then Felix flipped on the blender, and she stopped talking. *What an ass!* she thought, her palms burning.

I heard that, he thought. *Anger opens your mind like massage oil.*

Sayblee clasped her hands tight and sat down on the couch, her face flaming, and watched him finish making the drinks. He turned off the blender and took down two glasses from the cupboard and filled them to the top.

"Let's go and sit in the lanai. If business is going to ruin my pleasure, the least we can do is be comfortable."

Sayblee stood stiffly and followed him outside. Felix didn't turn on the outside lights, but the moon spun bright silver through the palm fronds, ferns, and vines. A gecko scuttled up the mesh that enclosed the lanai, and toward the shore, a seabird called out, swooping in front of the moon's face. She could hear the lap of the waves, the rhythmic motion of the water against the shore, the lull for a second relaxing her.

Even at night, this was paradise, Sayblee thought, and she could see why Felix stayed here. This was the perfect place for him, with his tanned, beautiful body—she shook her head and closed her eyes, checking again the clamp on her thoughts.

Felix sat down at a wooden table, and Sayblee took a seat as well, feeling how boring and plain she seemed with her white blouse and blue skirt. Besides the lovely pink bra, what had the wild Roxanne been wearing before she hadn't been wearing anything at all? Something wild and flowery and full of flounces and lace? Sayblee could see the kind of woman Felix would like to be with, tan and thin and wrapped

in sterling silver, her long dark hair hanging in loose ring-
lets, her dark eyes full of excitement. Did she wear red lip-
stick? Black eyeliner? Blue eye shadow?

In the years before Rasheed had left them, in the time before Roya blamed Sayblee for all the emptiness surrounding
them, Roya pleaded with Sayblee to try some girly things,
holding out bangles and hair combs and earrings. She
swooped up armloads of makeup from Harvey Nichols and
Harrods, imploring Sayblee to try just a bit of blusher. She
bought dresses from Madame Berton Granie's shop *Voilà*,
on the *rue Moufftard* in Paris, walking into Sayblee's room
with bundles of linen and silk and satin.

She would put the dresses and skirts on the bed and sit
down, crossing her legs and telling her a story, the one that
Sayblee had heard since she could remember.

"You have always been your father's child," Roya would
say. "You are thoughtful, and yet, you can, as we know, explode. Just Like Hanif. There is passion inside you, and I
wish your father was with us now, to see how you have
learned to hold in your fire until it is needed. To see how
smart you are. If only he had lived, he would be so happy to
see what a beautiful woman you are becoming. But, my
lovely Sayblee, you must use what you have on the outside
as you have learned to use your passion. Look at you. Look
at your skin! So pink! So beautiful," Roya had said, standing up and walking behind Sayblee. Together they looked
into the dresser mirror. "And your hair!"

Roya would stroke Sayblee's hair, running her palm
down the long, smooth sheen. "Hair from your father's side
of the family. From his mother, who was an amazing *sorcière,* who fought with Adalbert Baird himself at the battle
at Jacob's Well. She had the fire like you do, my sweet, wild
plum. No one has had hair like that in my family for years.
Decades. Maybe a hundred years or more. Gold! And your
eyes! So blue! You must try on the blue dress. A complete

match. Or what about the yellow? Or the pink? At least a scarf. *Lotifãn, Anuj!*"

Please, Wild Plum, Sayblee thought. How long had it been since her mother had called her anything, especially called her anything in the family language, Farsi? How long had it been since she'd bought anything for Sayblee, traveling through matter from London to Paris just to pick out dresses for her daughter? After Rasheed had left them, her mother had collapsed into herself, becoming pale and small, not wanting to engage in life, her hair turning as white as her thoughts. No longer did Roya use the *charme de beauté* to keep her chestnut hair deep and rich in hue or her skin soft and supple and unlined. She hadn't been herself or even half of herself. Not since Rasheed had swirled away from them in an instant of upset, too quick for Sayblee to catch him, to stop him with her fire.

Sayblee sat still, no longer looking at Felix, the drinks, the gecko, the silver light that moved on the stone pavers like a soft hand. No longer—for a moment—caring about the mission or Quain.

"Sayblee," Felix said quietly, and then she felt his mind pull away from hers. "Have a drink. They are my specialty. And we'll talk about the mission. You know I'd never turn Adalbert down. Not after what he's done for Rufus. For Sariel. For my entire family."

She breathed in, blinked away her upset, and put her hand around the cold drink. Felix must have used some magic because before she'd even taken one sip, she felt better, lighter, her memories of her mother and Rasheed disappearing like smoke, her chest feeling full of air instead of regret.

"Thank you. A very clear *charme d' équilibre,*" Sayblee said, sipping a smooth, cold piña colada, the pineapple piquant on her tongue.

"You always were a good student," Felix said. "Every

time I saw you, you had your nose in a book. Reading history and whatever. Reading everything. We all used to think you actually slept in the library so you'd always have something to read before bed."

"I was just trying to get good grades."

Felix put down his drink. "I don't think you had to try. Plain smart. I was always desperate to get your notes. I knew just one page alone would do the trick. As good as magic."

"As good as cheating," Sayblee said, smiling, wishing that a ridiculous sense of happiness wasn't washing through her as he spoke. And it wasn't his damn *charme*. How was she supposed to work with him for weeks if her body kept jumping ahead of her brain? How could she concentrate on the mission if her skin rose in gooseflesh each time he moved, each time he exposed a wonderful slice of chest, each time a strand of hair fell in front of his face? She took another sip of pina colada, making sure from this point on to keep her thoughts away from his, her body under control.

"So what is it? I haven't heard anything from Sariel or Rufus, not that I hear anything from those two and their respective Brady Bunches except for reports on babies and pregnancy stages. I've been keeping radio silence for months."

Sayblee nodded. "Miranda is huge. Her healer—"

"Her healer? Isn't Sariel taking care of her?"

"No, she fired him when she was in her third month. He kept trying to keep her from traveling through matter, even though her pregnancy has been fine the whole time. He's a little . . ." Sayblee shrugged, knowing that Sariel was just a little wonderful, totally in love with Miranda, and worried about his first child. Not even Rufus and Fabia, who were expecting their first child as well, could convince him to relax. Miranda complained that he was constantly checking in with the baby, using magic to communicate with the little creature from the moment it was possible.

"The baby is already going to need therapy by the time

it's born," Miranda had said. "Talk about father issues! Freud would have a field day."

Finally Miranda put her foot down, using her newly found magic to trap Sariel in the house one day so she could go visit Sayblee in London. When she returned, Sariel agreed to lighten up and relax, but Miranda confided, "I know he's got his hands on my stomach when I'm asleep. What do you think he's telling this baby? Maybe he's feeding it algebraic algorithms. He's probably already gotten the poor thing through grammar school. I tell you, I don't know how any *Croyant* manages to grow up sane."

Felix sipped his drink. "He's a little nuts. So is Rufus. I tell you, I just hope all this reproduction isn't contagious."

Sayblee opened her mouth to say something, but Felix kept talking. "So you must have something hot off the press. What are we going to do? What was so important that you couldn't wait until my date was over?"

Picking up her drink, Sayblee sipped and then thought of a comeback that Rasheed would have been proud of, something like, "I don't think it would have lasted that long." But she didn't say a word, didn't open her mind to let the thought free, laughing instead a tiny bit into her glass. Enough was enough. She had to be serious. They had to be serious, because what they were going to be doing was truly serious. Adalbert had put an intense spell around Felix's house before Sayblee had left that would allow no thought to enter or leave. What she was going to tell him next was that crucial to them all.

"We're going to Paris," she said, putting down her glass and sitting up straight.

"Oh, is there a big meeting? Usually they don't invite me to those."

"No. In fact, we won't be going to any meetings there at all."

Felix sat back, crossing a leg, his ankle resting on his

knee. She tried not to notice his perfect quadricep, the solid roundness of his knee, the length of long shin under his Levi's. She blinked and turned away, but not before noticing that even his feet looked good, tan, hairless, the toes perfectly shaped.

"So why go? Who's there?" he asked.

"Quain."

"Quain is in Paris? Why would he hide there? Where there are so many *Croyant?*"

"Why would he have hidden in London last year? There are many of us there as well. The fact is that bad magic is easy to hide in a big city, a city full of *Croyant.*"

Felix unfolded his legs, stretched out, and Sayblee watched his thighs flex under the denim. She shook her head slightly, knowing that she needed to get them both out of this house as soon as possible.

"Good point," he said. "Fine. I hate cities, but we're going to Paris. At least the food is good. So, is Adalbert ready to go after him again? Who is he assembling? I'm sure Sariel and Rufus—no, Sariel is probably sacrificing his all for the good of his unborn king- or queen-child, the most perfect baby to ever be in *utero*. So who? Who else?"

"I don't know yet. We won't know until everyone is all assembled. For a couple of days, it's just you and me."

"What are you talking about?"

"I just don't know, Felix," she said, feeling a bubble of exasperation pop in her chest. "I know the plan, but I don't know who exactly will be involved. For all I know, we could be the only two *Croyant* ready to go right now."

Felix shook his head and sat up, leaning his elbows on the table. His eyes were dark now, the moon a tiny square of light in each. And as she stared at him, she realized the moon shone also in each strand of his long, loose hair. *Help,* she thought to no one. *Help me, please.*

"You have got to be kidding me, Sayblee. You and I are going to go fight Quain by ourselves? This must be a joke. Did Rufus set you up to it? He is always trying to kick my ass in some way or another."

Sayblee played with the water drops the glass had left on the table and managed to take a breath. "Rufus has nothing to do with this right now. And I'm serious, Felix. Quain's slowly been building up his followers again. He'd lost most of them during his last siege, but he's changed course. He's become quite a salesperson. He's going after people who don't really have too much power or position. No one like Kallisto this time. No one like Cadcyrn Macara. Sort of your average *Croyant,* the *sorciers* and *sorcières* not involved in Council work, the types who live quietly, practice little magic, live mostly in the *Moyenne* world. He's working toward building up a critical mass."

Felix looked at her, his gaze steady and focused now, all the humor in the way the evening had begun gone from his expression. "So what do we have to do? Is there a new spell? A new way of deploying it?"

Sayblee shook her head and leaned forward, her elbows on the table. "No. In fact, there's not going to be any magic at all."

Felix blinked. "What?"

"That's right. No magic. At least for a while. Adalbert and the Council decided that we were going to start a critical mass of our own. They've found the general spot where Quain is and where he's been moving his new group. It's around the 7th Arrondissement in the Rive Gauche, which is a pretty strange place to start a revolution. Sort of fashionable, upscale. A little conservative."

"I get it. It's smart. Hiding in plain sight. Moving in these average sort of folks. People who've been used to using magic, who can probably afford to live there, who look like they belong. They won't be noticed. If he'd moved them to somewhere around Pigalle and all the junkies and the prost—well, you know what I mean."

"Not really," Sayblee said. "But, well, that's where we are going."

"Pigalle?" Felix asked, smiling and pretending to stand up. "Great. I'll go pack my drug paraphernalia and neoprene suit. Please don't let me forget my crack pipe."

"No, not Pigalle. Don't be a jerk. We're going to the 7th in a little apartment on the Champs de Mars. And the Council is moving in other couples—"

"Couples?" Felix said. "What do you mean, *couples?*"

Sayblee's mind shut tight, her face again aflame in the darkness, and she forced herself to keep speaking. "The plan is to move in people to the neighborhood. Couples. Make us seem like we are just regular people who live and work in the area. Nothing special. And the Council is planting us all around the 7th in a way that no one will notice us. Why would Quain spend too much time wondering about *Moyenne* couples? We won't be using our magic; we'll keep our minds completely shut, our magic hidden. The Council will also keep protective spells cast on the area. But then, when the time is right, we will be there, in the exact place where we can take on Quain."

Felix finished off his drink and put down the glass on the table. "And then what? We were all around him last time and he still escaped. I was really quite the performer in that scenario, dead to the world." He shook his head. "How will this time be any different?"

"There is a new spell."

"What is it?"

Sayblee shrugged. "Adalbert wouldn't tell me. He told me that they would let us know when we needed to know. They don't want us to have information that might be used against us in case—"

"In case this plan fails, too."

For a moment, neither of them spoke. The gecko moved along the ceiling, its legs and body in a constant bending, twisting rhythm. The moon fell behind the house, the lanai all in darkness now. Sayblee felt time grow long, could hear Felix breathe, could feel him trying to work into her thoughts. She was relieved that once they moved into their apartment on the Champs de Mars they would have no magic, no ability to look into each other's thoughts. At least that way, she wouldn't have to work so hard to keep her feelings about him hidden.

"So, no magic. None? Not even to get anywhere?" Felix asked finally. "You mean I will have to take the Métro?"

"That's right. No magic. None. We will be just like the *Moyenne*. Cooking, cleaning, taking the Métro and the buses, driving a car."

"A car?" Felix asked.

"Maybe. But for sure you'll be washing dishes. And clothes. You'll have to go shopping."

"Sounds like prison," Felix said.

"Oh, but wait just a second," Sayblee said. "Didn't you just tell me in the kitchen that some things without magic are just better?"

"Funny," Felix said, pushing away from the table and standing up. "Ha, ha. And I was lying. I'm going to get my things together. I'm going to go use a little magic while I still can."

He stood over her, looking down. "Don't tell me we have to fly there on, what? Air France?"

She nodded. "We have a flight out of Hilo on Aloha Airlines in the morning. We go to Kona and then Oahu and then to San Francisco on Air France and then—"

He held out a palm, shaking his head. "Connecting flights? How many hours is that going to take? How am I going to sit still for that long?"

"And then JFK and then Charles de Gaulle. It was the best reservation I could make. I guess if you want to fly straight through, you have to call a long time in advance. I don't really understand why. Anyway, we arrive like the average person on French soil using our best French accents."

Felix put down his arm and smiled. "Finally. I knew that Madame Lakritz's French lessons would finally pay off."

"It better. She kept you after class enough times," Sayblee said. And when Felix laughed, his head flung back, his hair a fan behind him, she suddenly understood why Madame Lakritz's door was always closed and locked on Thursday afternoons. Once when Sayblee knocked a few times, Madame Lakritz opened the door, her glasses slightly askew, her hair a gold, fuzzy mess. Peeking into the classroom, Sayblee saw Felix sitting on Madame Lakritz's desk, smiling, and when she tried to work her way into either of their minds, she found nothing. But she should have known. She didn't need magic to know, even then, Felix was a . . . a . . . she didn't know which word to pick. Lothario, cad, Casanova, creep. Maybe she should just go back to animal terms. Pig seemed to work just fine. She shook her head.

"God, Felix! Did you ever have a limit?"

"Not that I could see," he said. "Okay. I better go pack all my knives so that I'll have options when I finally decide enough is enough. When the diesel from the buses finally pushes me over the edge, I'll be ready to end it all."

Felix took their empty drink glasses and walked into the house, her eyes on that cute, yes, so cute, rear end. She sighed, watching him walk away, and then turned back, looking up to the ceiling for a moment, searching for the lizard. But the gecko was gone.

She smoothed her skirt again and then crossed her arms, wishing for stillness. Her body was tingling, and it wasn't from the rum in Felix's very tasty concoction. Her palms itched, and it wasn't that she needed to burn something to a crisp. She closed her eyes and took a deep breath. This was a mission, she knew that. And she shouldn't be so excited about it. She should be nervous. Even afraid. It would be dangerous and hard, and without magic, anything could happen. But her body still tingled, and she breathed coconut and pineapple, heard Felix moving about in the house, and smiled.

Chapter Two

His ass felt like—felt like—well, Felix didn't know what his ass felt like because he couldn't feel his ass. He shifted uncomfortably in 28B, his economy seat on the Air France 767, and tried to look out the window. Along with the innumerable plane changes and airport delays, Sayblee's flight plans had landed him in a seat where he was not only next to a very long-legged, tall, sleeping teenager from Belgium but the window looked out over a huge expanse of steel wing. He turned the other way again, bumping into Sayblee's small shoulder.

"Will you stop fidgeting?" she said, speaking quietly, in perfect French, her accent just north of Paris. She put down her gigantic book, some enormous tome about Thomas Jefferson. "It's not going to make time go any faster."

"Look, I could make time go faster," he said, replying in an accent from the exact center of Paris, like French Madame Lakritz had taught him in their many sweaty after-school tutoring sessions. "Just let me do a little magic. One second. I'll have us in the limo taking us to our apartment."

Felix hadn't been without his magic for this long ever, and it reminded him of the time he found his birthday presents, under his mother's bed three days before the celebration. He ached to have the comic books, knew that he could materialize them in a second, and then sneak them back under her bed without her noticing. But it would hurt Zosime's feelings if she found out he'd ruined the surprise. So, instead, he'd twitched his way through the three days until he could open the presents and finally have the comics to himself.

But this twitching? It might last for months. Everything he wanted—a long shower, a king-sized bed, a pina colada, another date with the tasty Roxanne from the gym—was just outside his grasp, and he couldn't have it.

"We're not taking a limo. We're taking the RER from the airport to the Metro. There's a stop just at the corner of *avenue Bosquet* and *Motte Picquet.*"

"Oh, please, Sayblee, just kill me now. Give me my knives this moment. Before they serve the flipping breakfast. I can't handle one more cheese log or another, tiny, stale, French-bread torpedo. And, please, no more damn yogurt." Felix rubbed his face, wondering how it was going to be possible to take four pieces of luggage and two carry-ons onto a train. That seemed more magical than speeding up time.

"Don't you ever do anything the normal way? They told us in school to use magic only when we had to, not for everything. We do have to live in this world. The *Moyenne* world. We can't always be casting spells."

"Sure. I put my clothes in the washer sometimes. And . . . well, yes, sometimes I do things the normal way."

"What else?"

"Things," Felix said, wishing he had a list. He wanted to say shopping, but even then he realized that if he did shop in the conventional sense, he did it on-line. And wasn't that magic in and of itself? Didn't that technology come from *Croyant* minds, after all? "Lots of stuff, okay? It's just that I don't travel like this. Why would I? And I certainly don't keep myself from making magic for longer than . . . oh, I don't know."

Sayblee looked at him, her blue eyes steady. She looked so composed, her hair neat and smooth, her blouse and skirt unwrinkled even after the twenty hours that had elapsed since they had taken off from Hilo. For a second, he wanted to listen to her thoughts, to see how horrible he actually seemed at this moment, a total whiner, and a pain in her probably-numb ass, too. She had always been a straight arrow (except for her little flares of fire temper tantrums), the smart one in their class at Bampton, the one that he'd always known he couldn't impress, couldn't win over with a smile, or a compliment or twelve. The one he'd tried to please with tricks and teases and *charmes,* but to no use for years and years. And here she was, sitting placidly beside him, barely tolerating his small rant.

"I told you to take a sleeping pill," Sayblee said. "I was able to get some just for this reason."

"*Moyenne* medicine is poison," he said. "Sariel always told me—"

"Well, Sariel isn't here annoying everyone. In fact, I bet he'd push the pill down your throat himself."

Felix smiled, breathed in. Sariel *would* probably cram the pill down his throat, wanting to keep Felix out of the way, out of trouble. Felix knew that's what he often felt like, the little brother being pushed aside so that his older brothers could do what was needed and useful. So this mission, this thing that he and Sayblee were doing, was important. Sariel and Rufus weren't going on the mission. He was, and he had to follow the rules because so much was at stake. The *Croyant* world, the magical world they all had worked so long to protect, was still at risk, and Felix had a chance to save it. He had to behave, even if it meant never feeling his legs again.

"Fine," he said. "Let me out of this damn seat. I'll go talk to that flight attendant. The one with her hair pulled back."

"All of them have their hair pulled back. Except Jeremy, of course. But I don't think you are going to talk with him."

"Okay, smarty. The one with her hair pulled back and the big—"

"I know, I know. Go." Sayblee unbuckled her seat belt and stood up, letting Felix move out of the row and into the aisle. "Just try to not cause trouble. We're only two hours out of Paris. And remember, you're a 'married' man, now."

"A married *French* man," he said, stepping on one foot and then the other, trying to get some blood flow going. "And you know what that means. You know about that lovely double standard. I've always thought it was a practice the entire world should adopt."

"Felix," she said, and behind her calm expression, he saw something, some feeling in her eyes and mouth, but then she seemed to catch herself and the feeling disappeared.

"All right, all right," he said, wondering how long this mission would go on. How long he would go without a little womanly contact. But, more importantly, he wondered how long it would be before he could feel his lower extremities. "I'll behave. I'll ask her for a Perrier or about the weather in Paris."

"Good," Sayblee said, all business now. "And don't be long. They're getting ready to serve breakfast. And I know how you love cheese logs."

He thought he finally understood why people thought Europeans smelled. It actually had nothing to do with their hygiene. Europeans were just as clean as Americans. No, it wasn't about soap or antiperspirants or perfume. It was all about the trains and the subway. Hot, crowded sweltering trains that everyone rode, the same kind of subway train that he and Sayblee were now crammed into with their four suitcases and two carry-ons, the huge load that made everyone who got onto the 8 Métro headed toward Balard give them a dirty look.

In fact, his head was pressed against a man's torso, and the man had clearly been on an un-air-conditioned train since St-Denis. To pass time, Felix tried to imagine what spell would work best on the slightly garlicky, oniony smell the man exuded. Perhaps a *charme de parfum?* Or maybe a *charme de baignoire?* That would do it. Suddenly, Felix would be leaning into a man who smelled like fresh water and castile soap. Then again, it very likely was he himself who smelled, all the travel and sitting not only making him uncomfortable but a little ripe as well. God knows how long it had been since he'd taken his shower before he and Sayblee left for the airport. What time was it? He was unable to add the twelve-hour time difference from Hilo to the travel time to France. What day was it? Where in the hell were they?

"Felix!"

"Huh?" Felix turned to Sayblee, who was suddenly standing up. He looked at her, wondering how she could still look so good, so fresh. She must be using magic, he thought, knowing that her soft pink skin could not look so, well, pink, unless she was doing something amazing to keep it that way. And, he thought, *I bet she doesn't smell like onions*. In fact, he started to drift, imagining that Sayblee smelled like something that started with *S,* something soft, something sweet, something succulent, but he couldn't think of the perfect *S* word that would do Sayblee credit.

"Felix!" she said again, frowning.

"What? What is it?"

"Our stop."

Felix sighed, stood, jolting against the onion man and unfortunately taking in one more sniff, and then he grabbed the handles of his bags, pulling them by inches to the door.

"Pardon, pardon. Excuse moi! Merde," he said, knowing that in about half a second, he could clear the entire train with magic. In a half a second more, he could have them both already in the apartment, unpacked, drinking a piña colada. In another half a second, he could . . . well, no, not that. Not with Sayblee Safipour, though, as he stared at her sleek hair in its perfect ponytail, her beautiful, calm face, he knew that wouldn't be so bad. Actually, it would probably be great. But there was no way she'd ever let him get past her button-down blouse that fit her like armor. Before this mission, she never even wanted to be in the same room with him, unless they were fighting Quain. And fighting the forces of evil wasn't a very good time to talk about a little romp.

"Don't even think about it," Sayblee hissed as she yanked on the handle because the door refused to open, whacking him out of his thoughts. Even before they managed to get out with their suitcases and carry-ons, people started to press into the train, looking extremely irritated and pinched by the way Felix impeded their progress.

"Don't what?" he asked, embarrassed, trying to erase the whole ponytail/sex scenario from his mind. "Are you reading my thoughts?"

"I don't have to. I know what you are up to. I bet you had us somewhere drinking one of those drinks. Just come on."

They banged their bags down to the platform and stopped, letting the train doors close and watching the train whoosh away into the tunnel. Felix closed his eyes, enjoying the sudden and temporary wind from the movement, and then the air fell still and silent and hot again on his skin. But for a moment, the Métro stop was quiet, the crowds passing and disappearing up the stairs.

"Stairs," Felix said. "Stairs?"

"That's right," said Sayblee. "Lots of them. Just be thankful we aren't living in Montmarte. You should see the stairs at Abbesses station."

"There's an elevator at that one," Felix grumbled, remembering the time that he, Sariel, and Rufus flew up the seemingly never-ending spiral of stairs to the street surface and back down again, over and over until Zosime cast a *charme d'immobilité*. The three of them hung suspended in the spiral until she let them fall down, one by one, complaining the rest of the day about how she had to enchant so many *Moyenne* to make them forget her three insane boys, whirling around like tops in a major tourist area.

"Can I take you anywhere?" she had asked, adjusting her robe in a huff. "Do you think I can let you out in the world for one minute without expecting some kind of disaster? Will there ever be a time I don't have to watch you every hour of the day?"

Maybe Zosime was still right, Felix thought. Here he was, still troublesome. But really! How did Adalbert expect them all to adjust to this life just like that? Airplanes, the Métro, baggage, and stairs? They should have had some kind of class before they left: *How to Live Like the* Moyenne: *A Crash Course*. Or at least a book called Moyenne *Living for Dummies* or *The Idiot's Guide to* Moyenne *Culture*.

"You'd think they'd put an elevator at every station," he said, yanking one of his suitcases closer to him. "What about the Disability Act or whatever?"

"Are you disabled?" Sayblee asked, adjusting her purse on her shoulder. "Do you have one thing wrong with you?"

"Well, yes, I think I am, actually. Half of what I use to get around is gone. I finally see what it's like for the *Moyenne*. In fact, when I get home, I'm going to become an activist. I'm going to join Fabia's brother, Niall, in his quest for *Moyenne* rights. I might just work with Cadeyrn Macara and his group. I may go renegade and become a healer to those *Moyenne* in need, *Croyant* secrecy be damned."

Sayblee shook her head and stared moving toward the *Sortie,* following the last of the commuters rushing home. "You are beginning to hallucinate. You're obviously delirious. Let's just get to the apartment. You can have a drink. But first," she said, turning back to him, smiling, and crinkling her nose a little, "you can have a nice, long bath."

"Okay," Felix said many hours later, a bath, a long nap, and one glass of Sancerre later. "I overreacted."

Sayblee looked at him from the kitchen. She was organizing something, pushing bowls and pans and pots around on their shelves. For a moment, he listened to her movements, feeling somehow content. The kitchen sounds began to lull him, bringing him back to a place where sleep was just around the corner.

"I think you still are," she said suddenly, peering at him and then stooping down so that she disappeared behind the cupboard. "Wasn't it about fifteen minutes ago that you freaked out because there was no coconut cream in the pantry?"

Felix sighed. It had been a long time since he'd been pulled out of his comfort zone. In fact, he lived his life so that he didn't have to leave it. Only his brothers could lure him away from Hilo and, usually, those calls lead to some kind of trouble. Last year's event with Quain at the Fortress Kendall had done just that. He'd spent most of the attack against Quain and Kallisto on the floor with a concussion and under a spell, though he hadn't been alone in terms of being overcome. Sariel had barely survived. Before that, he'd fought against Cadeyrn Macara and Kallisto in a cabin in Truckee, California, and again, things hadn't gone well. He'd had to recuperate at Sariel's for a week before he could get back home to the waves and sun.

The good news from those fights was that Kallisto and Cadeyrn were no longer working with Quain. The bad news was that here Felix was again, trying to find Quain. The man was like a terrible virus that was immune to antibiotics, popping up stronger and more intensely each time.

It wasn't that Felix didn't want to fight. He felt he had been in battle since graduating from Bampton Academy. Always on the lookout for those who would do bad magic. Finding *Croyant* who would use *Moyenne* to serve their own greedy purposes. Trying to do the right that would undermine the wrong that had given Quain power, that had led to the death of Felix's father, Hadrian. So he fought. But this plan already seemed flawed and slightly ridiculous. How did lugging a ton of baggage up and out of a Métro station and then up into a fifth-story apartment lead to the end of Quain? How could Quain detect the slightest, tiniest bits of magic? Had Quain somehow become omniscient, able to pick up vibrations from any spell in the area? That's what Felix wanted to know. That's what he wished he could talk to Adalbert about.

Felix put his glass down and leaned forward. "I—" he began, but then the doorbell rang. He stood up, looking toward Sayblee. "Are we expecting someone? Are we having a little get-together with our other 'couple' friends? Is someone bringing a petit Brillat-Savarin and a bottle of champagne?"

Sayblee put down a bowl, rolled her eyes, shook her head, and walked to the intercom near the front door. *"Allô?"* she asked, putting a finger to her lips when Felix started to speak.

"Ah, oui. Entrez," she said, pressing the red button, which opened the door downstairs. She took her finger off the button and turned back to Felix, her hands on her hips.

"It's not about cheese and wine."

"Well, you know what they say about cheese," Felix said.

"No, I don't know what *they* say about cheese." Sayblee turned to the mirror in the hall and pushed her hair away from her face, smoothing the neckline of her T-shirt. For the first time since he'd awakened from his nap, he realized that she'd changed clothes, her light blue shirt following the sweet shape of her body. He was surprised to notice she actually had some shape after seeing her in that ugly blouse for what seemed like two days. And this new skirt hugged—well, it hugged her ass, and she had one of those, too. Why hadn't he really noticed that before? Sure, he'd always thought she was kind of pretty in a serious-type way, but, wow, Sayblee was kind of built.

"Well?" She turned away from the mirror and stared at him.

"Well what?"

"Cheese."

Felix swallowed and took a breath. "Oh. They say a meal without some cheese is like a beautiful woman with only one eye." And then he stared at Sayblee again, looking into her eyes, so blue, so clear.

"Maybe a meal without cheese is like a man with no damn brain, which seems to often be the case." Sayblee flicked her hair behind her shoulder. "Lots of meals without cheese for everyone. But listen, Brennus and Philomel are on their way up. They'll be here in a second."

"Unbelievable," Felix said as he brought his glass to the kitchen. "Don't tell me they are one of these so-called couples? This I can't wait to tell Sariel about."

Brennus Fraser was an older *sorcier,* who had been a trusted friend of Hadrian Valasay and had appointed himself surrogate father to the Valasay brothers after Hadrian's death. Brennus hadn't been one for coddling any of them, and he sometimes took the Valasay brothers' business a bit too personally. He and Sariel had often had words over the years. Brennus was a good man, but to see him act as part of a couple with Philomel Holly—a very good-natured but slightly eccentric *sorcière*—would be the limit. And with no magic? Felix couldn't wait for this cheese soiree.

"Are you sure there's no cheese?" he asked, smiling just as there was a knock on the door.

"Would you please shut up?" Sayblee asked. "And try to be good, will you? Remember that this is serious."

"I promise," Felix said, enjoying watching Sayblee walk to the door. *Damn that skirt,* he thought. This mission might not be so bad after all.

"You understand the importance of keeping all magic completely under wraps," Brennus said. His dark eyebrows seemed to push down on his eyes, giving him a perpetual scowl. This was the disapproving face Felix knew well, the one always turning around at Council meetings to give the Valasay brothers the what-for.

"Cheese?" Philomel asked at the same time Brennus spoke, handing Felix a piece of crusty baguette topped with a delicious slice.

"I certainly don't mind if I do," Felix said. "What type is it?"

Philomel smiled. "Oh, it's a lovely little Chambertin. I know you'll just adore it."

Felix took the bread from Philomel, noting as he did how her floppy purple hat sat on top of her wild gray hair rather than on her head. She watched as he took a bite, and Felix almost sighed, the taste smooth and mellow on his tongue.

"I'm glad you brought it. Sayblee and I were having a truly interesting talk about cheese just before you arrived. Weren't we? It's amazing how the French feel about cheese."

"Are you listening to any of this?" Brennus slapped his hand down on the table.

"We are," Sayblee said, giving Felix a swift, dark look. "And Adalbert told us about the mission."

"He told you," Felix said. He took another bite of his cheese and smiled at Philomel as he chewed. "Delicious."

"The point is—" Brennus began.

"The point is that it doesn't make sense." Felix wiped his mouth with his napkin and sat back, an ankle resting on his knee. "There are thousands of *Croyant* in Paris, including those Quain has recruited. How can little bits of magic from a few couples even make a blip on his radar? Why all the hiding? Moving into the area, great. Marshalling our forces, yeah, I get it. But how is Quain going to know that I created a *charme de temps* in an underground Métro station?"

Brennus shook his head, mumbled something that sounded like, "Just like his brother," and then sighed. "It's not enough that Adalbert wants it this way. No, not enough that the Council has determined that this is the best way to finally get to Quain."

"The Council has agreed to a lot of things," Felix said. "The Council makes big decisions for everyone and then expects us all to just follow along." He pushed himself up off the couch, wanting nothing more than to whirl into gray and stay there. At least there was space and freedom in the gray . . . matter like an ocean he could dive into. He was so rarely cooped up in his house in Hilo, either working on Council business or in the water or hiking along a path of a river that wended toward the coast. When he wasn't doing any of that, he would move into the gray and head toward his mother's house, or Sariel's, or Rufus's. Or he was with some lovely lady, watching his wooing work on her, allowing him to move toward her slowly, feeling that first kiss like a promise. But at this moment, anything would be better than sitting in the room with Brennus, even being stuck in the gray forever.

He turned back to the group. "This is ridiculous. Putting us in a situation where we can't even take care of ourselves, living in this . . . living with . . ." He moved his hand to indicate the room, the apartment, and then realized that

Sayblee was staring at him, her face with that bit of feeling he'd seen in the airplane, something like hurt. Like upset.

Felix shook his head. "No. I didn't mean . . . It's just, well—"

"You've been on your own for too long," Brennus said. "You don't know how to work with anyone. It wouldn't matter where you were or who you were with—"

"Now, I say," Philomel began, smiling nervously. "More cheese. And a little more Bordeaux." She poured a glass of wine and held it out to Felix.

Felix sat down and took a glass from Philomel and swallowed it in one gulp. "What I want to know is how long will it go on? And will we ever be able to use our magic?"

Brennus took in a deep breath, his lined face turning a little red under his beard. "We are going to be your last *Croyant* contact. From tonight on, you are going to be living your life as a *Moyenne* couple." He pulled a piece of paper from the pocket of his shirt and handed it to Sayblee, who began to read it.

"There are your work contacts," Brennus said. "You have tonight and tomorrow to acclimate, and then you are to report to these people tomorrow. They are trusted *Moyenne* allies, but they've been enchanted so that they will think you are just a typical new employee. They will be briefed when this is over, but for now, they know nothing about *Croyant* or you or any plan. If you have any typical troubles here with *Moyenne* life, they are the people you go to. You are not, under any circumstances, to contact any *Croyant*. You will live your life quietly, but notice everything, and when we are ready to fight, you will be contacted."

"By you?" Sayblee asked, as she folded up the paper and put it in her pocket.

"By who is closest," Brennus said. "There may not be a

lot of preparation time, depending on what the Council scouts find."

"What are they looking for?" Felix asked. "What are we waiting for Quain to do this time? He already went after the Plaques de la Pensée," Felix said, knowing that there was nothing more powerful and sacred to *Croyant* than the *plaques,* the representation of all that was magic and sacred in the world. And when the three *plaques* were put together in a triangular form, they were powerful enough to create life. Or destroy it. And while no one had been able to subdue and capture Quain, *Croyant* had managed to keep the plaques safe and out of Quain's hands.

"Maybe he's not going for anything, dear," Philomel said. "Maybe he's just going to destroy everything. Everything we know."

They were all silent, and Felix understood. Quain had been trying to conquer so that he could *have.* Now, he could want to *take* so that no one could have anything at all. So that he could destroy the very people, places, and objects that had been denied him. Power.

Brennus stood, strangely normal in his button-down shirt and gray slacks, a regular *Moyenne* gentleman. "I know how hard it is for you Valasay boys to stay in the lines. But this might be our final chance to stop him."

Philomel stood as well, her hat bobbing on her hair, her blue dress a terrible mismatch with the purple, her orange tights even worse. Sayblee and Felix stood up as well, and then both she and Felix walked the older couple to the door. And even though Felix was often irritated with Brennus, for a small second, he didn't want this man he had known for so long to leave. When Brennus left, there went the answers. When he left, there went *Croyant* life. When he left, there went all that Felix had ever known.

"Just remember," Brennus said as he walked out the door, his dark eyes looking directly into Felix's.

Felix nodded, the word tingling in his mind. But then as Sayblee closed the door, he thought, *Remember what?* The question buzzed in his head for a moment, and then it was gone, nothing left in front of him but Sayblee's angry face.

"What?" Felix asked.

Sayblee crossed her arms and then shook her head, walking into the living room.

"What? What are you mad about?"

She ignored him, picking up the tray with the cheese and bread and wineglasses and carrying it into the kitchen, the glasses and plates clinking and clanging as she clipped through the apartment. She banged down the tray on the counter and turned on the faucet.

"All right, what is going on?" Felix asked, walking into the kitchen and leaning against the doorjamb. "Did I say something wrong?"

"Never mind," Sayblee said. "Just forget about it."

"If I knew what to never mind or forget, I'd never mind and forget it. But I can't read your thoughts, and I don't have a damn clue what you are in a twist about. So just tell me and we can both forget about it together."

She turned to look at him, her blue eyes almost navy with irritation. "You're just such a . . . all this about living, you know, with me. Like it's some terrible punishment. Well, it's no great treat living with you. You complained all the way across the country, across the Atlantic, all through Paris, and you haven't stopped since we got to this apartment. I didn't know you were such a baby. You want to have exactly what you want when you want it. Food, drink . . . sex. Yeah, I know you are mad about that woman and how I ruined your date. But you just need to get over it." Sayblee exhaled a loud *Ah*, turned the water to cold, and then ran her hands under the faucet.

Felix stepped back quickly, knowing what that cold dousing of palms meant. Once, after he'd teased Sayblee at school, she'd had to dunk her hands in the fish pond in the school courtyard, saving Felix from a scorched head, or worse, he was sure. "Look, you're right. Okay. You're right. I had hoped that Brennus would tell us something more specific about Adalbert's plan, but it doesn't look like we are going to need any answers."

Sayblee glared at him, but then she turned off the water and dried her hands on a towel. "Then just stop complaining, will you? It's not like this didn't interrupt my life, too."

Nodding, Felix realized that he hadn't thought about her life at all. Maybe she had a boyfriend in London, someone she was serious about. He hadn't seen her with anyone at Council meetings, and neither Sariel nor Miranda had ever mentioned anything about her having a boyfriend, but maybe it was new love. Maybe Sayblee had found someone special. He shook his head, surprised by a strange little balloon of disappointment sputtering in his chest.

"I know. I'm sorry. Look, let's get organized around here and then get some sleep. I promise to wake up tomorrow a changed man. We can figure out the neighborhood and get busy with our *Moyenne* lives."

Sayblee turned away from him and went back to the dishes, a lock of her gold hair hanging loose in front of her face. Felix resisted the urge to tuck it behind her ear. He realized he was resisting the urge to do more than touch her hair. Maybe, he thought, he should douse his palms. Or some body part.

"So where am I going to work?" he asked, stepping back and putting his hands in the back pockets of his Levi's. "Some kind of office?"

She started to giggle, and then laugh, shaking her head and looking up at him with her wide blue eyes. "No. Not an office."

"What then? A store? A manager of some kind?"

"No, not a manager."

"Oh, great. Brennus is finally getting his licks in. What? Am I working at a theater taking tickets? A market? A marché?"

"Sort of a market. A butcher. A *boucherie.*"

Felix was silent, staring at Sayblee, whose eyes had lightened to a powder blue, her face pink and smiling. "A butcher," he repeated.

"Just down the street, too, so the commute is easy."

"A butcher."

"Yeah. You know, lamp chops, pork butt, cow brains, kidneys, giblets, sweet breads."

Felix closed his eyes. Sure, he liked a steak every so often. Chicken more often. But that was it. And he was not a healer like Sariel, did not understand anatomy of any species, and didn't want to learn now. "Great."

"I'm going to be down the street, too."

Felix breathed in and opened his eyes. "Where are you working? A nice swanky office?"

"No. A perfume shop. A little *parfumerie* just across the street from you."

"So you can keep an eye on me, I suppose. You can arrange the little bottles while—"

"Yeah, while you are up to your armpits in—"

"Gore. Great. I—"

He interrupted himself, knowing that all he was going to do was complain, proving case-in-point that Sayblee was right about him. "Fine. I'm glad I brought all my knives with me after all. I won't be doing myself in but cutting up critters instead."

Felix knew he could go on and on, teasing himself silly, complaining about the work conditions until Sayblee hit him over the head with the bread board. So, instead, he turned away from the kitchen and started back toward the living room.

"I'm going to figure out this fold-out couch now. If I can't use magic, I'm going to need at least an hour. I've heard tell that such couches have eaten people alive."

In the living room, he stood over the couch and smiled to himself, not because of his joke but because of Sayblee's laughter that floated toward him. He wanted this second to last, to step inside her pleasure at his words and enjoy it. But this time wasn't magic, not at all, and her laughter ended, replaced by the sound of running water and the click clack of silverware in the sink.

He crossed his arms and stared at the green couch. Back at home, he'd say, *"Ouvrir,"* and watch the contraption spring up, unfold, and settle down to the floor, the mattress out and made up, the pillows fluffed and ready to go. Better yet, he'd command, *"Changez,"* and watch as the fold-out became—for the night—a king-sized bed with 300-thread count Egyptian cotton sheets and a goose down comforter. But, as Felix was truly figuring out, he wasn't at home nor would he be for some time.

He sighed and kept his eyes on the couch, focusing hard. *Moyenne* sometimes bent spoons with just their thoughts, and maybe, just maybe, he could use an ordinary channel to figure out the couch. Or to destroy it. Then he'd have no choice but to move into the bedroom with Sayblee, and then? Well, who knew? He didn't think she'd throw him on the floor. Her reaction to his comment about living in Paris with her had been too strong. Maybe there was something there. Maybe . . . Felix stopped thinking and breathed. There was no use thinking about it. Sayblee would no more invite him to her bed than do headstands in the middle of the *Champs-Elysée*.

So Felix focused on the couch. He waited and thought hard, imagining the ugly piece of furniture turning into a speck of dust, but despite all his nonmagic wishes, the ugly green couch refused to disappear.

Felix opened his eyes and turned to look back toward the

kitchen, trying to catch a glimpse of Sayblee, but she was busy with the dishes, seemingly enjoying all this "normal" work. She was actually humming something, a melody he couldn't catch, something light and soft. He turned back to the couch and pulled off a cushion and then another. It was going to be a very long night.

Chapter Three

Sayblee was flat on her back in bed, staring out the window. There wasn't much of a view, just the apartment windows across the street, but she'd spent at least an hour watching them, excited when a light turned on and then off. Once, one light even flicked on again, and she sat up, wondering what could be going on at three A.M. across the street. Certainly Parisians were more of a late-night crowd than even the Brits, and most certainly than the Americans, but a light on and off at three? Maybe she and Felix were actually living across the street from one of Quain's followers, a *sorcière* sneaking out of the apartment building in a whirl of light and magic. But then the light went off, and since then, nothing. And more than likely, the light was just a light. On and then off. Nothing even before it was nothing.

"Oh," she said, putting her hands on her eyes. She couldn't believe she was suffering from jet lag. She'd read about it, of course, and had felt sorry for all those *Moyenne* travelers who came home from faraway places and thought night was day and vice versa. But now, here she was, her body telling her that she'd gone to bed far too early. *Get up,* her body was saying. *Let's go for a walk. Let's have another meal. Let's watch television. Let's go into the living room and curl up next to Felix and see what he has in mind. And you know you don't want his mind. There are other fine parts. All of them. So let's go! Maybe he's dreaming of you.*

Ugh! As if, she thought, slapping a hand on the mattress. She must be crazy, delirious like Felix had been on the Métro.

Traveling through matter never created this mess. She'd pop in at Miranda's in San Francisco, stay for a couple of hours, and then go home to London. No big deal. If she stayed longer—a day or two or three—she adjusted quickly, not having had to endure the long travel time. If things became dire, she'd always known she could whip up a quick *charme de santé* or schedule a visit to a healer.

She turned on her side and stared at the clock. Felix had been right to complain, and maybe she would have joined in if it hadn't been so entertaining to listen to him. How fun it had been to watch him lug his suitcases up the apartment building stairs, swearing the whole time, his long hair coming loose and hanging wild around his face. And then he'd thrown himself onto the couch and fallen into a deep sleep for a couple of hours, looking like the dead, his arms dangling off the side. With the surprise of Brennus and Philomel's visit, she'd forgotten to tell him that he snored, a little, a few times. *So cute,* she thought now. *Even his snores are cute.*

The couch. Sayblee sat up and leaned against the headboard. How strange that Felix was sleeping out there in the living room. All her careful years of keeping a clear distance between them, and now, here he was, not twenty feet from the walls of her room. *What would she do if she was any other woman?* Sayblee thought. Would she push aside her comforter, walk into the living room, and slip in beside him, running her hands up his smooth body? What would she do if she was that woman from Hilo, what's-her-name? Roxanne. Would she just saunter in and sit astride his chest, bend down, and kiss him hard? And not stop?

As she thought about the way his skin would feel, her

palms began to itch, and her head seemed to fill with the smell of pineapple and coconut. Gritting her teeth, she clasped her hands tight, pressing them together. This couldn't keep happening. Every time Felix started in with complaining or teasing, or when she watched him for too long, her palms began to burn, the fire licking up and through her skin, the feeling pulsing in her head. No matter what she did, her magic was just below the surface, and she almost told Brennus, worried that her incipient flares could somehow alert Quain. But, so far, she'd kept the fire inside, not letting one bit out. How would Quain know about that?

And she had to remember who Felix was. What he was like with women. How he had always been with women. What had Miranda told her? She'd looked at Sayblee with one eyebrow raised and told her Felix had a "revolving-door policy of women. They come in and then they go out just as easily." That's not what Sayblee wanted from any man, much less Felix, no matter how beautifully warm his skin looked, how sexy his smile was, how much she wished she could run her hand along the smooth sheen of his wonderful hair.

Sayblee slipped down from the headboard and back onto the mattress and pulled the blanket over her shoulders. She had to stop thinking about him. Otherwise, the mission would be a failure and the whole apartment might go up in smoke.

Focus, she thought. Focus. She slowed her breathing and, after a few moments, her palms quieted, the burning pulling away from the surface. No fire tonight. No need to call the *pompiers,* needing hoses and ladders to put out her lust. She closed her eyes, and willed herself to not think one more time about Felix. Not once more about his long black hair and his smile. She flashed to how he turned to her when they were on the airplane, asking her about the mission, his shoulder pressed against hers. No! Not one more thought. No green eyes. No lovely round ass. No perfect white teeth. No! Not one more idea. Not even his attractive feet. Nothing. Not a thought. None. She focused on her breath, in and out, in and out and, eventually, finally, thankfully, she fell asleep.

The next morning, Sayblee woke up to the smell of coffee. She opened her eyes and yawned, the sun streaming in the unshaded window. Turning to the clock, she gasped when she saw it was ten o'clock, but then realized she didn't have to start work at the perfume shop until tomorrow morning. This was the settling-in day. A day to assess the neighborhood, scan for *Croyant* who might be aligned with Quain, blend in. A whole day with Felix.

She pushed aside the comforter, grabbed her bathrobe, and put it on as she walked out the bedroom door and into the living room. Felix was sitting at the small table in the living room, holding up an espresso cup and reading *Le Monde*. On the table were a baguette, cheese, and a sliced melon. He looked up when he heard her walk in and put down the paper.

"I tried to find a copy of *Libération,* but I suppose it's too socialist for our neighborhood stand. But this melon makes up for it." He picked up a fork, speared an orange chunk, and held it out to her. "Just taste it."

Her palms pricking, Sayblee walked over to him, acting as natural as possible, and tried to grab the fork. Felix pulled the fork back and shook his head. "My fork. Take the melon. Come on, just bite it off."

He waggled the fork and then brought it closer to her. Keeping her eyes from his, she bent down and bit down on the melon, pulling it off the fork, a little juice running down her chin. She would have cared about looking silly, but then the melon's flavor took over, bright and clean and sweet, tasting exactly like a spring morning.

"Oh," she said. "Oh. That's amazing."

"Isn't it? Here." He handed her a napkin, and then she blushed as she wiped her chin.

"So what do we have planned?" she asked, sitting down hard on the chair and tucking the napkin in her lap. She picked up the bread knife and sliced a piece of bread. *Don't look at him,* she thought. *This feeling is going to pass. Like a cold or something. Like the stomach flu. It's going to go away.*

"I've already done some early recon. The *boulangerie* to the right is better than the one at the corner. The *tartes des framboises* are superb. I would have brought you one, but I ate the last they had. The fromagerie wasn't open yet, but it looks good, too. And you know how I feel about cheese."

Sayblee bit down on her piece of bread and chewed as she chanced a glance at him. He was smiling, the sun shining on his hair, his lips a dusky rose.

"So," he went on. "I think we need to go to the *supermarché*, buy our supplies, and then, because it's in our neighborhood, we need to go to the Eiffel Tower. I've never actually walked up it."

"That's a real surprise," Sayblee said, shaking her head. "You work out daily in a gym and yet you won't carry suitcases without a fight or walk up the Eiffel Tower."

"Have *you* walked up the Eiffel Tower?"

"I haven't ever been to the Eiffel Tower."

Felix sat back. "You haven't ever been?"

"No."

"Why not?"

Sayblee shrugged. "No need, I guess."

"Well, that settles it." Felix stood up and walked into the kitchen. "Espresso?"

"Don't you think we should really do some scouting? Sort of check out the neighbors? I saw a light go on late last night a couple of times, so who knows? We could be right across the street from a Quain follower."

Felix filled the machine with water and coffee. "There's plenty of time for that. We'll be working down the street for weeks. And you know about lunch around here. From one to three everything shuts down, and we won't be working anyway. Lots of time for sleuthing. We can sit at a café and watch for magic." He ducked down and looked at her from under the cupboard. "So do you want this coffee or not?"

Sayblee smiled and nodded. "Yes, I want the coffee," she said, picking up her fork and spearing another piece of melon. "And make it a double."

After breakfast, Sayblee and Felix left the apartment and walked out into the warm May morning. She couldn't see the Eiffel Tower from the street, but after turning right onto *avenue de la Bourdannais* and then left on *avenue Joseph Bouvard*, there it was, rising up in front of her like . . . like . . .

"A giant erector set," Felix said.

"Felix!" she said. "Are you reading my thoughts?"

"No. Not at all. It's the only thought there is to have at this particular moment, though. What a contraption."

"The Parisians called it a 'metal asparagus' when it was first built," she said. "And the rest said it was like the Tower of Babel."

Felix shook his head. "Did you read that somewhere?"

Sayblee turned away from him, blushed, and said, "Yes." She wondered if this was what her life was always going to be like, knowing information about things she hadn't even bothered to explore personally. She knew all about the Eiffel Tower, how it was built, what the public thought, and how, finally, the author Guy de Maupassant made the structure acceptable by eating lunch in the restaurant and calling the view "very fine indeed."

They stopped on the corner *avenue Anatole* and looked up at the length of the structure. The sun hit the metal frame, the bright glint making Sayblee blink.

"I've been to the very top. And I mean, the very top," Felix said, putting a hand on the small of Sayblee's back as they continued walking. Even through her blouse, she could feel his warmth, his pulse, the way his fingers cupped her muscles and spine so gently. Her breath caught like a bad zipper somewhere in her throat, and she forced herself to keep her eyes on the tower.

"They let you? How did—Oh, I have a feeling this was an unofficial tour. A magical mystery tour."

"Exactly. Rufus, Sariel, and I, well, we had this habit of taking little trips at night when my mother was asleep. First we hit all the tropical islands we could think of, which weren't many until we found a map of the world. After that, we visited the pyramids, the Great Sphinx of Giza, the Eiffel Tower here, St. Paul's Cathedral, the Leaning Tower of Pisa."

"You three must have been a menace."

Felix laughed. "My mother figured it out after a couple of months. After that, there was so much protective magic around us and the house at night, I could barely move the blankets off my toes. But before she caught us, we even made it to Antarctica. For about one second. Talk about weather issues."

"Did you know the emperor penguins . . ." Sayblee began, and then stopped, knowing that throwing out another ridiculous fact was going to make her feel even more freakish than usual. "That must have been intense."

"We saw the emperor penguins," Felix said, staying with her, "when we opened our eyes. I don't know how they stay out there in that cold. I don't even think the word *cold* can explain what it feels like there. But there wasn't time to visit with them. I think we were standing around in shorts. We never made it to the Arctic, though. Mom had us figured out by then. So no Santa Claus for us."

Sayblee let out a little laugh and then bit back her information about global warming and the melting Arctic ice shelves. After a few more steps, Felix moved his hand, and the space where his palm had pressed against her skin now felt like the Antarctic, cold and barren. She felt like a penguin, wobbling alone on the frozen ground.

"That was the best time, I think. When we were finding out about magic. It was like each day was something new. Rufus would figure out a spell, and then he'd tell Sariel, who would tell me. I'm not really sure how my mother did make it through."

Felix laughed, and she could hear his pleasure in his family. And the space she still held for Rasheed in her heart echoed with his absence.

Felix brought his hand back to her back, and she wanted to stop walking and let him hold her, long enough to forget about Rasheed. Or long enough for her to be able to believe that Rasheed was all right. But she didn't. They kept walking, moving together down the street.

"Three boys," Sayblee said finally. "Three very active, magic boys. She deserves some kind of award."

"Well, I bet you were a handful, literally, all that fire in your hands. You and your brother—"

Sayblee sighed, listening to Felix's sentence die in the air. That's what always happened. People forgot, and then they remembered, Rasheed was known best for the last thing he did in the *Croyant* world: leaving it.

"I'm sorry," Felix said.

"No," Sayblee said. "It's okay. We did—I mean, I got us both into trouble. When I first realized I could make fire, I almost set him completely ablaze. I was about four, I think, Rasheed, five, going on six. He had taken the book I was reading, was holding it over his head, and I just got so angry. He wouldn't listen to me. He wouldn't do what I said. So I held out my hands, and his shoelaces burst into flames. He was so surprised he dropped my book and ran into the bathroom and jumped in the tub, turning on the water, forgetting about magic altogether. By that time, his pants were starting to go."

She laughed, pushing her hair away from her face. "You'd think he would have been afraid of me at that point, but all he did was make me promise not to tell my mother or father. At night, we'd practice. He'd collect things during the day, and at night we'd see if I could light them, when we were supposed to be in bed. I'd work on leaves and sticks. Then he'd bring in rocks or bits of brick. I was just getting to aluminum when my dad discovered us."

"How did your parents handle your gift?" Felix asked, moving his hand from her back again and taking her elbow as they joined other jaywalkers crossing the *avenue Gustave Eiffel*. A Mini honked as they jumped onto the curb, flashing by in a whir of red and silver.

"Oh," Sayblee said, "carted me off to Adalbert's. He loved to have me light his fireplace logs at night and keep them going when he told me stories. But he really did show me how to keep things from bursting into flame at odd moments. Well, mostly."

"Are you really under control?" Felix asked. "What about those palms of yours?"

Sayblee looked up at him. *No,* she wanted to say, *I am absolutely not in control. Not with your eyes and smile and hands and . . . everything.* "The last time I blew was when someone teased me about burning things down."

Felix raised his hands in mock surrender. "I'm begging you. No fire. Not by the Eiffel Tower. It would cause a general panic. We'll end up arrested by the *gendarmerie*. And there won't be any magic to free us."

Sayblee held out her palms in a quick promise, but there

already seemed to be a general panic at the tower, May tourists in long lines by the giant pillars, waiting for access to the elevator or the stairs. Hawkers walked up and down the line, selling water and sodas, and one man sold toy birds that actually flew for a short time. He would wind up the bird and then set it soaring, the plastic parrot flapping until it landed still on the ground and children grouped around it, amazed.

"That thing needs a little magic," Felix whispered. "What if I made it keep going, all the way across the Seine?"

Sayblee smiled, shrugged, and looked up, the tower rising over her, seemingly, weightless, a crisscross of light and metal against the blue sky.

"I've never really looked at the tower from this perspective," she said. "Mostly, it's just been scenery in the background."

"It's ugly but, really, lovely," Felix said, and his words made her somehow sad. She wasn't sure why, but something about not being recognized, not being seen—or being seen for the wrong reasons—made her want to walk across the sandy floor of the esplanade, cross the street, and head back to the apartment all by herself.

"At night," she said, trying to keep her voice steady, "it's beautiful."

"I've seen it. Flashing lights. Sometimes fireworks. I think it's all for tourists, though, the locals hate it." Felix took her arm again and they walked to the line for the stairs, getting behind a German family with three squirrelly children, who all wanted a mechanical bird, *now, now, now.*

Felix let go of her arm and they moved forward slowly. "Okay, we walk the first two flights, and then it's the elevator to the top level. No other choice, unless you want to misbehave and move through matter to the top. And I mean the beacon. We can grip ourselves steady on the girders.

Maybe we can throw all caution to the wind and have a little fly."

Sayblee laughed, her melancholy lifting. "I knew you'd work in an elevator somehow. Can't bear to pull your own body around by foot, can you?"

"I am nothing if not consistent," he said. "And I hate to disappoint."

She thought of a hundred comebacks, one-liners that she might regret having said later but that would sound so good now, the kind of quips Rasheed taught her all those years ago. But she couldn't bring herself to say one of them, knowing that no matter what Felix did, no matter how annoying he was, how self-centered, how lazy, how just plain testosterone-ridden, he didn't disappoint. Couldn't. There was no possible way.

The best part of the walk up the stairs was being able to stare at Felix's rear end the entire time. At first, Sayblee didn't realize she was staring at the perfectly formed mounds of flesh, focusing on the pockets of his Levi's (he carried something small and square in the left one), noticing his waist size (30), the length (34). She stared at the worn spot just under his rear, a crease of white fabric from continual wear. Clearly, these were his favorite pants, worn and washed often. From time to time, she looked down at his shoes, then let her eyes move up his legs, making sure to keep his same rhythm lest she trip and fall flat on her face. And then she followed the line of his back and waist, noticing how his lats (she thought that's what the muscles were called) flared and how he didn't even have an inkling of love handles under his just perfectly and slightly tight T-shirt. Not that he needed handles; women were happy to grab him and hold him tight without them.

The stairs just kept coming, one after the other and, eventually, Felix stopped turning back to talk to her so he could concentrate on the climb, and the next thing Sayblee knew, she was watching the round smoothness of his ass, how tight it was, how she could probably cup her hands and hold it. And if the rest of his body was any indication, it would be firm and nicely developed. She let her eyes drop a little to his thighs, imagining his hamstrings, which were undoubtedly strong and lean and tight. If she just had some magic, she could make herself invisible, swing around to the front and really get a look at him, watch all sorts of muscles flex. And then if she activated her *vue de transparent,* she would see through his jeans—

"Sayblee," Felix said.

She looked up and knew that he'd seen her watching his—him. "What?" she asked, stopping abruptly and looking just to his right so she wouldn't see the amusement in his eyes. Why did she imagine she was any different from all the other women Felix met? How did she imagine she was immune to his charms, when no one else seemed to be, *Croyant* and *Moyenne* alike, the old, the young, the in-between? She was sure he expected nothing less from any woman.

"We're here. But there's a little traffic jam. I think one of our German kids is scared to go out onto the platform."

And, in fact, one of the children was crying, holding on to his father's shorts, gripping so tight and hard on his father's waistline that the man was in danger of exposing himself.

"*Nein, nein!*" the child cried, but the parents managed to pull to the side, letting the crowd behind them move out onto the platform.

"They should take him back down," Sayblee said as they passed by the family.

"I bet they want him to have the experience. To see Paris

from the Eiffel Tower. A once-in-a-lifetime event. Now, instead, he'll be traumatized for life," Felix said. "He'll be complaining about this moment to therapists for years. 'They forced me to do everything.'"

"I would never do that," Sayblee said, turning away from the crying child. "I would never make my child do anything she didn't want to."

"Really?" Felix said. "Never make her do her lessons or go away to school or treat people with respect?"

"No, that's not what I mean," she said. "And you know it, Mr. Smartie. I mean, make her live up to some impossible expectation of mine. Make her live up to what I think she is rather than who she is truly."

Felix nodded, looked at Sayblee for a second, and then started walking along the Champs de Mars platform. People were sitting on benches, looking out, pointing at landmarks.

"I bet we could find our apartment building," Sayblee said.

Felix nodded but kept walking, taking her arm again as he did. "Maybe we can find the exact spot what's-his-name proposed to who's it."

"Huh?" Sayblee asked.

"You know. That actor and his much taller actor girlfriend." Felix looked at her, his eyebrows raised. "Some publicity stunt to promote his upcoming movie."

Sayblee laughed. "Do you read the tabloids? *Moyenne* tabloids? Felix, you've outed yourself."

"Okay. Okay. But no tabloids. Just a bit of late-night television. The show with the woman with the big blonde hair and the big—"

"A little edifying viewing after your dates have left?" Sayblee pulled her arm from his. Felix started to say something, but she cut him off. "Let's go up. Let's go to the top level."

"We have some more stairs. But I warned you. We have to take an elevator to the top level. If there were stairs, I'd take them."

So would I, she thought. *And not for the view of Paris.*

"Well?" he asked. "Come on. Let's make sure to beat the German family to the line. Junior is probably hysterical by now. By the next floor, he'll be catatonic."

Sayblee laughed, and they began to walk toward the stairwell. For a second, she let herself be filled with something she would describe as happiness. The feeling was light and filled her chest, made her feel like smiling. In fact, she could feel her cheekbones under her skin. In a weird way, she could feel everything. But even as she felt her lightness, the smile on her face, the way her body seemed to be moving perfectly to a natural rhythm, her strides matching Felix's, she felt the truth hit her like a mechanical bird losing altitude fast. She bit her lip and forced her thoughts front and center: *This is not a date. I am not one of Felix's dates. Not one of his typical women. This is work. He wouldn't be here with me unless he had to be.*

Felix reached the line for the stairs first and then turned around to smile at her, and she smiled back but then turned away to look at the view, to keep herself from looking into his almost-green eyes.

"We're going all the way up," he said.

"Yeah," Sayblee said, her eyes on the wide expanse of grass in front of the tower. "Up. All the way."

"I'm glad it's Sunday," Felix said, as they left the Casino *supermarche.* "The store is closed on Monday. I don't think I could have made it to work at the animal-hacking store without coffee and lots of it."

"Can I remind you that you enjoy eating hacked animals? I do believe I saw you consume an entire chicken this afternoon. Not to mention all the *pâté* and *jambon* you've just purchased. We'll be in duck liver and ham for weeks."

Felix shrugged, the only thing he could do with so many bags in his hands. "I know. Hacked animals are among my favorite foods. But I just like to imagine my meat selections come from nowhere. Sort of appeared on my plate, roasted, dripping juice, smelling like rosemary. I don't want to think about their animal lives. Sad months of living in a cage, that kind of thing. And then, I like to avoid their little deaths."

"Sort of like magic, huh? Chickens only exist on a china plate. Cows exist for months like New York strips? Basically, animals live and die in tiny Styrofoam containers covered in Saran Wrap?"

"Exactly," Felix said. "So no more animal talk. I have a feeling I will be overwhelmed with the subject shortly."

Sayblee stopped talking and followed after Felix. It was late, almost eight o'clock. After making it to the top of the Eiffel Tower, Felix had persuaded Sayblee to walk in the *Jardin du Trocadéro* and then up *avenue Kléber* to the *Arc de Triomphe,* actually insisted on it once Sayblee admitted she'd never been to the top of that structure either.

"I've been on the Ferris wheel in the Tuileries and to the top of the Parthenon, so no more ideas. No more stairs," she had said, finally as tired as Felix had seemed to be in the Métro.

"There's no excuse for this. I have to help you make up for a terrible lack of cultural study," he'd said, holding her hand all the way up the stairs. "You can't just read about things, you know."

And after climbing the stairs there and admiring the Champs-Elysées from the heightened vantage point, they'd eaten at a street-side café on the *rue Galilée* then and walked back toward home. Sayblee's feet felt like wooden blocks, and if she wasn't so sure that Felix would tease her to death, she'd complain. But she hadn't dared, not even when Felix pulled them inside Casino and purchased everything he missed from home plus everything he longed for from Paris. Sayblee was praying that the plastic bags she was carrying now wouldn't rip and, as they headed toward the apartment, she was wondering how to conjure a *charme d'intensité* to keep the plastic whole until she could drop them all on the kitchen counter with a sigh of relief.

"I can't believe we have to go to work tomorrow," Sayblee said, as they unloaded the groceries and stocked the cupboards. "And I can't believe I even said that. One summer home from Bampton, I found a job at an ice-cream parlor. My mother thought it would be a good place for me to work, to learn to fit in with *Moyenne,* and it was also an easy place to cool my palms. Whenever a customer stepped on my last nerve, I just opened the freezer and stuck my hands in."

"I'm sure people wondered why their cones melted so quickly," Felix said. "Hottest ice cream in town."

"Anyway, it was the only job I thought about going to. Now, I just go. Then, it was, well, like work."

Felix nodded. "I know what you mean. I've always—well, felt sorry for *Moyenne.* Having to do everything by hand that I can do by thought."

"We're lazy. I'm surprised there isn't some *Croyant* obesity epidemic."

"We have spells," Felix said, as he put the lettuce into the refrigerator. "We have healers. We can lose weight in two seconds."

"Is that your secret?" Sayblee teased. "You have a food/spell disorder, huh? You eat the entire contents of a store and then whip up a *charme de disaparition* and the contents of your stomach vanish?"

Felix stood up straight and patted his flat belly. "No. This is all about surfing and working out with weights. And

I don't use magic at all. Not even to keep my balance on a board. I actually can stay on all by myself."

"That I'd like to see," Sayblee said, gathering up the plastic shopping bags.

"When we get home," Felix said. "I'll take you to the beach. Better yet, I'll teach you how to surf. I think you'll be a natural."

Sayblee turned away from him and shoved packages and cans into a cupboard, her palms on fire. *When we get home.*

She swallowed, breathed out, and turned back to him. "So what's for dinner? Instant chicken on a plate? Magic pasta that flies in from Italy all by itself?"

Felix put his hands on her shoulders and, for a moment, she looked up into his eyes. What was inside his gaze? Humor? Compassion? Was he feeling sorry for her? Was he trying to be nice just to keep her mind off the mission? Was he trying to keep her distracted so she didn't think about Rasheed?

Sayblee couldn't tell what he was thinking. All day, the stillness in her mind, the lack of any input from the outside—no voices, thoughts, messages from anyone—made her realize that without magic, she didn't understand anything. There was nothing in any book that would help her figure out what to do next.

"Go take a bath," Felix said. "I'll make dinner."

"But—"

"Don't argue. It might be the last time I do. After tomorrow, I could be off food for life."

"To the mission," Felix said, raising his glass of Pouilly-Fuisse. The candlelight shone in the burgundy liquid, the sound of their glasses clinking was almost like a bell in the darkened apartment.

"To the mission," Sayblee said. She brought the glass to her lips and sipped. She felt how serious her expression was and, while trying to keep a serious look, Sayblee put down her glass and looked at her plate, keeping a laugh inside her mouth. She couldn't believe the scene. She'd come out from her bath in her robe, her long hair combed but still wet, to find Felix had made a dinner of green salad, bread, cheese, and olives. The lights were turned off, the entire apartment was illuminated with white tapered candles he must have bought at Casino.

With the wine and the music on low, she almost laughed then, and now she could barely contain herself. What was this? Some kind of sad seduction scene? Was the compassion she'd seen in his gaze really a mask for a good-old go for sex? This was, she realized—finally able to figure out something without magic—how he moved.

"What?" he asked, putting down his fork. "What's so funny?"

"Nothing." She burst out laughing.

"What?" Felix sat back and crossed his arms.

"It's nothing, really. I'm just tired," she said, spearing a cherry tomato and popping it in her mouth.

Felix stared at her, silent, waiting.

"Oh," she said. "It's just this." She waved her hands, indicating the dark apartment, the intimate café-style table, everything.

"Dinner is funny." He still had his arms crossed.

"No, you. The sort of . . . the whole scene."

Felix raised his eyebrows but didn't say anything. Sayblee felt herself blush, her palms twitch, her heart pound. She had a feeling she'd have to jump up and run for the kitchen sink and the faucet any minute.

"I mean, dinner is great. Thank you."

He cocked his head, shrugged, and then uncrossed his arms and leaned forward, picking up his fork and starting to eat again. "So tomorrow—"

"Tomorrow," she said, and she glanced at him as he ate his salad, watching him for as long as she could without being noticed.

Again, Sayblee was in bed, awake, watching the apartments across the street. Her body was telling her all sorts of things tonight, all of which had to do with Felix. Her stomach felt full of jungle drums, the pulse steady and strong. Her fingers flicked with unmade fire; her lungs seemed small, unable to catch breath.

There's plenty of room on the fold-out bed, her body whispered. *Just go on out there. He wouldn't be surprised. Think about that little dinner party. The candles. The wine. You know he'd like it.*

Spinning on her side, Sayblee watched the light from last night turn on and then off again, twice. She leaned over and looked at her alarm clock. Three A.M.

Maybe someone was getting some action, she thought, pushing her pillow into shape. Maybe someone was having some fun.

Go on, her body said. *Just give it a try.*

Sayblee sighed, blinked, and then closed her eyes. If she was still awake in ten minutes, she'd get up and take a piece of a sleeping pill. Just enough to get her relaxed. But she remembered Sariel's words about *Moyenne* medicine, so she decided to try her technique from the night before. Getting comfortable, she promised herself she wouldn't think another thought. She would keep her mind completely blank, open, clear. No ideas or images or whispers from her body. Nothing. Not another thought.

In her dream, Felix was sitting on the side of her bed, stroking her hair with his hand.

"I wish you'd come into the living room. Wake up and

walk to my bed. Push back the covers. Slide in. That way, I would know you really want me, that way, I wouldn't have to guess."

"Of course I want you," Sayblee said, pushing herself up and touching his knee, his thigh. His skin under her hand was warm, firm, soft.

"Laughing at me is a terrible way to show it."

He leaned over her and, for the first time since she whirled into his Hilo house, Sayblee allowed herself to breathe in deeply, to taste the pineapple and coconut and ocean breeze of him, to put her hands on his shoulders, his face, to run her hand very slowly down his hair.

Felix laughed, pulled her closer, and kissed her softly on the cheek, his breath like night. "Making fun of my dinner. When I tried so hard to please you."

"I didn't know what you were thinking. I never have," she said, but, finally, her body was able to do what it had wanted for two nights. For longer than that. Since forever.

She relaxed, and he slowly moved closer to her, his lips just above hers.

"I have no magic," she said just before he kissed her.

"Oh, yes, you do," he said. "Believe me."

And then he kissed her again, and again, until Sayblee realized that she was dreaming and there was nothing in the room but the lightening sky and stillness.

Chapter Four

Felix's fifth customer of the day left the *boucherie* with a strangely wrapped chicken and a perplexed look.

"*Au revoir,*" Felix called out, sighing. He turned to the sink behind the counter and slowly washed his hands in warm water and soap. What was he going to do? How was he going to get through this? The only thing he was good at here was smiling. The customers seemed happy until he grabbed a chicken or lamp chop and stared at it.

Felix turned off the water and dried his hands before picking up his knife, waiting for the next customer. He'd been on the job for four days, and only today had Jean-Noël allowed him behind the case, but only to sell chickens and chops. Nothing too fancy. No roasts or duck.

"Maybe next week you are ready for the full job," Jean-Noël said, his hands on his hips as he looked at Felix's work on two chickens. Felix could tell that his new boss had no idea why he'd taken on Felix as an employee. And, obviously, there was no way Felix could explain to Jean-Noël that he'd been enchanted weeks ago and promised a complete stranger to hire Felix enthusiastically and on the spot.

So here he was. Felix felt like some sort of cliché. He wasn't exactly sure what cliché he was, though, some kind of French food dude, wrapped in a white apron, wearing a little white hat, holding a sharpened cleaver in one hand and a towel in the other. He felt like he should amplify his French accent, making it completely over the top, and start flinging food around the small boucherie as he yelled out commands and disdain. On the other hand, he felt creepy. Wasn't there a French movie about a butcher, a man who killed a young woman? He shuddered, looking down the long line of animal flesh in the case. Actually, the French did a nicer job with their dead animals than most of the butchers did in the United States, the meat resting artistically on the white paper that lined the case, parsley interspersed in between the sections. And the meat itself came from smaller producers, the beef and chicken and even pork free range. *So*, Felix thought, *Californian*.

"*Ca va?*"

Felix turned to Jean-Noël, nodding. "Yes. Thanks. I think I've almost got the chicken-wrapping thing down."

"I see," Jean-Noël said in a tone that suggested anything but clarity, his business instincts straining against the magic that kept him from firing Felix *tout de suite*.

"I'll come back early from lunch to practice again," Felix said. "I'll keep at it until everything is completely *parfait*."

"Very well," Jean-Noël said, sighing and going to the back room. As he left he said, "Make sure you ring the bell when someone comes in."

Felix shook his head. He wasn't ready to be alone with a customer. That was clear enough. And until he figured out his job, he wasn't going to be much of a spy. For all he knew, every customer that had come in so far was a Quain follower. Felix was too busy freaking out about how to tuck each roaster's legs together and then tie it all up with string to notice if a customer was wearing an "I Love Quain" button. Meanwhile, the *Croyant* world could be falling down all around him because of hard-to-tie chicken wings.

He walked to the front of the store and looked across the

street to the *parfumerie*. Bending down a little, he could just see Sayblee inside the store. She was talking to a woman, pointing to something. Then they both moved to a case, and there Sayblee was dabbing some fragrance on the woman's wrist. He could almost hear her, the way she would enchant the woman with words.

"Oh, Madame! This fragrance reminds me of the oranges from Persia."

She would stare into the woman's eyes earnestly, nodding, showing the woman with her gaze how she needed to smell like citrus and cinnamon. The woman would bring her wrist to her nose, close her eyes, and breathe in deeply, smelling orange groves in Babylon.

Felix watched the sale play out, the woman and Sayblee moving back to the register, both of them laughing. He stood up, and pictured Sayblee's blue eyes, eyes the color of . . . the color of . . . Well, all Felix could think of were the waves in Hilo, how they sometimes looked when the weather was calm and the sun came from behind a cloud and struck the water just so. Aqua with a hint of the deepest blue, a cold current in an ocean of warm.

A woman walked into the store, ignored Felix's *bonjour,* and Felix sighed, hitting the bell. Jean-Noël came immediately out from the back room, and he and the woman began a long, detailed conversation about the exact and perfect marbling of a pork roast.

Felix crossed his arms and listened for a while, but then his mind began to wander. The past few nights, he had been dreaming about Sayblee. At first, he thought he was dreaming about her because he was on a woman diet, forced into fake coupledom and thus celibacy because of the mission. So the dreams were only diversions. But as the plot lines became more intense, Felix started to wonder. In the beginning, the dreams were innocent enough. A kiss or two, the fantasy ending just as the sun came up.

But last night. Oh, last night! As Felix pretended to listen to Jean-Noël, he let the dream open in his mind, just a bit. It wouldn't serve to let it play out all the way because then— well, he couldn't stand behind the counter at a *boucherie* in a state of arousal. The pork-marbling woman would be scandalized or, even worse, excited. The *boucherie* would end up with customers for a whole different reason.

So he let himself think of the end of the dream. Just the end, the part where he pulled out of Sayblee's warmth and held her tight against his chest, kissing her forehead, her soft hair spread out all around them. Her body felt so good against his, her long, smooth arms and legs wrapped around him tight. He could still see her gazing up at him, her eyes wide. In the dream, she'd allowed herself to let go, to let down her defenses, that steel wall he'd felt from the minute he'd walked into his living room in Hilo and found her standing there, her arms crossed. In his imagination, she wasn't sarcastic or cold or abrupt. She wasn't irritated with him or scared of him or worried that she'd said something wrong. She didn't tease him or laugh at him. Her palms weren't itching with the fire she longed to burn him with. No. She was completely with him, the whole dream, her movements matching his, her breath against his ear, her voice saying only "Yes."

Felix sighed, loudly enough for both Jean-Noël and the woman to turn to him. He blushed, and turned away, picking up a towel and cleaning the glass over the steaks. That was it. No more thinking about the dreams. He couldn't think about them during the day, especially when he was around Sayblee. What he needed to focus on was chickens. Picking out the plumpest ones, tying them up neatly, and selling them to everyone who came in. Chickens all day and, if he was lucky, Sayblee all night, at least in his dreams.

* * *

"I know I waited on *Croyant* today. I know it!" Sayblee said. She looked at him, her eyes thoughtful and dark blue in the shade of the large park oak. Every time she moved an arm or pushed her hair behind her shoulder, Felix was hit with a waft of fragrance, flowers and spices and fruit. He held back a sneeze, rubbing his nose and turning away, taking in a deep breath.

"This woman came in for a bottle of *J'Adore*. Or maybe it was *par Amour*. Or *Addict*. Anyway, I can't remember. She seemed so confused about the order of buying something. She wanted to pay before she even smelled the fragrance. She reminded me of you on the Métro. Sort of clueless."

His sneeze in check, Felix put down his sandwich on his napkin and stared at Sayblee, who was now smiling. "Very nice words."

"Well," Sayblee said. "You were having some difficulty navigating *Moyenne* terrain. But I'd say you are improved."

"I haven't been fired, have I? I am still very gainfully employed, thank you very much."

Sayblee laughed. "You can't be fired with such a strong spell on your employer. You could burn down the whole place and he'd keep you on the payroll."

"So, about this woman," Felix said, ignoring her comments and plucking a big green olive from the container. "Do you think she's with Quain?"

She picked up a strawberry and popped it in her mouth. Felix tried not to stare at her lips as she chewed, but he thought of last night's dream, what those lips had done to him and his body. The way she'd taken him in her mouth.

"So, do you think?" she asked, and Felix blinked, choked a little on his olive, swallowed. He looked down at his sandwich.

"Huh?"

"Pay attention," she said impatiently. "Listen. Now, should

I try to befriend her if she comes in again? I keep thinking about that apartment across the street and the light going on and off."

"If she's one of the couples the Council has set up, you could be interfering with her attempts at being normal. Maybe yesterday was her day off, and she thought she'd try her hand at shopping. So just keep an eye on her. If she starts walking around with a man who doesn't seem to know how to buy a parking ticket from the *horodateur*, then you know they're on our side." Felix felt his blood calm, and he picked up his sandwich and took a bite, staring at a woman walking a little white dog along the path in front of the bench he and Sayblee sat on.

"Won't Quain's people be trying to live, too?" she asked. "How will we tell them apart?"

"They can do magic," Felix said. "They don't need to buy *J'Adore* at a counter. They can conjure it up."

"Of course," Sayblee said, flushing. "I'm just—I just want to start building up information. I don't want to waste any time. I think I'm going to have to go and check out that apartment tonight. I want to see what's going on there. Every night at three, there goes the light. Off and then on."

"If you are up at three every morning, I take it you're not sleeping very well?" he asked, his dream unfolding again in front of him.

"No, no," she said, her voice a bit higher than before. "No. It's—I'm still so jet-lagged. I can't seem to get back on schedule. And I'm having these weird . . . I'm having dreams."

Sayblee turned away from him a little, looking out over the small park at the end of the Square Denys-Bülher. For an instant, Felix hoped that she and he were actually having the lovely sex they were having in his dreams, meeting in the gray together. Or making some kind of alternative apartment with a spell. These things were possible.

Rufus told him the whole story of what had happened with him and Fabia, both of them cast into a spell by Kallisto during their battle and thrown onto a deserted tropical island. At first they were separated by some kind of weird time/place disturbance, both on the same island but not at the same time or space, but eventually, they found their way together through their imagination.

However, Felix knew that a magic island or a shared dream was impossible because neither he nor Sayblee had the ability to do magic right now, stripped of their spells and abilities entirely, all their magic completely buried. And in Rufus's case, someone else had created the island. No one was creating anything for Felix and Sayblee, the entire 7th *Arrondissement* a magic no-fly zone.

"What kind of dreams?" he asked, his skin pricking as he asked.

Sayblee waved her hand, her face still turned from his, but he could see her blush on her neck. "Nothing, really. I think it's because I'm so tired. I probably should take one of those pills Sariel thinks are poison."

"No," Felix said, too loudly. "I mean, don't. They *are* poison."

He didn't know what he was doing or saying. Who cared if she fell into a deep, dreamless sleep? He could still have his own dreams, couldn't he? And he wasn't even sure she was dreaming about him. Probably, she was creating some kind of story about the apartment across the street. Or she was creating a scenario where she was able to save her brother in some way. To at least find him. To bring him home. This wasn't magic. These dreams were just their minds throwing off daily thoughts. *Brain garbage,* his mother used to say when he had a frightening dream. All that was going on here was that he was missing his women. He was, well, just ready for some woman flesh. And Sayblee was there every day, right in front of him, with her lovely ass and breasts and bright blue eyes and her—Felix shook his head.

"I'll go with you," he said quickly, looking down at his mostly uneaten sandwich.

"To the apartment?"

"Yes. Tonight. Set your alarm for two, and we'll go check it out." Felix stood up and began packing up his sandwich and the remaining olives.

"Where are you going? You're not even done eating," she said, looking up at him the same way she had in his dream, her eyes wide and full and waiting.

But Felix had to go. All he wanted right now was to get away from her. To stop thinking about her.

"I promised Jean-Noël that I'd come back early from lunch and practice on the chickens. I have some, well, issues."

"Practice?" she asked.

And Felix knew he couldn't tell her he was all thumbs when it came to tying up chickens. He wasn't all thumbs when it came to other things. That he could have corroborated by many women. He wanted to tell her how his hands had touched her body all last night. In fact, he wanted to give her a little demonstration right now, in the park, bringing her toward him and kissing her, pressing her body against his, feeling her breasts, her hips, her thighs. But instead, he grabbed his bag and said, "Bye," walking back, almost running, to the *boucherie*.

Felix yawned, leaning against the apartment building, waiting for Sayblee to lock the door. It was 2:00 in the morning, Sayblee shaking his shoulder just as a dream he'd been having slipped away from him. He'd been trying to pull it back, almost able to recreate the softness of Sayblee's smooth face against his palms, when there she was, leaning over him, whispering for him to wake up.

He yawned again, and then stood up straight as she put the keys in her pocket. "So, did you see the light go on?"

"Shhh," she whispered. "No."

Felix put his hands in his jeans pockets and followed her across the street. Paris was still slightly awake, taxis periodically hurtling down the *avenue Bosquet*. A siren blared in the distance. A block over, a dog barked twice. In an apartment somewhere, a telephone rang, the loud whine of the wireless ring cutting through the relative silence. But there was no one walking on the street, and a light breeze blew cool, late-spring air around them. Felix shivered, wished he'd brought a jacket or that Sayblee would turn around, forget her mission, and let him hold her. She would warm him up in an instant.

Felix shrugged. *The dream's over, Bro,* he could hear Rufus say.

Get a life, he could hear Sariel add.

Once on the other side of the street, Felix and Sayblee stood next to the doorway, staring at the three brass locks that glinted in the dim streetlight.

"So how are we going to get up there?" Felix asked. "We don't have a *charme de libérer*. We can't just incant *Ouvrir* and expect the lock to open. I, personally, have never had to break into a house."

"No," Sayblee said, her voice a slight hiss. "You are let in wherever you go, aren't you?"

"Don't be nasty."

"Well, it's true. Anyway, I have a lock-picking kit."

"You brought a lock-picking kit with you?"

Sayblee nodded. "I thought it might come in handy."

"So you are just going to pick the lock right here on the street? Don't you ever watch *Moyenne* television? Burglars usually dress all in black, wear little black-knit hats, and slink around like cats. They actually call them cat burglars. I'm not kidding you. Sometimes they are successful, but usually all sorts of alarms go off or they are snared in laser beam sensors, and they are caught, thrown into jail, and can't post bail. They rot in prison, sleeping next to large, beefy characters, who have more on their minds than sleep. I should also remind you that you are wearing a bright blue sweater. Easy for a *gendarme* to notice."

Sayblee crossed her arms and stared at him, her eyes unblinking. "I have been practicing, you know."

"When?"

"Oh, for goodness sake!" she said, her whisper turning into a slight yell. She shook her head and lowered her voice. "Listen, I can do this. I just need you to keep watch, okay?"

"Okay. Go for it, my little cat burglar."

Sayblee sighed and shook her head a little as she stared at him, but then she took the kit from her pocket and turned back to the locks on the door. Felix stepped out to the edge of the sidewalk and looked toward the *avenue Bosquet* and then toward the *rue Cler*. He wasn't sure what would happen if he and Sayblee were arrested. Maybe Adalbert and the Council were keeping a magical eye on them somehow and would whisk them out of their cells with a spell, but since the visit from Brennus and Philomel, life had become so ordinary, so average—if it wasn't for the dreams, the chickens would be driving him crazy.

Felix turned to take a look at what Sayblee was doing and then turned away, knowing he would start looking at her rather than watching out for predawn pedestrians. He could imagine her hands, the long, slender but strong fingers. Oh, how she touched him, her palm moving up and down his back, over his—

"*Voilà! Ici!*" Sayblee said.

Felix turned quickly and moved toward her and watched the door click open, the tumblers all working free.

"Very impressive," Felix said. "Perfume is not challenging enough for you."

Sayblee put the kit back in her pocket and took his arm. "Come on. It's about the time the light starts going on and off."

Closing the door lightly behind them, they walked down a long, narrow corridor and then started walking up a flight of stairs.

"What floor?"

"I was thinking it's the third or the fourth, depending which way you count it."

"So, third or fourth?" Felix asked. "You know the French have a whole different system. So it might even be the fourth or fifth."

"Just follow me," Sayblee said, and Felix smiled as he stepped in behind her. If he reached out, he could just touch her lovely ass. He knew that Sayblee had been staring at his posterior as they walked up the Eiffel Tower. She turned bright red when he turned around suddenly and caught her, and then for the rest of the day, she'd looked at him carefully from the corner of her eye. But if he reached out now, when she was so intent on finding out who was turning on and off the light? He'd get knocked down the stairs for his efforts. So he dropped his gaze and focused on his feet, careful to make silent steps as he walked up to the apartment with the flickering light.

They made it to the fourth-floor landing. Sayblee turned to him, her eyes intent. She nodded, grabbed his arm, and they walked down the hallway. She seemed to be counting off apartment doors and, then, when they reached the fifth door, she pointed, mouthing, "This one."

Felix knew that with magic, all he'd have to do is send his thoughts under the door, into the rooms, searching out for the person working the light switch. He could have managed this from his bed, finding out in short order that a six-year-old with a sleep disorder was trying to get his parents' attention every night. The kid was just bored out of his mind and wanted his mother to come read him *Casse-Noisette* or *L'oiseau de feu* for the hundredth time. In a second, all of this could be over. But now? Felix scratched his head and lifted his hands in a "what now?" move.

Sayblee pulled him to the sixth door, and then brought her mouth close to his ear. "This apartment is vacant."

"How do you know?"

"I've been watching. No one in or out. We go in here, out on the balcony. Or there might be a connecting door. Or the walls are thin."

Felix sighed. "Fine," he whispered, and then he pointed to her pocket. "Start picking the lock. Use your amazing cat powers."

Sayblee rolled her eyes and took out her kit, but as she leaned over the doorknob, the door creaked, shuddered, and then opened on its own.

Felix felt the movement in his chest, in the raised hair on the back of his neck. That, he knew, was too easy; it was too cheesy, in a horror-movie way. Whenever a door opened like that in a movie, the killer/monster/ghost/psychopath was just inside, waiting for the stupid B-actors to come and get what they deserved. And, of course, what did the hapless characters do? They walked in, making sure not to turn on the light. He grabbed Sayblee's shoulder.

"All right," he said. "That's enough."

"Someone just left it open," she said. "An estate agent was showing the place, I would suppose."

"Sayblee," Felix said. "Aren't we here looking for Quain supporters? Why would the obvious answer be the likely one?"

"It's just a vacant apartment."

"Listen, if you really—" he began, a bit loudly.

"Shhh," she said, moving forward. He kept his hand on her shoulder and pulled her back again.

"If this light is bothering you, I'll find a way to contact Adalbert. Or Brennus. I'll take the TGV to Provence or even Italy and kindle up the magic and put out an all points bulletin. But we are not going in that apartment."

"We are." She tried to shake off his hand. "Or I am. You can't . . . You aren't—"

"I should be," he said.

"What?"

"The boss of you," he said.

"I don't need a boss. I mean, I don't need anyone telling me what to do. I can take care of myself. I always have." She grabbed his hand, almost getting free, so he slipped his other arm around her waist and pulled her to him. He could feel her heart pounding, her body a rhythm of excitement and fear. She smelled and felt so familiar, the moves of his dream between them somehow, like a shared memory. But how? It didn't matter now, though. He had to stop her.

"I'm not letting you do this. Remember, I'm the one who's been knocked out of his mind twice by Quain. I know what I'm talking about. This looks too easy."

"But the light going on and off!"

"It's probably nothing. You're just anxious for something to happen right now. Well, trust me, something will happen. Just not this."

"Just not what?" a man said. Both Felix and Sayblee turned, to look at a man standing in front of the fifth apartment door. He wore a bathrobe and strange pink slippers that must belong to a woman—not only because of the large yellow flowers on each toe, but because his heels hung over the edge. His dark hair flopped in a messy tangle over his eyes, and he yawned once and then again, stifling the sound.

Felix stood straight. "So sorry to have disturbed you.

My—my wife wanted to see this apartment. But I don't think it's the time. Clearly. A little late, wouldn't you say?"

"How did you get up here?" the man asked, yawning after he spoke.

"It was open," Sayblee said a bit too quickly. "I heard from a friend that it was vacant, and I wanted . . . I wanted . . . "

"To hear what the street noise was like at night. But I told her, you know, that we could arrange it with the real estate agent. I'm sure people ask that kind of question all the time. How many cars go by—what is the café scene like. You know." Felix felt his words overtake him, almost as if he was in a spell, the lie becoming a story he could see. "But she insisted. I couldn't get her to stay home. So here we are."

The man shook his head. "The only noise around here comes from our new baby. Two weeks old. And the reason I heard you was because she wakes up about this time every night. That might turn you off from this place more than anything."

"The good news is that babies grow up," Felix said. "They eventually sleep through the night. Traffic tends to stay the same. Don't you think?"

"Good point," said the man, yawning again. But even knowing their story, he didn't go back into his apartment. He finished his yawn and then stood a bit straighter, and crossed his arms. He began to tap his left foot, the yellow flower jiggling.

"We'll call the agent tomorrow," Felix said, pulling Sayblee gently away from the door. Sayblee was compliant, finally, letting him take her down the hall past the man. "I'm sure she can give us the information in a way that won't disturb anyone."

The man nodded, pushed his hair off his forehead, watching them carefully, his eyes dark and intense, taking in everything. As they walked by, Felix realized that he was holding himself taut, rigid, closed, his magic pushed so deep inside him that he wondered if he would be able to find it later. He hoped Sayblee was doing the same thing, but he couldn't warn her or tell her anything except through the tightening grip on her arm.

"Good night," Felix said. "Again, our apologies. I hope you get some sleep tonight. You and your baby."

"Thank you," the man said. Felix waited for the sound of the man's apartment door closing, but it didn't come. It took all he had not to look back.

Together, he and Sayblee walked down the hall, into the stairwell, and quickly padded down the stairs until they were out the door and standing on the street. Felix took in a deep breath and took her arm again as they crossed the road to their apartment building.

"I guess you were right," Sayblee said. "Nothing but a baby waking the parents up. That's what the light was all about."

Felix took the keys from her, opened the door, and almost pushed her into the foyer. He put his hands on her shoulders and looked at her. "No," he said. "You were right. There's something wrong there. I could feel it without my magic. We're going to have to go back tomorrow night."

She stared at him, looking up at him with surprise, and without thinking another thought, Felix bent down and kissed her.

Chapter Five

Sayblee had always imagined what Felix would taste like, would feel like. Her dreams had given her a bigger clue, shown her his whole, lovely body, let her feel what they would be like together. And now, in the real, waking world, she knew she hadn't been wrong one bit. In fact, she'd underestimated everything. He tasted sweet, salty, lovely. His shoulders were hard and strong under her hands. His lips were soft and smooth, asking her questions, which she answered by opening her mouth a little, just enough for their tongues to touch.

May I? he seemed to ask.

Oh, yes, she answered back, putting her hand around his neck and bringing him closer to her. She breathed in his warm skin, the ocean that had seemingly followed him from Hilo, the tart smell of pineapple, the tang of dark rum.

She allowed herself to bring her fingers through his thick, soft hair, loving the texture, the feel of it under her palms.

She had never kissed a man without being able to slide into his mind, and now, only her body and mouth giving her impressions, she felt blank, every sensation new somehow, this kiss painting a picture she would remember forever. There was the first stroke, his hands on her back, pressing her to him; next was her neck tilting up, letting their tongues meet more fully; finally, the line of energy running from the thoughts in her head to the desire in her belly, so much instant heat, she almost felt embarrassed, knowing she was wet the moment he first bent toward her.

"Sayblee," he whispered, and she knew she had to feel more of him. She ran her hands down his back and slipped them under his shirt. Oh, she almost could feel his tan line, he was so warm, and she stretched out her fingers, touching his soft skin, his hard body, feeling him pulse under her palms. She let her fingers run down the column of his spine, feeling the smooth pearls of bones under her fingertips, letting her hands fan out along the arches of ribs, slide down till she could feel the beginning of his fabulous ass, the one she had stared at all those many *up, up, up* stairs of the Eiffel Tower. She ran her fingers along the edge of his waistband, loving how his body shook slightly to her touch.

She heard Felix's slight moan in her own mouth, her body beating out a rhythm along with his. He brought his hands down to her rear, pulling her in a sudden tug to him, and she felt his erection rub her in just about the perfect spot.

If they had their magic, they could whisk to her bed through matter, naked already, and she wasn't sure how she would manage to let go of him now, waste the time it would take to get upstairs, into the apartment, and undressed.

Felix brought his lips, his tongue to her neck, and whispered, "You smell so good."

Sayblee smiled, leaned her head back, but then something started to bother her, pulled at her memory, yanked at her thoughts. She opened her eyes, straightened up, her hands falling away from his back. She smelled so good? Where had she heard that before? It wasn't a line she remembered from the few men she'd dated and the fewer still she'd slept with. *Smell so good? Smell so good! Smell so good?*

Then she remembered the pink bra dangling on the arm of the couch, her search for the imagined thong on the carpet, the giggles from underneath the bedroom door. She could almost taste the sugar and rum, feel the warm breeze coming in from the window. That was it. The woman in Hilo. Felix's seductive line to her. *You smell so good. I can't breathe enough of you in.*

"Oh," Sayblee said, putting her hands on his shoulders, pushing. "No! Enough!"

"What?" he asked, his voice against her neck.

"Stop," she said. "I can't believe I'm this stupid. God!"

Felix stepped back, his face still full of their kissing, blissed out, eyes half-closed. "Stupid?"

"I can't believe—I'm not going to let you do some one-stop shopping with me." She pushed again and walked past him and up the stairs. "I'm not a *supermarché.*"

"Sayblee, wait. I don't know what you mean," Felix said, following her as she clomped up the staircase.

"Revolving door? In and out? I know all about your system. Everyone does. It's common knowledge. People actually talk about it, Felix."

Felix didn't say anything until they were at their door. Sayblee checked her pockets, but then remembered Felix had the keys.

"I'm so stupid," she repeated, turning to him slowly, scared to take a tempting glance at him.

"No, you're not stupid. Not at all. Let me explain—"

"No. I don't want to hear it now. Let's just go inside and forget about this. We have work tomorrow and then we'll do whatever you think we should do tomorrow night about the apartment."

"Sayblee," he said softly. "It's diff—"

"Don't *even.*" She held up a hand and then breathed in and forced herself to look him directly in his wonderful almost-green eyes. "Look, we have to work together. We can't get involved like this. It will confuse things."

"How can it confuse things? It will help things make

more sense. I know what you've been thinking about me. About us."

Sayblee opened her mouth, her tongue heavy with words and surprise. He was so . . . so conceited. That was it, the word the girls at Bampton always said just before they went behind the dormitories and kissed him . "Felix is so conceited," they'd say, coming back hours later with red lips and messy hair. But then Sayblee had a worse thought.

"You haven't been using magic, have you? You haven't been letting yourself into my thoughts?"

"No, of course not," he said, moving a little closer to her, enough so that she could breathe him in again, almost taste the salt and rum of his skin.

She pressed her back against the apartment door, wishing she could use a *charme de faiblir* to break herself into pieces and press through into the living room on the other side. It was unbearable to stand here so close and not desire him, not to want the energy and passion she'd just experienced. She pressed her hands against her sides to keep herself from touching his face as well as to stop the tingling she was beginning to feel inside her, the clue that always led to fire. Her palms twitched with flame.

"Because if you do—if you have used magic," she said, her voice low, "Quain could find us. It's like a beacon. You know that. And he can't capture me. Not until I find my brother."

"I know that. I do." He looked at her without blinking. "And you have to know that this time it's diff—"

"No!" she said loudly, looking down the hall as if she could catch her sound and pull it back. Her fingertips began to tingle, and she pressed them hard against her sides, willing the fire down, back, inside.

"Sayblee."

"Let me in. I want to go to bed. I have a lot to do tomorrow."

"Sayblee," he said, his voice low and soft and warm.

"Now, now, now!" she said, loud again. Felix shook his head and sighed, pulling the keys from his back pocket.

"All right." He put the key in the lock and pushed open the door, waiting for Sayblee to go in before he did.

She didn't turn to look at him, and walked right into her room and closed the door, leaning back on it with an enormous sigh and closing her eyes. For a moment, she thought he was going to come to her—his footsteps on the floor outside her door—but then they faded, and she heard the bathroom door close and then the sound of running water.

Sayblee shook her head and pushed off from the door, walking to the window. Across the street, the man's apartment was lit up, and she saw a shadow on the wall, moving back and forth. He was walking his baby, back and forth, comforting his child back to sleep. It all made sense, no matter what Felix picked up as they left. What harm could a man who wore his wife's slippers pose to *Croyant* life?

Turning back to her bed, she sat on the edge and then lay back, her eyes open. Her heart beat out a wild pattern, two beats when there should be one, a *bam, bam, bambam.* Then it seemed to stop for too long before it beat in a triple rhythm, a *bambambam.* Why had she moved into his arms? She'd told Miranda once that she wouldn't touch Felix with a ten-foot pole, and she should have listened to her earlier self. If she had her magic, she could go back to her earlier self and warn her about this very night. She could whisper in her younger version's ear and say, "Just say no!"

But, oh, his lips! And his arms, so strong and tight around her. She'd never felt the way she had for five minutes in Felix's arms with any other man, even those she'd gone out with for months or years. Not Raúl, the *sorcier* from Madrid. Not Billy, the taxi driver from Bristol. Not even Edmund, her sweetie from Bampton, who laughed when she burned things to a crisp. Not Cyril, who had been there for her so completely in the time after Rasheed betrayed everyone. No one. That five minutes with Felix had given her the most pleasure she'd ever had, save for the dreams she'd been having. But those were Felix, too.

"Oh, no," she said, turning on her side, her hand under her cheek, and she stared at the wall, watching the light move across the plaster, until she finally fell asleep.

The dream picked up where the action had stopped in the apartment foyer, but now Felix and Sayblee were in her bed, naked, Felix hard and deep inside of her. They kissed and then their mouths parted, moving toward other flesh: necks, chests, ears. For a second as they moved together, she wondered if, in fact, this was happening. What was so dream-like about this dream? Nothing weird was happening. No one from her past sat in a corner smoking a pipe. Neither her father nor Adalbert nor even Brennus was lecturing her on the appropriate use of magic, imploring her to hold back her fire. Her mother wasn't crying, pressing her face into a puffy dress. Her brother and she weren't running down the sidewalk, laughing. No flying lizards. No balloons. No strange chronological shifts, the scene jumping suddenly from the bedroom to the Sahara or Mt. Everest. The setting was completely real, they were real, her desire for Felix was real, and yet, she knew she was asleep. Time was slow and floaty and still, everything only this lovemaking, the bedroom an egg of light, nothing visible except the bed and Felix.

"I'm sorry I can't do this for real," she whispered, putting her arms around his shoulders.

"What's not real about this?" He bent close to her ear, biting her lobe and then sucking it slightly. Sayblee closed her eyes and put her hand on his head, feeling the softness of his hair on her palms, which were so quiet now, no tingling, no twitching, no fire. Instead, all the fire was in the center of her body, ready to burn her up and take her away in smoke and flame.

"It's a dream."

"Yes, it is," he said. "These are the best dreams I've ever had."

Sayblee brought her mouth to his, pressing her hips up, feeling him pulse inside her, loving the length of him in and out, the hardness, the passion. *Oh, yes,* she wanted to say, *this is the best dream I've ever had, too,* but she couldn't because they were kissing, and they kissed and made love until it was no longer night, and Sayblee finally woke up, the alarm an annoying cricket in her ear.

Madame and Monsieur Durant clucked when Sayblee walked into the *parfumerie* at 8:10, late, her face pink from her hot, quick shower, hair still slightly wet. She'd barely been able to drag herself out of bed, and she'd skipped breakfast entirely, not because she wasn't ravenous but because she couldn't bear to see Felix sitting at the small table. Not after last night, the real and the fake last night. Either way, she could feel her face burning as she ran to the apartment door, saying, "See you tonight. No time for lunch today," and then left, almost slamming the door behind her.

On her way to work, she'd grabbed a croissant at the *boulangerie* and a peach at the fruit stand, eating as she walked down the street. But now, she had to work, keep focused, pay attention to the business in the store and out. They were on a mission, and she couldn't forget that, not for all the lovely kisses and fabulous dreams in the world.

"My dear, do something with your hair," Madame Durant said, shaking her head, her mouth pursed in a way that made her lips look like a sea anemone. Sayblee could almost see the criticism forming in the woman's mouth before the spell she was under took over her behavior. "But. Well, of course, you look *très bien.*"

"I'll put it up, Madame. *Je désolé*" Sayblee went into the back room and hung up her purse on a hook and stared at herself in the mirror. Women who worked in Parisian shops did not look messy, not like the tourists everyone complained about but so eagerly wanted in the stores buying up French items.

"Hair," Madame Durant had explained Sayblee's first day, "should be pulled back. A chignon, *s'il vous plait*. And the clothes, well, a skirt, of course."

As she stared at herself in the mirror, Sayblee could barely recognize herself. It wasn't her wet hair or her pink skin. It was something else, something inside her that felt unleashed, freed, given permission. Allowed to come out. Fire had always given her that feeling, especially when she burned something down on purpose. In battle, fighting Kallisto or Quain, she'd felt more alive than ever, all of her energy and power let free.

Last night in the foyer and then in her dream, she'd connected her mind and her body in a way that was new. She could almost see the beating on one point in her belly, the straight, hot line that led to her mind, the burning gold current that connected everything. As she looked at her reflection, she wasn't sure she would ever be the same. And wasn't it just too bad that the man who had helped her release her feeling was Felix Valasay, the charmer from Bampton, the ne'er-do-well from all those years ago. Mr. Revolving Door, Mr. Hilo, Mr. Piña Colada himself. It wasn't safe to let him into her heart. She'd end up like the poor woman in Hilo, who probably wondered where that darling man from the gym went off to, an emotional wreck.

"That's it," she said, pulling her hair back tight and cinching it into a *chignon*. She smoothed her plain white blouse, adjusted her fashionable but ordinary black skirt. "No more Felix. Not now. Not later."

"Oh, Sayblee, *mon chéri*," Madame Durant called out.

And Sayblee looked at herself one more time. She was ready now to do business, ready to battle the one thing she'd never had to before: her own heart.

She'd looked out the window once toward the *boucherie,* seeing Felix behind the meat counter, his arms up over his head, the customer gesticulating, the boss, Jean-Noel, rushing toward them. She smiled, wished she could go over and help him with the blasted chickens, but then breathed in and stood up. If she went over to the store full of her feelings for him, the *meat counter* might take on new meaning. So she turned back to the perfume and forced herself to focus on her customers and the scents they wanted to waft.

"This smells so wonderful," she said, spritzing a thin white arm, fanning the place on the skin where the perfume had dried.

But at seven that evening, after the last of the shoppers had left the store, Sayblee knew she had to leave, even though she asked Madame Durant if she needed any help closing up.

"Oh, no," Madame Durant said, looking into the office where Monsieur Durant sat reading *Le Monde.* "It is all taken care of."

So Sayblee had to go home. There was no other choice. She didn't even have any wonderful observations to tell Felix. Nothing that would take her mind off their kiss. No interesting customers came in the store. The woman Sayblee was sure was *Croyant* didn't even walk by on her way toward other stores. No magic trickled by the windowpanes, no disturbing evidence of bad magic, no Quain spottings at all.

Sayblee waved to the Durants, said her *Bonsoirs,* and pushed out into the evening. Outside, the rue Cler was still full of people headed home, baguettes and shopping bags in one hand, cell phones in the other. Sayblee walked slowly, but even with her measured gait, she was at the apartment house in no time, staring at the door.

"*Pardon moi,*" a woman said, pressing past her to unlock the door.

"*Je vous en prie,*" Sayblee replied, sorry for being in the way, sorry she didn't know how to handle Felix or herself. Sorry that they were on a mission that she seemingly couldn't help. A man in slippers was their enemy? An on-and-off light was a sign of something gone wrong? She shook her head and followed the woman into the foyer and then walked up the stairs.

Get over yourself, she thought. *Go home. Deal.*

Sayblee took in a deep breath and let herself into her apartment. Their apartment, hers and Felix's.

The surprise inside was that Felix had started dinner, and he wasn't just cutting up a baguette and arranging cold cuts and cheese on a platter.

"Oh, no. After subduing chickens all day," he said as she stuck her head in the kitchen, "I am going to seal my victory with a perfect roasting of one."

"Have you ever roasted a chicken before?" Sayblee asked.

Felix smiled and shrugged, his eyes gleaming. "No. But I've watched Sariel do it, and Jean-Noël gave me some hints. He was worried about it, though, offering to come up to show me some tricks. But I told him, 'No way.'"

Sayblee walked over to the oven and opened the door a tiny bit, happy to note that the chicken looked fine, good, really, covered in rosemary and garlic and browning solidly in the roasting pan. She stood up and put her hands on her hips.

"Well, I'm impressed. It's a breakthrough."

Felix cocked his head, moved closer to her. For a second, everything in her body seemed to stop, and she was overwhelmed with all of him—his eyes, his scent—rum and spices, and the lemon he had squeezed on the chicken. She could almost feel his arms around her, just like last night, and she wanted to walk to him, lean against him, lift her head, and let him kiss her all the way into tomorrow. But she'd promised herself, and she closed her eyes, took a breath, and backed away, right into the counter, the wood pressing against her hips.

"I suppose so," he said, noting her movements, shrugging again, and turning back to the green beans he was trimming.

"I'm going to go get changed," Sayblee said, too quickly, pushing past him. "I know I'll need another outfit for tonight. For our spy mission."

Felix nodded but didn't turn back to her. She sighed, and left the kitchen, stopping when she noticed what she hadn't paid attention to before: the dining room table set, folded cloth napkins, candles, crystal wineglasses. He was trying, she thought. If the door was revolving, he wanted it to stop, at least for a little while. Sayblee's palms itched.

"Could you turn on some music?" Felix called from the kitchen.

And Sayblee blinked and walked into the living room. That's all she needed. Music, a wonderful soundtrack to her confusion.

"Okay," she said, flipping through the stack of CDs. She needed something harsh, long tracks to prick her brain with reminders of her promise to her reflection. The Cure. Or, if it was classical, maybe some Wagner. Or Nine Inch Nails. Or something really horrible, like that rap artist Dirty Bastard.

But all the CDs in the apartment were calm and nice, and before Sayblee went into change, she put on Norah Jones and wished for magic to block her ears, knowing that it wouldn't take much more than Norah's sweet voice to ruin everything.

*　*　*

"This was really amazing," Sayblee said, putting down her fork. On her plate were nothing but bones, a rosemary sprig, and one green bean. "You might not be doing so well at the *boucherie,* but you can roast a chicken."

"What do you mean not doing so well?" Felix sat back in his chair and crossed his arms.

She was about to say something about the scene she'd witnessed from her window, the flailing customer and Jean-Noël rushing to save the day. But Felix was looking actually hurt at her comment, so she shook her head. "I mean. Training and all. You should have seen me the first day, and today. Well, let's just say Madame Durant was not pleased with my hairstyle."

Felix smiled, the annoyingly perfect candlelight flickering in his green eyes. As he watched her, Sayblee felt an absence of air everywhere in her body—her chest, arms, legs, head. It would be easier to simply disappear than to stay one more minute with Felix in this apartment, she knew that. After tonight, she had to find a way to contact Brennus. It was only a matter of time before she burned something into cinders, alerting Quain and his followers to their whereabouts with her flare. And the dreams? What if they were some kind of magic? She knew she should ask Felix about them, but just the thought of talking about the subconscious lovemaking pushed a whirl of orangey-red shooting through her middle. Nothing was safe. Not a conversation. Not this dinner.

"When do we go?" she asked suddenly, turning to look toward the apartment building. "What's our plan?"

Felix pushed a potato wedge across his plate with his fork. "During my solitary lunch, I scoped out the apartment across the street. And I found out that there's a courtyard behind the building. And there is a flight of stairs that goes up the entire outside."

"But that wouldn't be the side the flat is on. What are you going to have us do? Climb the roof with ropes and crampons?"

Felix raised his eyebrows, and Sayblee shook her head. "Oh. Oh, no!"

"Yes. What else?" Felix asked. "It's the only way to get to the top without magic. And, there are skylights. You can see them from the top floor of our building. One smack on top of Mr. Pink Slippers's apartment."

Sayblee shook her head. "There has to be another way. We could go a bit more quietly into the hall. Not make a fuss about going into the flat."

"If what I felt is true, he'll be looking for us. We can't make the same mistake twice."

Sayblee sat back and looked at the wine, wishing she could have one more glass. If not for this idiotic idea, she could go into the living room and watch some mind-numbing television and fall asleep lulled by Sancerre and the whine of bad dialogue. Then she could wake up in the morning and search out Brennus. But this plan was ruining that lovely idea.

"Felix, really." She held out her hands, and then stopped moving, seeing how serious he was about his plan. This was no joke. He really had felt something. So that meant she would be scaling walls and clinging onto roof tiles.

"What is it?" she asked, leaning in closer, really looking at him, seeing him for who he was, outside of his sordid dating life, tropical drinks, lovely kisses, and sexy eyes. In the still part of her mind, she could find the man who had fought at her side before, who wanted to find Quain as much as she did, who had lost family, a father, to bad magic.

"It's a feeling. I suppose you could call it intuition. A gut feeling. With magic, I would have known for sure, but he made my skin crawl, right up my spine. It was all I could do not to pull you down the stairs in a hurry." Felix paused and pushed his hair away from his forehead, and as he moved, Sayblee could almost touch Felix's reaction to the man, could sense the fear.

"Maybe he's just an evil *Moyenne* man," he said. "A criminal who is lying to us about his baby so he can cook up pots of methamphetamines or traffic in teenaged girls. There are enough bad people roaming this planet, that's for sure. But I just have a feeling. I just know—"

"When do you want to go?" Sayblee asked, pushing back from the table and picking up her plate and then his.

"You're up for it?" Felix said. "Ropes and all?"

"I believe you," she said. "I always should have."

Four hours later, Sayblee was clinging to a chimney, watching Felix scale up to the roof's pitch. When he made it to the apex, he tied his rope securely around another chimney, looked back at her, signaled that he was about to toss her the second rope, and then did. This time, she managed to catch it on the first try, and she gripped tight, hoping that she wouldn't end up pulling Felix loose and thus herself. She looked behind her and then down, seeing the square of the courtyard, a cold, flat expanse of brick and cement, which would crush them both. She turned away and tried to focus on something else.

Noise swirled around her, cars and buses from the *avenue Bosquet,* airplanes headed for Charles de Gaulle overhead, voices from the street below as people headed home from late-closing cafés. The air was soft and slightly cool, flicks of wind on her cheeks. But what she felt most of all was her heart, pounding against the stairs of her ribs. She'd never known heights before. Not really. Not even the Eiffel Tower prepared her for this, the safety of the metal rails keeping her from vertigo. And with magic? Well, one thought, and she was safely on the ground.

"Sayblee," Felix said, his voice soft and invisible in the night.

She gripped the rope and turned toward Felix, noticing that from this height, she could see the Eiffel Tower perfectly, lit up and glowing in the Paris night. Too bad she wasn't just up here for sightseeing, she thought, as Felix jiggled the rope to get her complete attention.

"Come on," he whispered.

Sayblee nodded and, holding onto the rope, squeezed it tight, using her feet to push her up the tiles, grabbing on to what she could with her free hand. They'd made it all the way up the roof this way, and she wondered again how *Moyenne* managed to get anything done. Making the Eiffel Tower? Impossible. Skyscrapers? What about the pyramids and the Great Sphinx?—oh, no, she remembered. Those had been *Croyant* constructions. But the rest? All the tall and large and massive structures that involved lifting their bodies up and over and around? That was magic. Danger was everywhere, in a little tile that could be wet with dew or loose, in a rope that could fray, an arm that could weaken. Just getting to work in the morning was a miracle, battling each other in tons of steel or crammed all together in a train. How did they survive?

"Concentrate," Felix hissed. "Pay attention!"

Sayblee focused on the tiles, watching one after the other until she felt Felix grab her free arm and pull her to him.

"I made it," she said, letting herself lean against him, as if they were opposing magnets and contact with him would keep her locked and immobile. And safe.

Felix put his arm around her and, for a second, she allowed this further touch, almost forgetting she was on the very top of a building in Paris. He felt so good. He smelled so . . . well, she found herself almost saying aloud Felix's clichéd line that had infuriated her last night. But it was true. He did always smell so good, like something she could lean into forever. Maybe—Maybe he'd actually meant what he'd been saying to her. It was all she could do to keep herself from putting her nose against his neck, burrowing in, acting like the cavewoman she felt she was when next to him, pulling in his salt and spice and rum and tang. She could almost feel her tongue reach out, lick the strong line of his jaw. And what would happen? They would kiss and slip down the tiles to their death.

"Okay," Felix said, interrupting her olfactory moment. "There's the skylight."

He pointed to a flat patch of glass about seven feet away, light glowing from the flat below.

"So what's the plan?"

"We lean over and watch."

"That's it?" she asked. "We watch?"

Felix adjusted the rope in his hands, moving away from her. He tugged on it a few times, adjusting his hold, and then looked at her. "There is the possibility that Mr. Pink Slippers is just a dad walking a screaming baby, so we can't break the glass and slide down without proof. We'd blow our *Moyenne* life, spending a good few weeks in jail. Or, at least, we'd have some huge explaining to do to the gendarmes and the landlord and Mr. Pink Slippers and his angry wife. Not to mention the baby. So we'll watch. And wait."

Sayblee nodded. "All right."

Felix started to loop the second rope around her waist. "Lift your arms."

She did, biting back a smile, remembering her mother dressing her for family parties. As Felix put the rope around her, she looked up, wanting to tell the story of a particular red dress to Felix, but she caught him watching her, his eyes serious, full, wide-open, truly seeing her. In that second, neither of them seemed to breathe. Even the air stopped moving, the sounds of Paris disappearing.

"Sayblee," he said after a moment. "I'm sorry about last night."

"Sorry?" she asked, hoping he didn't mean about their kiss. Hoping he didn't mean about the dream, but, of course, he didn't know about that. "Why?"

"I wish I hadn't said the wrong thing."

She shook her head. "I—I overreacted. But I did, I do think that we can't . . . We shouldn't . . . You know."

"No," he said. "I don't."

And he bent toward her and kissed her lips, not softly like last night, but firm, strong, knowing her mouth now, the conversation between them already started. It was as if they'd shared not only that wonderful kiss but all the dream moments in bed. There was his hand behind her neck the way she liked it, there was his sigh as she ran her hand through his long, thick hair. How well she knew the feel of his lips against hers, the taste of his breath, the wisp of his eyelashes on her cheek.

Sayblee held him, pulled him to her and, for a weird second, for a moment of strange time, she actually felt them together on the bed. No, saw them. No, was on the bed. There, in her room, on the bed, together, naked, as in all the dreams. And then, just as quickly, they were pulled out, back on the roof, held together by ropes.

"Oh! Did you see that?" Sayblee pulled away, breathed in, blinked.

Felix was watching her, his mouth slightly open. "Did that really happen? Were we really there?"

Sayblee swallowed. "Yeah. We were. The room."

"Yes," Felix said. "Your room. The dreams. You."

She blinked, took a deep breath. "You've been having the dreams, too?"

"Since we got here," Felix said.

And Sayblee felt her skin flare, her palms twitch. Had it all been real? Had they really done what they had done? Had she . . . Had she? She pressed her hand against her sternum, forcing herself to speak.

"So . . . So we have been . . . We've been . . . and we've been using magic."

Felix brought his hands to her face, looked at her, silent and still. She wanted to look away but couldn't, not even when she felt the tears come. Not just because they'd managed to break the rules and endanger the mission, but because she'd done something in dream magic that she wanted to do in real life for so long, something she'd begun to think about when she was only a girl and Felix Valasay teased her in the school corridors, winking at her and giving her his killer smile as he begged her for her homework. She didn't want the fog and the forgetting and the fuzz of the dream, but Felix in the world where he was Mr. Revolving Door and he stopped the in-and-out traffic just for her. In the world where he would have had to ask her permission. Where he would have to change who he was if he wanted to be with her.

"I think it happened because I wanted you so much. I couldn't wait for the mission to end. And because you must have wanted it, too." Felix kissed her nose, her lips, her forehead, and then wiped away her tears with his thumbs. "It wouldn't have worked otherwise."

"But," Sayblee managed to say.

"No," Felix said. "Nothing has happened to the mission. No one found us. No one knows. From now on, all we have to do is be who we are—to do what we want to do without the magic. We won't need the dreams then."

"But," she said again, and Felix shook his head.

"No buts," he said, and bent down and kissed her again. And this time, they stayed on the roof, in the waking world, the place where the real magic happened. *This is real,* Sayblee thought. *I won't wake up. It's not a dream at all.*

Chapter Six

Felix could not believe that he had Sayblee Safipour's willing, sweet face between his palms, his lips pressed against hers, her body pushing toward him. After two weeks of travel and life in Paris and a lifetime of her ignoring him, he had her taste in his mouth, her smells in his nose, her soft sounds of pleasure in his ears. He couldn't get his mind around the fact that he had all this right now, here, on the tiptop of a roof. Underneath his ass, he felt a tile slip, grind against grout, slip away and slide down, hitting the chimney on its way down. Bracing himself with his legs and feet, he pulled away from Sayblee and listened, waiting for the little *clink* of sound on the stone courtyard below.

"Clink," Sayblee said, hearing it hit when he did. "We're going to fall. And at the height of pleasure. Seems very mythological."

He looked down, knowing that they had to stop this kissing. There would be much more time for this now, now that they both realized the dreams they'd been having were shared. Or had they even been dreams at all? God, when he'd awakened just this morning, hard and throbbing, her taste on his tongue, he'd thought he'd go insane. If it hadn't been for the long, hot shower, a matinee of nice memories of their kiss in the hallway, and the dream itself, and his hand, he would have busted down her bedroom door and done something he might have regretted.

Felix had managed to compose himself and be calm and collected when he went out to shop for bread, milk, and fruit before Sayblee even woke up, thinking of casual things to say to her, such as, "Incredible croissants," and, "Read the top story on the front page." But then she had run right out of the apartment, barely saying good morning. After that, even the fresh coffee seemed stale.

Felix opened his mouth, ready to say, "I've already fallen."

But he didn't say a word, knowing that Sayblee had a shit detector that scanned a hundred miles in every direction. Not that anything he was saying was shit. He knew he'd said every conceivable line at least once, and some lines more times than he could count. How could he tell her, though, that now, this time, he meant every last syllable?

"We better do what we came here for," he said. "Let's find out that absolutely nothing is going on and go home. I have some plans for you."

She looked up at him, her face free of her typical distrust of him. He didn't blame her for any of her feelings. He'd earned the Mr. Revolving Door nickname that Miranda had given him, after he once mistakenly told Sariel his theory about dating. And it wasn't that he didn't enjoy the women he'd been with. He loved them all, in the way that he could, but always there was something missing. Last year at Adalbert's house after the battle with Quain and Kallisto, he'd turned to Sayblee and seen what he'd been missing in all the other women. And it wasn't really her body, though he loved that. It was her mind and her sense of humor and her wicked comebacks. It was her voice and her literal firepower and her magic. It was just her, all of her.

But she'd refused to really even look him in the eye, leaving before he'd even had the chance to suggest they meet somewhere—Nevus, Portugal, Madrid, Rejivak—for dinner one night. *Poof!* she was off into the gray, swirling away from him, Miranda looking at him with a slight smile. What could he have done? Follow her and have her ignore him some more? So he'd gone back to Hilo and his life. And the women.

"Felix?" Sayblee asked.

"Right," Felix said, kissing her forehead and pushing a strand of fine blonde hair away from her face. He meant to kiss her lips one more time, loving how soft they were, amazed by how she opened herself to him, parted her lips, let her soft tongue touch his.

"Enough!" he said as he forced himself to move away from her lips.

Sayblee laughed. "Oh, come on. Just one more."

She ran her fingers over his bottom lip, and Felix thought of the dreams, of Sayblee's lovely body next to his, how she'd touched him on his lips, touched him everywhere. He could feel himself grow hard at the thought, and he took in a breath, and pushed himself a littler farther away from her. Swallowing, he picked up one of the ropes and then the other, pulling each to make sure they were secure. "Okay. I'm going over to the skylight and then you follow. But wait until I tell you that it's safe."

Sayblee smiled. "I don't think it's safe up here with you, and I'm not talking about the ropes."

"I have done many things in my life, but lovemaking on a rooftop rife with loose tiles is not one of them. I want to live to enjoy the experience. In fact," he said, meaning it, "I want to savor it." He winked at her and started to slowly crawl away from Sayblee, holding on tight, following the roofline as he headed toward the light, keeping the rope taut between them. As he got closer, he started to notice the light change from white to yellow, the color pulsing, as if there was a power surge in the apartment below.

"That's weird," he said.

"What?" Sayblee asked from behind him.

"The light," he said, nearing the skylight. "It's—"

Felix stopped talking and turned to Sayblee as he felt the rope go slack behind him. He wanted to tell her to stop moving, to stay put, but Sayblee was gone. He looked around, his heart starting to beat fast, but then everything around him was the same yellow as the light pulsing from inside the apartment. *Sayblee!* he called out, pulling his magic out from the box he'd hidden inside himself when they started the mission. *Where are you?*

But then everything was light, hot light, and Felix lost consciousness.

"Well," the voice said above Felix. "This is so very interesting. So very interesting indeed."

Felix tried to open his eyes, but they were just too heavy to move. He tried to open his mouth to ask the voice what in the hell it was talking about, but he was just too tired to do so. The only thing that seemed to be working in his body was his brain, but his thoughts seemed slightly distorted. He actually felt he was by a river somewhere, hearing the sound of water outside. And the air itself seemed different, not like Paris, which had been slightly humid with a light May breeze. The air around him now was crisp and hard, cutting at him with cold. He wanted to know where he was, where Sayblee was.

"You don't think we really were in Paris, do you?" The voice—Felix could now tell that it was a man's—laughed. "Oh, Adalbert is getting so old. The Council is ridiculous to keep him in power. But this just shows that it is finally my turn. After all that I have endured, it is my turn."

Felix's heart started to pound again, and he tried to open his eyes, but still he was trapped inside the silent darkness of his body. He searched around for his magic, but he couldn't find that either. He had to get out of here: his body, this place, this being stuck. He had to find Sayblee. What had this man—this man? Who was he? Trying to focus, Felix thought about the voice, reimagined his words. *My turn. My turn.* The voice. That voice. Who else? It was Quain Dalzeil. Quain was right here, talking to him. Quain knew the Council's plan. He knew everything.

"Oh, of course I know," Quain said softly, and Felix heard Quain's footsteps walking near his head, the floorboards creaking lightly as he moved. How was this possible? Felix was in a room with Quain, a cold room, seemingly so far away from Paris and from Sayblee. He tried to bring forth an image of Quain, but the only thing he could see was Quain's terrible cold eyes, black as wet dirt, reflecting no light at all. Ugly, unforgiving eyes, eyes of a man long dead to any kind of love.

"So complimentary, my dear boy. I am so pleased I've left a lasting effect on you. The last time I saw you was under very similar circumstances, I'm afraid."

Felix breathed in, tried to concentrate, taking in a lungful of air chilled by water and ice. How far had he come? Where was he? And, more importantly, where was Sayblee?

"You needn't worry so much about where you are or where your beloved is, Valasay. Valasay. Oh, how I hate that name."

Felix wished he had some power, any power, magic or otherwise. Use of his arms and legs would be a great place to start. How wonderful it would be to get close enough to Quain to deck him, send his scrawny body back against a wall. But all Felix could feel was his heart beating faster, adrenaline and involuntary muscles the only things working in his body. He was useless. He couldn't redeem himself or take his revenge. Quain killed his father. Quain needed to be punished for what he'd done to Hadrian Valasay and to thousands of others, *Croyant* and *Moyenne* alike. Look at what he'd done to Rasheed Safipour. But what could Felix do? He was no more use than a corpse. As usual. Here he was again, unconscious, powerless, worth nothing, the way he always was when fighting Quain. The only good news was that his brothers weren't here to see him like this.

"Now, calm yourself. Try to keep your knickers out of a twist," Quain said.

And Felix knew the man was reading every one of his thoughts. He tried to shut down his mind, but he couldn't find a way to shield himself from Quain's attention. He was broadcasting on a wide bandwidth, open to everyone.

"Do you think I left you any magic? It was all so simple. You really made it so easy, hiding everything away like that, putting it all in a tiny little box. Or, at least, so you thought. You and Ms. Safipour were like two pigeons, squawking about on the roof. One spell, and you were just *Moyenne*, ripe for the taking. Now we just have to go and round up all the others. They will make wonderful recruits."

Or so you thought? What did Quain mean by that?

"Oh, please. You realized it yourselves. Those sexy little dreams you were having. My, my, my. I guess routing women runs in your family. I'll never forget how your father talked about that . . ." He spit out the last word and then sighed. "Zosime. And we almost had Sariel's little peach last year. Disgusting woman."

Inside his body, Felix's veins and arteries pulsed to each of Quain's words. He knew he should calm down or he'd have a heart attack. It was as if his heart—knowing it was the only thing that could move—was trying to bust out of his body and go for Quain. His stomach flared with acid, and his head pushed out thought after thought: his father, Sayblee, Sariel, Rufus, Zosime, Miranda. Quain in the same room. Quain laughing at him.

"This is exactly what I'm trying to do to you," Quain said. "It's just too easy. You are quite the hamster in the cage. I've put you on the wheel, and you will *spin, spin, spin* away."

Quain was right. Felix was reacting to every single word. There was nothing he could do, so, instead of imagining beating Quain to a pulp with only his heart, he relaxed, focused on how his heart was still keeping him alive, focused on trying to follow his breath. He once dated a woman who dabbled briefly in Zen Buddhism, and he remembered the meditation she'd forced him into. There they'd been in his living room in Hilo sitting on these little round cushions she called zafus, breathing in incense that made him want to sneeze. After about ten minutes, his folded legs fell asleep and his back ached, but he remembered now what she'd told him.

"You don't have a mantra or anything, but just focus on your breath. In and out. In and out. You can think of the sound of breathing as so-hum if you want, but breath is all you need. That's all."

Felix had tolerated this meditation, thinking the whole time about the sex he and the woman would have later, but now, he remembered. He stashed Quain in a corner of his thoughts and breathed in and out, focusing only on his breath. Standing above him, Quain laughed at him, said something about how ridiculous he was, but Felix kept breathing and, slowly, his heart stopped racing, his blood calmed, and he felt a small measure of stillness spread over him. He had to stay calm. He had to find a way. For Sayblee.

"Oh, do try, dear boy. Do try," Quain said.

Felix ignored him, breathed in a few more times.

"Quite valiant. A remarkable achievement without magic. Bravo!"

What about Sayblee? Felix thought, releasing his breath. *Where is she?*

"Don't you worry about her. We have plans for her that

don't include you. She's rather important to our cause. You just happened to be in the way. Just like all the rest of the *Croyant* hiding out in Paris. But when I was told by my followers that you were with her, well, it just made me giddy. I thought I'd work a little magic on you before I killed you. Just for kicks."

You need me, too, Felix thought. *I can help you. I have information. I know about the plan.*

Quain laughed, a horrible, loud sound, croaky and full of sarcasm. "Really. Oh, really. You have been such a fighter, Felix Valasay. I'm sure you are the exact person Adalbert Baird would entrust with 'the plan.' The last time I saw you, you were enchanted and unconscious. Flat on the floor. Was that Kallisto or me who did that? A wonderful bit of work. In any case, I won't be needing your staunch support. Maybe if you were your older brother, Sariel, I could use you. He is one the Council would trust. Or even Rufus, perhaps. He gave me a bit of trouble a few years back. But you are just a tagalong, aren't you? Showing up when needed and not able to produce. I hope you remember all your glorious achievements as you die."

Felix almost shot out a response in a burst of thought, but then a word Quain said stopped his mind, made him hang in the small silence that followed the sentence. As he tried to hear it again, recreating the sound in his mind, something silent and cloaked moved into his thoughts, unfurling like a tiny magic carpet. He knew he was remembering something, and this something was hidden from Quain. Listening only partly to Quain's words as the man began to rant again, Felix watched as the thought opened up, and he could see Brennus Broussard, could hear him whisper, "Remember."

When Brennus had first said the word as he was leaving their Paris apartment, Felix had been confused, thinking that Brennus had lost it somehow, a man too old to be on a mission of any kind. *Finally,* Felix had thought, *retirement is on the way.* But now the memory of the word beckoned, and Felix followed it, concentrated on the sound flushing through his brain, unleashing something from him that he knew rose up and over him, a signal, a flare of thought, a vortex of energy that Quain could not see or feel or push through.

Felix followed the thought as long as he could, raising it, bolstering it, pushing it up with his hopes and with his need to find Sayblee, to make sure she was safe.

"Oh, I will be sorry to finally put you to rest," Quain was saying. "Indeed I will. I had hopes of you as a doorstop, but you do have this annoying tendency of coming back to life. But there's another thing. Yes. It has been my hope of a Valasay triptych over the mantelpiece at home. Of course, the Council took my home and my lovely stone mantel, for that matter. But I will have it back and more. Much more. And wouldn't that be a fine decoration?"

Felix wondered why Quain always talked so much before killing someone. It was his trademark show, the ramblings of a loquacious sociopath. Miranda told him how he went on and on as he was readying to kill her. But all Quain's jabber would buy Felix's rising thought some time.

What would you title the triptych? Felix thought.

"Oh, something like, 'The Sad Little Valasays.' I think it will be quite poignant." Quain chuckled, amused at his little funny.

Maybe you can get it into the Musée Croyant. *When you take over the world, I suppose you'll be in charge of everything. Museums. Banks. Mental health clinics.*

"Quite humorous. Extremely," Quain said, his voice now flat and soft, joking over. Then there were footsteps, the sound of air swirling overhead, the smell of something acrid, burnt, dangerous. "But I think I've tired of you. Time for you to go."

Felix cast about in his mind, but the unfurled spell had totally vanished, and all that was left in his head were the sounds of Quain's slow footsteps moving closer to him.

Sayblee, Felix thought. *I'm sorry.*

Quain laughed, and the moving, fetid air around Felix began to grow warm, and he could feel something leaving him slowly, his energy drained from him as if sucked out by a hose. *Very smart,* Felix thought just as he began to lose consciousness. *A charme d'évacuation,* an emptying of everything that made him who he was: memories, thoughts, ideas, feelings.

He felt dizzy, faint, his head and body filled with white light, his mind slowly sailing away into a pure field of warmth that beckoned to him. How easy it would be to just hand himself over to that airy, soft light, let himself go and not have to think about anything, all of it so meaningless, really. Here was the place he felt the best, here was where he could truly be at peace. Felix was about to let himself collapse into nothingness, his body almost weightless. But something pulled at him, nudging him ever so softly backward. And, as if from a great distance, he heard a crack, as if someone had snapped a plate of steel in two.

What could that possibly be? he thought, turning to look longingly at the lovely light, seeing the very spot he would let himself fall into. *Who cares? Who needs the sound when there's the light?*

But even as he thought that, he was yanked back into his body, his bones heavy on the cold, wood floor. Voices seemed to be right on top of him, calling out incantations. People were yelling, throwing spells through the room like javelins. Magic whirled around him, whips of heat, lashes of ice. He tried to open his eyes, but Quain's bad magic was still closing him off from what was around him, keeping him from helping whoever was trying to save him. Disgusted with himself, his only hope was that he wasn't in the way of whatever was happening. Felix was, after all, a doorstop, just as Quain had suggested.

Before he even had a chance to wonder where Quain was, Felix heard his soft, slippery laugh in the room. Then there were more cries and then a loud crash, glass falling to the hard floor. Then, in a yellow flash Felix could see through his stuck eyelids, Quain must have disappeared.

"Shit," a man said, and Felix knew the voice instantly, and he wished he wasn't a lifeless, lumpy log on the floor.

"Go after him," another voice quickly called out, and Felix prayed for magic that would allow him to simply disappear, even if it meant being frozen like this forever. As Felix should have known, they were both here. Both standing. Both with all of their magic.

Someone cracked away into matter, and then there were running footsteps as people searched the room, the rest of what must be a house, looking for clues, information, evidence. The voices trailed off, more cracks as people moved back into matter. And then the inevitable. Sariel knelt down next to Felix and put his hand on his shoulder.

"Bro," Sariel said, laughing, the sound so familiar and so damn irritating. "You look a little stiff."

"That he does," Rufus said, now kneeling at Felix's other side. "Our wee brother is taking a nap."

You both suck, Felix thought. *Get me out of this.*

"I don't know that I will," Sariel said, "if you're going to be combative."

"Aye," Rufus said. "Send him to his room. Put him in time-out."

Goddamn it, Felix thought. *Sayblee! We've got to find her.*

At that thought, neither Sariel nor Rufus said or thought another word, and Felix felt Sariel's hands on his face, his brother smelling like spice and oranges, his known healing touch too familiar from the times Felix had been enchanted or hurt. Warmth spread throughout his body, and soon the grip of Quain's magic lessened, loosened, and then released, disintegrating into the air around them. In small increments, his body came back to him, and he could feel and move his legs and arms, could feel the embarrassment creep over his face. Taking in a deep breath and blinking, Felix opened his eyes and then tried to sit up, but Sariel held him down.

"Hold on, Bro. Just give it a second." Sariel wasn't teasing now, his manner that of a true healer. Rufus stood over Sariel, looking just as worried.

Felix almost sighed, wondering when he'd ever not be the object of such concern. Together, their long dark hair hanging free, his brothers seemed like a protective tent, one Felix wanted to jump out of and run screaming from.

"I'm okay," Felix said. "I'm fine. I haven't been under that long."

Sariel didn't move his hand from Felix's shoulder, and Felix brushed it off, and sat up, ignoring the quick and sudden attack of dizziness that made the room spin like a pinwheel. He took another breath from the bottom of his lungs and rubbed his forehead, hoping that he could cover his face that had gone from blush to stark-white in about a second.

"Really. I'm all right."

Rufus bent down, and he and Sariel helped lift Felix to his feet. "You're lucky the *signe d'alerte* did just what it is supposed to. We were prepared for it ever since the mission started. We have people waiting. Lutalo and Baris and Nala are going after Quain. Brennus has already traveled to Rabley Heath to inform the Council."

Felix was relieved to hear the names of *Croyant* he knew well. Lutalo Olona, Brennus Fraser, Nala Nagode, and he had worked together before. Hopefully, this was the last time they'd have to work together to capture Quain. But he wasn't hopeful now, not after being knocked out once again.

"Yeah, going after Quain always seems to really work," Felix said, finding his balance, feeling his blood flow again. He shook his head. "How could the Council have been so wrong?"

Neither Sariel nor Rufus said anything, and Felix looked around the small, cold, empty room. It seemed to be a living room of a small house, doors leading to a kitchen one way and a dark hall the other. There was nothing that suggested that Quain and his followers had made this their headquarters. Quain certainly would have wanted something more impressive than this shack.

"Where in the hell are we?"

"Alaska," Rufus said.

"Alaska?" Felix asked.

"Haines, Alaska, to be exact," Sariel said. "A very small town. A conveniently empty house. I don't even want to know what Quain did with the owners."

Felix didn't know what to say. He'd been all over the world, but the idea that Quain had brought him to Haines, Alaska, seemed ridiculous.

"Why here?" Felix asked.

"It's your guess. Who knows why here?" Rufus said. "But we didn't ask questions when we saw the signal."

"Sayblee was there when Brennus gave me the magic. She must have had the spell, too. Did she contact you? Did you get a signal from her?"

Neither brother said anything, looking at each other and then away. Sariel waved his hand in a small circle, and three chairs appeared out of matter. Rufus and he helped Felix into one and then they both sat down, leaning their elbows on their knees.

"No," Rufus said. "She must not have taken in Brennus's magic, or Quain figured out she had it. We don't know. All we know is that Quain breached your magic, the Council's magic. The vortex. The protections. He got through, despite everything."

Felix dropped his head into his hands. "It wasn't Quain," he mumbled.

"What do you mean?" Rufus asked.

"It was me. And Sayblee. Something sort of—we were doing magic. But we didn't know," Felix said, knowing he didn't want to explain with words. So he closed his eyes and sent his brothers a quick mental movie of the dreams, leaving out the more personal bits, the thoughts that Felix still couldn't believe belonged to him, were his memories, even if they were simply figments of his imagination.

Sariel shook his head and crossed his arms, sighing loudly. Felix heard his, *You and women* loud and clear.

"Aye, lad," Rufus said. "Why didn't you figure it out? Some dreams are too good to be true. Especially all of that lot. My God—"

"Don't you think I know that?" Felix asked, sitting up and glaring at Rufus.

"Maybe you didn't want to think it was a dream," Sariel said. "Maybe this time, finally, you've found—"

"You know," Felix said, standing up, "I don't really need this shit right now. For one, Sayblee is missing, with Quain, God knows where. In danger. And, for two, it's none of your damn business. And anyway, shouldn't both of you be back on the breeding ranches you call home?"

Rufus looked at Sariel, and they both laughed. "Don't worry. Fabia and Miranda are in good hands. Mom has taken over Miranda as her new special project, not that she doesn't come to visit Fabia whenever possible, too. But she isn't as needed there, as Xanthe has all but moved in," Rufus said, sort of grumbling through the part about Fabia's mother.

Felix shook his head and stood up, walking to the window that faced the bay. The town seemed to spread out to the left of the house, small houses and buildings leading to a large commercial dock. The sun was wide and yellow in the light blue sky, the almost-aqua-colored water full of rippled sunlight. Anywhere else, Felix would have guessed it was noon, but he knew it had to be at least eight in the evening. A cruise ship sat in the water like a bath toy, ferries chugging back and forth bringing tourists back to the ship.

His magic returned to him, Felix felt strangely full, as though he'd eaten a large, heavy meal, all his abilities sinking into his body, filling his blood and bones. He closed his eyes, taking in but not really listening to his brothers' thoughts, vague worries about Felix, questions and thoughts about what to do next, images of Fabia and Miranda and their expanding bodies. From outside the house, he picked up conversations from passersby and people standing on the dock, letting their words float through and then leave his mind. How could he have all of his abilities back and not have Sayblee? She needed her magic more than he did. How could she be with Quain and his followers and not have her fire?

He turned to his brothers. "So what are we going to do? Sit around here talking about our extended family all day? What about all the other *Croyant* in Paris? They're sitting ducks."

Sariel stood up and walked to Felix. "We're going to Adalbert's. There was always the chance that something like this would happen, so there was the contingency plan. Others have alerted the group in Paris."

Rufus nodded. "We got your message in time to warn the others. So don't worry about it. It's hard to tamp down magic in the best-case scenario, and almost impossible when there is strong feeling involved. I don't think that anyone imagined in a million years that you of all people would fall in l—"

Felix put up a hand. "I just need to know that she is safe. That's all."

"Whatever you say, lad." Rufus stood and walked to his brothers, put a hand on each of their shoulders, and, within seconds, all three were whirling through matter, on their way to Rabley Heath and the safety of Adalbert Baird's house.

"My dear boy," Adalbert said when he greeted them, but for the first time that Felix could remember, Adalbert was distracted, putting his hand on Felix's shoulder quickly and moving them all toward the large lounge. Felix glanced at Adalbert as they walked and noticed that his long gray hair seemed just a bit whiter and sparser than it had been just over a year ago, his face pale, his purple robe pulled crookedly on his shoulders. Even his beard seemed off, wild sprigs of grizzled gray making his face seem in spring bloom. The Armiger of the *Croyant des Trois* was rattled by this latest development, and Felix's fear about Sayblee pulsed in his gut.

We will find her, Adalbert thought. *Don't let my rushed, late-night dressing disturb you. And, alas, the beard needs a decided trim.*

Felix blushed, but before he could send Adlabert an apologetic thought, they were all in the lounge, facing a group of Council members. Some sat in overstuffed chairs talking, others stood in huddled groups; but they all stopped their conversation when the Valasay brothers and Adlabert walked in the room.

Brennus Broussard stood up, sighing, his face dark with disgust, a look Felix was familiar with from countless reprimands, either of him or his brothers.

"We should have never allowed you to work with Sayblee Safipour. Of all the *sorciers*, we picked you," he said. "And to lose her—with her abilities Quain has likely based his plan upon her."

"Oh, lighten up," Sariel said, moving past Felix toward Brennus. "Didn't anyone in the school yard tell you that 'I told you so' is rude and completely useless. What's done is done. Let's move on."

"Why is it that I'm always having to say the words to Valasays?" Brennus asked. "If your father could see th—"

"Don't be a bajin balloon," Rufus said. "Why dwell on what's past?"

In the midst of the arguing, Adlabert thought so loudly, that Felix didn't even know what words came into his head, only that Adalbert had his attention just as he had everyone else's. The room was silent, still, empty now of anything but the crackle of the tidy fire in the fireplace and the snoring of Zeno, Adalbert's Kuvasz that slept on the rug, dreaming dog dreams.

"As usual, it seems, Quain has gotten the better of us, despite our careful planning. And it doesn't matter how or who or where. As Sariel says, why dwell on the past. Wonderful advice. What matters is that we get close enough to Quain to work the magic we so carefully created for the end of the mission," Adlabert said.

"How will that be possible now that he knows our plan?" Brennus asked.

Sariel pushed an elbow into Felix's side, thinking, *He asks the question no one else does because it's flipping stupid.*

Adlabert turned to Sariel, an eyebrow raised, and then turned back to Brennus. "Fortunately, I have a plan. Perhaps ill-conceived and potentially futile, but I do think that it will work."

And then Adalbert's thought became pictures that Felix could see, images that he'd thought about before, Quain's version of the world, *Moyenne* enslaved, *Croyant* either dead or obedient. Magic restricted for the "deserving," the syco-phants that would crowd around Quain and curry favor. So much of what Felix had always taken for granted—leisure, peace, happiness, freedom—would be gone.

The vision faded, and the Council members began to speak and think, thoughts and words flowing through the room.

Felix stepped forward, unwilling to let another second pass. "But what about Sayblee? Why would he take her? We need to find her. We need to get her out of there be-fore—"

Adalbert held up a hand, and everyone was again silent. "Yes. We do need to do all of that, and desperately. But this time, there can be no room for failure. We've been lucky be-fore that Quain was not in full power or that we've man-aged to knock out a crucial element of his plan. Kallisto. Cadeyrn Macara. But this time, as you can see, he's really working alone, in full strength, without help from any ob-jects of power or people with special abilities. Certainly, he has his helpers, but no one acting as his agent. We need to create our own elements, our own power great enough to subdue him. That will take me some time to organize."

Adalbert looked at Felix, a long, direct glance and, some-how, Felix began to relax, to calm, finally sensing the *charme de serein* sliding over him.

"Will you be with me?" Adalbert asked, his eyes first on Felix and then moving around the room. "Will you help me finally capture our enemy?"

At first there were polite murmurs, but then Rufus pushed past people and walked toward Adalbert, stopping just in front of him. "Aye. That I will." Rufus turned to look at Felix and Sariel. "That we all will."

"He's right," Brennus said, keeping his gaze carefully away from the Valasay brothers. "We will. We have no choice."

The rest of the group agreed, and then there was hand shaking and back patting and further excited discussion. But

Felix couldn't join in. He stood quietly, looking at the fire, watching the red and gold flick across the logs. All that energy was inside Sayblee. She could burn down this entire house if she wanted to, and yet Quain had her trapped. Someone laughed, Sariel began a story about his battle with Quain, and Rufus started in on Kallisto. Felix couldn't handle it. Not one more conversation. All this noise. All this wasted time. He knew that if Sariel or Rufus even started in on the babies they were expecting, he'd lose his mind. What was everyone thinking? They needed to leave now, but Adalbert was as immersed in the conversations as anyone.

Felix bolted out of the room, into the dark hallway, and leaned against the wall. He didn't understand how they could spend one more second in this house. He didn't want to do anything but get to Sayblee, wanting nothing more than to fling himself into matter, to find her, wrap her in his arms, and carry her out of danger. And maybe, just before they left, she could burn down a few things.

Felix closed his eyes and thought her a message, knowing she had no magic and would never get it. He knew Rufus would have a shit-eating grin if he could hear his thought, so Felix made sure his mind was his own. He thought as hard as he could, needing Sayblee to understand that no matter what, he was thinking of her. Wanting her. Wanting her home safe.

Chapter Seven

She had no magic. Nothing. None in the core of her body or in her arms or legs or hands or feet. No magic in her mind. As she sat blindfolded and tied up tight in the hard-backed chair, she searched around in her mind for a spell, something simple that she had learned when she was a little girl, a *charme d'apparaître*. In her bedroom, she'd whisper the words, and ladybugs and butterflies and sometimes long, wet worms would appear on her carpet. Later, she'd take the worms into her brother's room and leave them on his pillow and then wait for his surprised yell and his angry footsteps heading toward her. Behind her locked bedroom door, she'd giggle, laughing still when he whooshed in front of her, his dark hair sticking out on end from his quick jump into and out of matter.

"You little brat," he'd say.

"No, no," their mother would say later. "She's just our Wild Plum."

So this magic should come to her now. Sayblee knew how to conjure anything without even thinking, could always bring what she wanted out of nothing. But as she sat in the chair, she couldn't even find her way into the place where she kept her ideas about spells and *charmes* and incantations. Something strong was keeping her from even beginning to think about her magic, and she was so confused, she couldn't find the first magic thought to think.

So she had to rely on her *Moyenne* talents, all that she'd been working with for the past two weeks. As in the Durants' *parfumeier,* she breathed in, sniffing for essence. Unfortunately, there was no Chanel No. 5 or Joy here but instead a damp, musty wetness, like a kitchen rag that had been left damp too long. She listened, but could only hear the drip of water in a corner, *a splat, splat* on rock or concrete. Her feet were on the floor, which was hard and slightly gritty, and the only other things she could feel with her body were the chair, the magic that must be holding her arms and legs in a tight, painful grip, and the heavy, sodden air against her face.

And what was worse was that she couldn't feel her fire. All her life she'd hidden her hot, twitching palms, shoving them in her pockets before she did something she would regret. Or not, reacting before she could think, lighting fire to friends' schoolbooks or cars that sped by too quickly, forcing her to put out the flames with even more magic. From as soon as she could remember, her feelings turned into a reaction inside her, her body wanting to shoot out energy, but now, for the first time ever, there was nothing. Her body was still and calm. Slow. Empty.

She yanked again on her bonds and cried out in frustration. Sayblee felt tears pulse under her cheekbones, but then she jerked up as words hit her mind and grabbed her. For a clear second, she heard the word *Want.* And then she was sure that he'd said something else. Something lovely.

Needing to hear more, she turned her head in the darkness, certain that someone had spoken to her.

"Who's there?" she asked. "Who's talking?"

Her words hit the slick walls, slid down, and died out with hardly an echo. Someone had said something to her, directly into her left ear. A man. Him. She could still feel his cry, taste his upset, smell the pain he was in. Even though it was impossible, she swore she could hear his heart beating as he spoke to her. But if he'd been in so much pain, why had he said what he had? And who was he to talk like that to her? No one that she could remember loved her enough to cry out in the night, send her such a thought. Yet there was something familiar about him, as if he was a part of her life. But so many things were unclear to her now, her thoughts a jumble of past and present, so much smeared away as though with a clumsy schoolgirl's eraser.

Sayblee breathed in and tried to remember, focusing on his voice, his sounds, his heartbeat, but the more she thought, the less she could pull forth, and in a minute she had nothing—everything but the words was gone.

I love you.

As she thought about the words, her tears came from behind the blindfold. What amazing words. Sayblee started to sob, leaning forward, feeling the chair tilt forward as she did, the legs wobbling. Ever since Rasheed had deserted them, no one had loved her, really. Her mother had given up on her, pulling inside her cocoon of resentment and depression, no longer calling her Wild Plum or buying her dresses.

Sayblee knew she had good friends, but at the moment, she couldn't really recall who they were; there was someone with red hair who made Sayblee laugh, but it wasn't a friend's voice who spoke to her just now. The men she went out with were fine, good company, but she'd never felt what she knew lay deep inside her body and mind. She never felt what the words whispered to her by a strange voice had made her feel, the tingle of recognition of—of her other half.

I love you.

Sayblee leaned back and started to laugh into the darkness. *How sad is this?* she thought. *I'm hearing imaginary voices. I'm bound, gagged, and weeping about lost love. A love that doesn't even exist.*

It was so funny, truly pathetic, and Sayblee kept laughing quietly, laughed until she fell asleep in her chair.

"Sayblee," someone said in her right ear, and she jolted awake, blinking into the blackness of her blindfold. She took in a quick breath of the wet air, letting her lungs fill, and then she held her breath, imagining that the voice from before was speaking to her again. She thought that if she waited, the words she longed for would sail through her mind, filling her with hope, reminding her of something she'd forgotten to look for.

"No one loved you," the voice said. "No one besides me. No one ever will."

She exhaled, letting her breath out in a sudden stab, unable to believe what she was hearing.

"That's right," the voice said. "It's me."

"It can't be," Sayblee said. "You're—we thought . . ."

He didn't say anything, letting her sentence trail away. She listened, following him with her ears, hearing his quiet footsteps, the *swish, swish* of his robes.

"Take off my blindfold. Undo this magic," Sayblee said. "Please. Please. I need to see you."

He kept moving, and Sayblee imagined him walking round the room, his face thoughtful, the way he used to look before an exam at school or when he played poker, cheating as he always did at cards. She wanted to stand up and run to him, even though she knew that he was no longer the brother she knew, twisted in some horrible way by Quain.

"That's not true, my little plum. I am the same brother you knew. The same brother you grew up with."

Sayblee shook her head. "How could you be? You've

been with him for five years. You've watched him kill all those people. You just let it happen. You didn't do anything to stop it."

There was silence and then he was at her ear again. "I did it for you. And for Mother."

"How can you say that? She's never been the same! She was destroyed when you left. How can you tell me that anything you did was for her?"

As Sayblee spoke, she saw her mother lying on her bed, her hair fanned out around her head, unwashed, uncombed, her eyes vacant and uninterested in food, talk, or Sayblee.

"We have to make sacrifices sometimes, in order for things to get better. Some losses are acceptable when it is for the greater good," Rasheed said, stepping away and walking the room again. "If you had come with me, you would know. You wouldn't be working for Adalbert and his idiots. You wouldn't be mooning about for . . ."

Rasheed stopped walking, his words held tight in his mouth. Sayblee waited, wishing she could move into his thoughts, but she was trapped in her own brain. He knew something about the voice who spoke to her before. He could give her the answers.

"Never mind that," he said finally, moving around the room, his robes making a velvet *swish swish*. "You're here now. You'll be with us when we finally can change everything. That's all I've been working on since I joined him. That's all I want. Then we will go to find Mother and bring her here, where she can truly live the life she deserves. She will live like a queen."

"She *had* a life she deserved," Sayblee said. "Before. When you weren't with him. When you were part of our family. Don't you remember, Rasheed? Don't you remember what it used to be like? All our family? How Mother laughed?

She even learned to be happy after Father died because she had us to be with. So just come home. Take me home, Rasheed. Right now. Undo this magic and let's leave."

For a second, Sayblee thought she could feel his desire, as if a memory floated between them, something warm, a thought that smelled like their mother's cooking, couscous and cumin and saffron, a thought that felt like laughter. But then it disappeared, and as she tried to catch it, Sayblee felt her own memories of home start to fade slowly, as if her thoughts were photographs left out in the sun, all the vibrant reds and blues and greens fading to sepia, to white, to nothing.

"No," she said, terror clawing at her throat. She thought of the voice she'd heard before, the way it sounded, but then she knew she couldn't remember what voice she was thinking about, couldn't remember what to remember. "Please don't take them. They're all I have."

"I have no choice," Rasheed said. "Maybe I will give them back to you later. But I need you to listen to me. To believe in me. To do what I say. And if you do, I'll give them back. When we win, I'll let you remember."

Sayblee held on, holding tight, but then there was nothing to hold on to. All she knew was that she'd been fighting against something, gripping something so tightly, it was hard for her to swallow.

"Relax," Rasheed said. "It's all right. Now everything is just fine."

Sayblee took a large breath, feeling the in and out of her lungs. Yes, he was right, wasn't he? Here was Rasheed, the brother she'd thought she'd lost. Here she was about to see him again. Nothing mattered, and there was nothing really to think about. Nothing but looking at him, smoothing his hair away from his face, looking into his eyes. How happy her mother would be! How pleased! How joyful!

"Why am I tied up, Rasheed?" she asked. "Let me free."

"Of course, little sister," Rasheed said, and then, in seconds, she was blinking into the darkness that slowly ebbed into light. There he was, a silhouette. No, there he was, her brother, kneeling down, his hands on her knees. It was him, his long black hair, his beautiful black eyes, the smile that no one else ever had, slightly crooked and wide. There he was, his smooth olive skin, his lovely cheekbones, the tiny silver hoops in his ears, hoops she had given him when he turned twenty, conjured from magic. The brother she'd assumed was dead. She leaned forward, pressing her forehead to his, closing her eyes, listening to her heart pound against her ribs.

Are you really alive? she thought.

"Yes, my little wild plum. I am."

Sayblee lifted her arms and put them on her brother's shoulders.

You're here, she thought.

Yes, Rasheed thought back. *Now you can be happy.*

Sayblee nodded, held him tighter. She would be happy. He was right. There was nothing else she wanted. Her brother was alive, and her mother would finally wake up, come back to life, smile. She would laugh and make her special magic, reading the future for them, telling them little snippets of what was to come. Then she would create meals that would bring them all together again. There was nothing else to ask for.

"How true," Rasheed said, pulling her gently off the chair and hugging her. "You don't need anything else. Come. Come meet him."

Sayblee smiled into her brother's soft robes, but as Rasheed took them into the gray, something pricked her mind. She realized she was leaving something important behind in the cold, wet room. Something she loved, like a beautiful earring or a favorite necklace. A gift, something so precious, she wanted to yank on Rasheed's collar and force him to take her back to the room so she could get on her hands and knees and scour the floor for it, needing to feel the gold on her fingertips one more time.

But even as she imagined the earring in her palm, Rasheed placed his hand on her head, and the thought evaporated, and they swirled away, on their way to meet with Quain.

"This little thing has caused me so much grief," Quain said. "I remember distinctly the intense singeing she gave me the last time we met. She's a very dangerous girl."

Sayblee stared at Quain, knowing that he was a leader, someone very important to all *Croyant*. He was going to save them—save them from something bad. Something evil. Rasheed almost had his head bowed in respect, and she knew she should do the same. But she couldn't get her muscles to cooperate, her eyes mesmerized by Quain's thin face, his dark, dead eyes, his quick, flicking movements across the stone floor, his body and legs whip-thin, standing straight in his black clothes and robe.

They were in a large, drafty room, kept warm by a fire in a fireplace that Sayblee could have walked into without having to bend down. The logs hissed and flared, waves of orange and red licking the wood. The ceilings were at least thirty feet high, and long velvet curtains hung closed at the windows. At the far end of the room were a desk and chairs and a table, but the rest of the cavernous space was empty save for the large wooden chair Quain had been sitting in when they'd arrived. He'd been reading scrolls when they swirled in from the gray, but he made the papers disappear with a pop when he saw them arrive.

Whatever building they were in had to be huge if this room was any indicator. A mansion. A manor. A castle. And they must be someplace in Europe—maybe France, maybe England, maybe Germany. Or, really, it could all be a spell,

Sayblee thought. A pretend castle in a pretend place. Maybe all of this was pretend, a dream, a nightmare.

Quain seemed so real, though, and the room wasn't as interesting as he was. He stared at her as she thought—a thin, barely there smile on his face. His energy felt like a hot, live wire, a strand so thick and powerful she could feel it wrap around her as he moved around the room.

"Yes, I am, as the young folks say, 'All that,'" Quain went on. "Truly, Rasheed, you needed to have put a bit more into her conversion. She is thinking just a bit too much for my taste. It's like watching a terrible *Moyenne* news show, flickering, constant, irritating images."

"I'll finish my work," Rasheed said. "I promise you that."

Sayblee turned to Rasheed, not really understanding what her brother was saying. Things were still confusing and difficult to understand, as if each of her thoughts was falling into a pot of glue. She had to struggle to pull each out in order to see it, and even then, the thought was covered in goo, stuck to her hands.

"I," she began, and then stopped, not knowing how to continue or what to say.

"Of course you don't," Quain said. "Just be still. Be silent. Listen to your brother and take my orders."

"Yes," she said, nodding.

Quain stopped in front of them, the fire blazing behind him. Sayblee felt the flush of heat on her cheeks, a slight breeze from his billowing robe. She knew that the fire and she were related, but she couldn't quite remember how at this point. What had Quain said about her? She'd singed him? She'd actually done something to him? And when? Had the nerve to . . . to . . . ? She swallowed quickly, her body starting to shake, but she couldn't stop staring at him. He was so powerful, so amazing.

Quain laughed. "Oh, this will be just too easy, Rasheed.

She is not quite like you, is she? Now, I have things to do. Finish your work."

He flicked his fingers, and Sayblee felt herself fling through matter, Rasheed at her side.

"What are we doing here?" Sayblee asked. "What does he want us to do?"

They had appeared in a bedroom that was actually comfortable, warm and filled with a yellowish light from candles that were lit on the dresser. There was a bed made up with thick blankets, an upholstered chair, and a window framed with velvet curtains. Sayblee tried to move her mind back into the room where she'd first seen Rasheed, but she couldn't quite see it. It had been wet, she knew that. And the next room had been warm. There's been fire. But the world seemed to close up as she passed through it, each second the only second that mattered, everything else like a story from someone else's book.

Rasheed walked over to where she sat on the bed and put his hand on her shoulder.

"He is the *sorcier* who will have the world."

"From what? From whom? Who needs to be saved?"

Rasheed sat next to her. "We do."

"Why?" Sayblee asked, the glue in her thoughts clumping all of Rasheed's words together. "What's wrong?"

Shaking his head, Rasheed leaned into her. And then, finally, she remembered something. They were children, together in her room, laughing over—over a fire. She'd started it, a little white, flickering flame on the carpet.

"Blow it out," Rasheed had whispered.

"No," Sayblee had said. "Let's watch what it does. Let's see what happens."

"It will burn down the house, and Mom will take away our magic for weeks," Rasheed had said.

"Uh-uh," Sayblee had said. "Watch."

And she'd lifted the fire with her thoughts and put it on a saucer on her dresser, making a spell that would keep it a tiny flame, unchanging, constant. She used it for a night-light for two nights before her mother finally found it and, in fact, had taken away her magic for weeks.

"The past is no good," Rasheed said. "The past is where we've let *Moyenne* rule us. Where we haven't made the rules. Where we are ruled. Quain will change all that."

"What is he going to do?" Sayblee asked, knowing some-how the answer. He was going to do what he had done be-fore, which was to kill.

"Oh," she said, but then Rasheed put his hand on her head, and the thought vanished, until all she could feel were his warm fingers on her forehead.

"You must sleep," Rasheed said. "We have a lot to ac-complish in a short amount of time. There's so much I need to show you."

Sayblee nodded, but then looked up at him. "I can make fire. I can burn things down."

Rasheed stood up. "I know. And that's one thing we are not going to let you forget."

In her dream, Sayblee was back in a room she understood she'd been in many times, but she didn't really remember being there before. It was small and square, with a window that looked out toward city lights, but toward which city she wasn't sure. Yet there the lights were, bright in a somehow-familiar landscape. The focus of the dream was the middle of the room, the dream's light on a bed in the middle of the room, the blankets thrown back, the pillows on the floor. Two candles burned on the nightstand, and as Sayblee stared into the scene, she now saw that there was a man and a woman on the bed, moving together, making love. She could feel herself lean toward them, wanting to take in all of this movement.

"Oh," the woman said in almost a moan, her voice full of pleasure.

The man lifted his head, his long hair falling around the woman so that Sayblee could not see either of their faces.

"Oh, yes," he said, kissing her, his body so close to hers.

His skin was so lovely in the candlelight, honey colored and warm. His shoulders were muscled, his ribs lean, the lines of his body arcing into the small of his back so smoothly. She wanted to put her hand there in that dip and then to trace the flesh line up his perfect rear. She almost felt as though she'd done so before, her imagined touch so real she could feel his muscles under her palms.

The woman under him sighed, her gasp of pleasure filling the room, and pulled the man even closer with her legs, her arms encircling his shoulders.

Sayblee wanted this, needed to push the man's hair away so she could see him. She wanted to look him in the eyes, to have him recognize her and tell her who she was, who they both were. She wanted the woman who was holding him so tightly to disappear, and Sayblee thought she might have the magic to make it happen. She hated the woman, envied her the grip she had on him, the way she welcomed him into her body, resented all the pleasure she was receiving. Sayblee wanted to be there. That was her spot, her place. He was hers, but as she struggled to move forward, the dream broke up, turned into a scattered collage of gray and white and black, and she woke up, blinking into the pitch of her bedroom. During the dream, she'd thrown back the blankets, and she was uncovered in the middle of the bed. But she was warm; she could still feel the man on top of her, as if she had been the woman kissing him so long and hard.

"Oh," she said, but there was no man's answer. No yes. No kiss. No skin. No love. Nothing but darkness.

*　*　*

Rasheed was teaching her things. Or trying to. Since early that morning, they had been practicing something he called *lancer*. They were outside of what was, in fact, an enormous mansion. Rasheed stood in front of her on a wide green lawn, staring at her with his enormous dark eyes, his magic coming from him and into her mind. They were behind the mansion, hidden not only by the house but by a vortex Rasheed assured her was in place, strong enough to keep the locals and anyone else, for that matter, at bay.

But why it was important to be so isolated, alone, safe, she wasn't sure. It had to do with Quain, but, again, everything was unclear.

At least the setting was real. The mansion was built of stone that had flecks of orange in it, the color making Sayblee think they were in the north of France, maybe Normandy, maybe Brittany. Normandy was more likely, the landscape all around the mansion rural and agrarian. Behind them was a stone paddock full of horses, sheep, and one small braying donkey that drove Rasheed crazy. Rasheed threatened the animal with magic but never did anything but call it *Burro*. Burro seemed to be lonely, and even now, he stood by the fence periodically braying and flicking his ears, ignoring the five sheep that clustered in a fuzzy circle next to him.

"Forget the animals. Pay attention," Rasheed said, sending her images of a wide, white flume of fire coming from her hands and entering . . . entering? She wasn't sure. And then there was the image of an explosion, a bright, white burst of intense flame.

Sayblee sighed and tried to focus on the magic he was feeding her, but it was so hard. She was sure that she knew what that word *lancer* meant, had felt the full force of fire launch from her body before. But Rasheed was coaching her to move through conduits, except, of course, the conduits were not here for the practice sessions. And what, exactly, these conduits were was completely confusing to her. She had a terrible feeling, though, that the conduits weren't *whats* but *whos*.

An incipient migraine beat behind her eyes.

"I don't understand," she said, her thoughts seemingly clogged with cotton, gummy and slow. "Why do I need to force the fire through them? What will it do? And how can I practice without conduits?"

"You don't need to understand everything right now," Rasheed said, his voice containing a slight strand of irritation. "And I promise you that we will have practice conduits for you soon. Sooner than you will want."

Sayblee turned to her brother, feeling, as she had since she had arrived, as if she was underwater. Her entire body was heavy, and she wondered if Rasheed was still enchanting her. But why would he do that? Maybe she was sick. Maybe he'd found her completely ill somewhere and nursed her back to health. He'd rescued her from certain death, but she was still recovering. Anything seemed possible because she could barely hold on to one thought, time turning liquid and invisible in her head. How was she supposed to learn like this?

Rasheed shook his head and walked to her, putting his hands on her shoulders, and looking at her. For a second, Sayblee thought she'd seen something behind his concerned gaze. Irritation. Anger. Or hatred. But then, as soon as she thought she saw the emotion flick yellow and ugly over his face, it was gone.

"Remember this is for Mother," Rasheed said. "Remember that Quain is going to make her life so much better."

She blinked, nodded, breathed in. He was right. This was for Mother.

"Can we go get her now?" Sayblee asked. "Can we bring

her here? She would be so happy to see you, Rasheed. She would want nothing more than to hold you and then make you *Khoresht Fesenjaan,* your favorite dish."

Somehow, she'd managed to say the name of Rasheed's favorite food, and the memory of the delicious chicken, pomegranate, and walnut dish made her mouth tingle, her brain thrum with memory. Oh, there was also *Tah-Cheen,* chicken with rice and saffron, and *Zereshk Polow,* rice with barberries. *Home,* she thought. *Home.*

But even as she imagined the table set with all these treats, the emotions Sayblee had seen earlier flared in Rasheed's face and then disappeared again. "No, my wild plum. We can't bring her here until everything is just right. Until everything is perfect. Until you have learned how to do the magic you will need to do to make everything exactly as Mother would like it."

Like everything since she woke up blindfolded in the wet, damp room, this sentence didn't make any sense at all. Sayblee knew her mother wouldn't care if things weren't perfect. She'd be overjoyed if she knew Rasheed was alive. She'd whirl into gray in a second, burst into matter at the mansion and grab him, holding him so close for so long that he might never take a clear breath again. She'd cry and alert all of the Safipour clan, bringing the party to Rasheed, everyone ready to celebrate and listen to his story. And then the cooking would begin, the feasting going on for days. Sayblee could almost see them all at the table, hear the toasts, taste the wine on her tongue. How could he think she would want things to be just so?

But even as Sayblee felt her doubt about Rasheed's statements, her confusion and questioning began to disappear. Rasheed was right. He made sense. He knew what he was doing. She had to trust him. Trust him totally. And then all she knew was that she had to make her fire perfect, exactly the way Rasheed wanted it. She would move it through the conduits, whatever or whoever they were. She would do as she was told.

"All right," Sayblee said. "I'm ready."

That night, Sayblee saw the man again, but this time he was alone, no woman under him or next to him or in the room at all. Somehow, she knew he was lonely or sad, even in his sleep. He lay on his side on the bed, and she came into the dream scene from behind, her eyes stroking his lovely side, her gaze running from shoulder to calf. His long hair hung behind him, a smooth, dark river of softness on the mattress.

She breathed in and smelled something she couldn't really recognize, something tangy with ocean, fruity and full of spice. She reached out and tried to move closer to him, but she was stuck, feeling the way she had since Rasheed had found her, immobile, sticky, trapped in the slow puddle of her own thoughts and body.

Then she tried to call out to him, but her voice was caught somewhere in her throat, in her lungs, all the words she needed to say caught between thought and sound. She tried to stamp her feet, to make some kind of noise to wake him up, but he moved only an arm, pushed a strand of hair back over his shoulder, moved more fully into sleep.

Wake up, she thought, her head full of only that one demand. *Wake up to me.*

But he didn't move again, didn't say a word. He just slept, and Sayblee watched him until the dream turned into morning.

Chapter Eight

After the meeting in Adalbert's lounge ended late, Felix, Sariel, and Rufus sat at the kitchen table, holding cups of tea which none of them sipped. Adalbert had long since whirled away, off to confer with other *Croyant*. Felix felt punched out, empty, and exhausted. Nothing felt right about the way things were going, especially the delay. He wondered if he would sneak out tonight and try to find Sayblee on his own. As he thought this, he realized that Sariel and Rufus were right there in his mind.

"Adalbert needs to get a plan together," Sariel said, putting a hand on his shoulder. "This is really our last chance to get to Quain."

"But why wait? Quain wouldn't expect an immediate response, so why don't we give him one?" Felix sat back and shrugged off Sariel's hand. "Why do what he thinks we will do?"

"Lad," Rufus said. "I—"

"Stop *ladding* me," Felix said. "I'm not your damn son, who you should probably be at home waiting for." He looked at Sariel. "You, too."

Sariel and Rufus exchanged the look they had been exchanging as long as Felix could remember. It was the, isn't-he-a-smidge-slow look that made Felix want to go to, and then eventually move to, Hilo and stay there for the rest of his life.

"Listen," Sariel said. "I know what it feels like to lose the person you love."

Felix started to protest out of habit, the way he'd protested all the long years he'd been the youngest brother. *No, I don't love Susan or Marie or Tiffany or Yvette. I don't believe in all that bullshit,* he'd thought and said. But now, the protest faded and disappeared even as he thought to voice it. He did love Sayblee. He always had. Ever since they were in school and she refused to even look at him, much less hand over her homework.

"But you really don't remember what it felt like," Felix said. "You forgot about Miranda. Your memories were gone."

"That may have been so," Sariel said. "But inside me, I knew something was missing. That there was something very wrong. Quain and Kallisto had captured Miranda, and it turned out all right. But I had agreed to the magic. I waited for direction."

"Aye, La—" Rufus began and then stopped himself. "Aye. The same thing with Fabia when we were on that island."

"At least you could communicate with her," Felix said. "At least you could see her."

"Footprints. The impression of her body on the sand," Rufus said, shrugging. "But yes, there was that."

Sariel put his hand back on Felix's shoulder and leaned forward, staring at Felix with his gold eyes. Felix tensed for a moment and then relaxed, knowing that, truly, he'd always been able to trust his brothers. They were his touchstones. They were with him for everything.

"Think about it," Sariel said. "Maybe you can communicate with her. Maybe those dreams have a magic that no one can detect. Or wouldn't be looking for now that she is captured. They may still be your way in."

Felix nodded, letting his brother's hand move warmth and healing into his body, a *charme de réparation* helping him relax. He took a deep breath, feeling all his muscles unclench. Maybe Sariel was on to something. Maybe he could dream his way to Sayblee. He hoped so.

"Fine," he said, looking up at his brothers. "I'll wait. I'll let Adalbert come up with a plan. But I won't wait forever."

"Nor should you," Rufus said. "If you did, you wouldn't be a Valasay."

"Now, drink your tea," Sariel said, and Felix shook his head, a smile on his lips before he realized it was there. No matter what, he was still the youngest, and for just a second, that seemed all right.

It wasn't until three days later that Reynaldo Arroyo, Cadeyrn Macara, Nala Nagode, Sariel, Rufus, and Felix sat around a back table of The Quaggy Duck, waiting for Adalbert, Akasma Saintonge, a longtime member of the *Croyant* Council, and Brennus to appear for the meeting.

Felix had barely been able to stand the tension the past few days, his worry about Sayblee like a boiling caldron in his stomach. Last night, Sariel had forced him to take a *potion du grand sommeil* before bed. Sure, Felix had slept through the night for the first time since arriving in England, but he felt confused when he woke up, his dreams in a jumble, images of darkness and confusion. He'd felt like he'd been running in glue through long, dark corridors, the walls wet and dripping. And there was a voice talking to him throughout the dream, forcing him to do what he didn't want to do, to shoot—well, he wasn't sure what he was supposed to shoot. But he knew he didn't want to do it. That if he shot whatever it was, the people would die. He didn't know which people, though, and when he tried to remember when he woke up, the sticky dream dried and flaked away like salt.

As he sat at the pub table, his head in his hands, listening only vaguely to the conversation around him, he vowed to never take anything Sariel offered him again. Clearly, Sariel's medicine wasn't any better than *Moyenne* pills and elixirs. Now Felix regretted that he hadn't taken Sayblee up on the sleeping pill she had offered him on their way to Paris in the airplane. He should have listened to her then. He should have taken her more seriously when she first told him about the flickering light in the apartment across the street. She had known, and he'd doubted her. Sure, he'd had a hunch later, but if he'd only let someone know right away, the minute she'd mentioned it. If he had, she'd be with him now. She'd be safe.

Reynaldo shook his head and put a hand on Felix's arm. "No, *mi'jo*. You did right. You were protecting the mission. It's what you needed to do."

Felix lifted his head and shrugged, deciding to shut down his thoughts, even though he was sure that everything he was thinking was written all over his face. Reynaldo smiled and turned to Nala, and Felix looked at him, a short, square man with thick, short, curly gray hair and the blackest eyes Felix had ever seen. Even inside the pub, Reynaldo wore a hat—cowboy hat, which was molded perfectly to his head. His cowboy boots probably made dogs nervous just looking at them, they were so thick-soled and pointy-toed. Not that Reynaldo would kick anything. In fact, he was the most serene man Felix had ever met. His very presence was like a balm, a *charme de paix*.

Reynaldo lived in a sprawling hacienda in Arizona, and was *Moyenne*, of a sorts. But like no *Moyenne* Felix had ever met before. Reynaldo could read thoughts, conjure magic, and create potions. The only thing he couldn't do was travel through matter on his own, so that was one of the reasons for the delay of this meeting. Rufus had traveled to Reynaldo's *hacienda* to get him—to tell him of the urgency of the situation, and bring him back. Likewise, Adalbert sent messengers for Cadeyrn Macara, who had been in Afghanistan and Iraq, doing magic, Felix assumed, that he shouldn't have been doing. Since Cadeyrn had been freed of Quain's influence and after studying with Reynaldo for two years, he'd returned to his mission of bringing *Moyenne* and *Croyant* together with even more passion. And he and Brennus had argued late into the evening the night before about how to end *Moyenne* conflicts.

"It's not our place," Brennus had said, his arms folded.

"Then whose is it?" Cadeyrn had replied, his wild red hair matching his passion. "How can we just watch this carnage? This ridiculous behavior? They are focusing on this while they destroy the planet. We must bring them in. We must integrate."

"And have our way of life discovered? Have the *Moyenne* rule us as they did in the past?"

"What's worse? Having to share magic or live on a desolate planet?" Cadeyrn had slapped his hand down hard on Adalbert's kitchen table. "Think, man! Imagine all the lives we can save."

On and on it went, an argument spiraling nowhere and in such loud repetition that Felix had left the room, wishing for a *charme de silence,* wanting only to think of Sayblee.

But now Cadeyrn sat quietly sipping his beer and talking with Nala Nagode, a powerful *sorcière* whom Felix had fought with before. She was swathed in her customary yellow robes, her perfectly smooth face a mask of concern and worry. Felix had never seen her worried before, not even when standing directly in front of Kallisto and Quain, firing off her strongest magic. Angry, yes, irritated, certainly, and infatuated, most definitely, when she looked at Rufus, for whom she had a true *thing*. Since Fabia's arrival on the scene, Nala had kept her longing gazes and thoughts to a minimum, but sometimes, she'd have a little whisk of a sexy Rufus image, enough to give Felix ammunition for teasing his brother, weapons he'd used at any opportunity.

But now Nala was concerned, no longing or desire for Rufus in her mind, even though he sat across from her. Both Rufus and Sariel were subdued, no jokes, no laughter, just quiet, somber faces and nods at Cadeyrn's words.

Felix sighed, shifted in his seat. In about five minutes he was going to bolt. He knew that. His thighs were jumpy, his feet twitched under the table. *Where in the hell was Adalbert?* he wondered, turning toward the door, hoping to see Adalbert push through the doors. Or at least someone who could do something, show up and take control.

But the pub was empty, the Council had protected it with a vortex. The only *Moyenne* in sight was the barkeep Freddie Stanton, who had long been a friend of the *Croyant* and who poured a fair pint. But Felix didn't feel like sitting or drinking, and he certainly didn't feel like waiting.

Just as Felix thought to swing his legs over the bench, excuse himself to the loo, and disappear into the gray to wherever—anyplace, someplace he might find Sayblee— Adalbert and Akasma Saintonge burst into space, appearing wild and ruffled from matter. A second later, Brennus appeared, accompanied by Philomel, who was not only wild and ruffled but puffy, her hair a giant gray halo around her head.

Freddie Stanton looked up from the bar, raised his left eyebrow, and went back to polishing glasses. The group around the table shifted, murmured, and Felix felt the first bit of relief he'd felt in days.

Adalbert pushed back the hood of his purple robe and then moved aside to let Akasma sit in the chair at the head of the table. She was a tall, imposing *sorcière,* who had been a member of the *Croyant* Council for over forty years. She sat down regally, her face stern and impossible to read. Felix sent out a tiny feeler into her thoughts and was slapped away, as if he'd been trying to sneak the best cookie from a freshly baked batch.

"I am sorry for the delay," Adalbert said, sitting down at the table and motioning for Brennus and Philomel to do the same. "We encountered a little trouble with . . . Well, it is of no importance now. However, all is well, and we need to quickly acquaint you with the plan."

Freddie Stanton walked over with four pints of Dragonhead Stout and put two in front of the new arrivals. Adalbert thanked him and took a long sip of his beer. Felix felt his internal pressure shoot up, his blood at some terrible overflow line on his forehead. If he were a cartoon character, he knew that the caption above his head would be unprintable.

"Yes," Adalbert said. "I am aware that this has taken longer than it should have. But let us now finally begin."

Reynaldo looked at Adalbert carefully and then nodded. "I can see that this is a careful plan," he said. "But I hope I will not be a deterrent to you. I do not have all the magic you need, my good friend."

Adalbert put down his mug and ran a hand through his long beard. "Oh, you have more than enough magic, old one."

Felix sat back and shook his head. "What plan are you talking about? I think the rest of us need to be shown."

All the group looked at Adalbert, and Felix could feel the thoughts firing across the table, zinging off each other in a blaze of neurons. *Yes, show us. Let us see. What are we going to do? Will the damn thing work? We have no time. It's too late.*

Adalbert turned to Akasma for a moment, a private conversation whooshing between them, and then he looked at each member of the group sitting around the table. He took his time, slowly making complete eye contact with each person, the energy in the communication so loud that Felix was sure he could hear crackling in the space over the table.

When Adalbert got to Felix, Felix almost breathed in at his intensity, feeling the light but complete scan Adalbert was making of his mind, despite the block Felix had cast earlier. Adalbert was a powerful *sorcier,* his magic the highest Felix had ever known, and all he could do was offer up his feelings and thoughts, his dismay over the delay, his yearning for Sayblee, his confusion on the roof in Paris, his fear and helplessness in Alaska.

All Felix could take in in return was Adalbert's commitment that Quain would not infiltrate anyone's mind here, that this mission, unlike the prior two that Felix had been involved with, would be with people untainted by Quain's bad magic.

Seconds after the scan began, though, it was over, Adalbert moving to Sariel before finishing his exploration.

Adalbert took in a deep breath, nodding. "I am in complete agreement with you, Felix. We do all need to be made aware of the plan. But I had to make very sure this time that we have no one enchanted or confused or full of mixed or contradictory feeling." Then looking again at each person very quickly he said, "All I can see here is a great intensity to have this finally over. To capture Quain and to end the threat. And, I must say, to save those he has in his grip."

Felix slumped a little, relieved, but then he felt a jab of irritation and impatience. He sat up straight again, his backbone feeling like it could push him into flight. They were all here. They needed to move on this, now.

"Of course," Adalbert said, holding out his hands. Together, in The Quaggy Duck, under the swirling, protective spiral of the vortex, they joined hands. And within seconds, his head full of images and plans and ideas, Felix finally understood everything.

* * *

Back at Adalbert's house, Felix stood alone in the lounge, watching the fire spit in the hearth, his arms crossed in front of him. The rest of the group he was part of—Cadeyrn, Nala, and Reynaldo—was taking care of last-minute plans, but within minutes they were going to leave for the staging ground of the mission. Sariel, Rufus, and Brennus had already left, whirling away from the pub. Adalbert had gone to collect the most important part of the plan, and the house actually felt empty without him.

As Felix stood waiting, he tried to connect to Sayblee, to let her know that he was coming. That he had not forgotten her, but every time he reached out with his mind, he found nothing. It wasn't nothing, really—more of a sticky wall of no thought that seemed to prevent him from moving closer to, well, what he imagined was her. He'd never felt anything like it except, he supposed, in the dream he'd had the night before.

He sighed, but then, at the sound of a slamming door and a known, irritated voice calling out for him, he breathed in and turned around to face none other than his mother.

Zosime Valasay pushed into the room, flinging her deep blue robe onto a chair, and put her hands on her hips. Her now-graying hair was pulled back in a thick braid, her face flushed ruddy from travel, as usual.

"End of the world again?" she asked. "Evil to be subdued? Problems that only Valasay brothers can solve?"

"What else?" Felix asked, moving closer and folding his arms around her.

Zosime hugged him tight, and he felt how small she seemed now, her body tiny against his.

"What?" she asked, pulling away. "You're turning me into a crone already? I have a few good years still."

"Mom," Felix started, but he could see that she was launching into one of her favorite topics.

"You know," she said, winking at him. "I've always thought there should be another kind of stage before crone. Something like, the most-fabulous-time-in-your-life stage. Maybe Diva. Maiden-Mother-Diva-Crone. Sounds good to me. Crone gets such a bad rap."

"I never said . . ." he began. "I didn't mean to say that you were a crone. I just thought—"

"Never mind," she said, interrupting him and walking in front of the fireplace. She rubbed her hands together briskly, her magic making the fire roar a little as she did. "I just don't understand why every time Adalbert gets a wild hair, it involves all three of you boys. All three. Not just one or two but all of you. Aren't there dozens of *Croyant* families with three boys he could pick from? Why always my sons?"

"Unfortunately," Felix said. "We seem to have more experience with Quain than most."

As he said the words, he wished he hadn't. The lightness in the room dissipated, the air suddenly thick with feeling. But it was true. His father, who had supposedly been Quain's best friend and colleague, had been killed by Quain. And then, in later years, all three of the Valasay boys had been caught up in Quain's plots. Either Quain wanted to do them in or the Valasays wanted revenge. Or both.

"Ridiculous," said Zosime turning to him, fixing him with her light brown eyes. "So tell me what happened. Adalbert tried to give me the details earlier today, but it didn't make any sense. I made him explain—"

"So you were the reason for the delay?" Felix asked. "You were what held up our meeting? It was you he had to deal with? What are you up to, Mom?"

Zosime walked to Adalbert's favorite overstuffed chair and sat down in it, crossing her legs and drumming her fingertips on the arms. "Oh, the man is stubborn. So clear on what's best for the entire universe. And can you believe it? He thought I wouldn't approve. I tell him all the time that

. . . Just the other day . . . Earlier . . . In any case, I don't understand how this imbroglio started."

Felix sat in a chair opposite her and sighed, confused by all the pauses in his mother's sentences. "Mom."

"Well, it just seems a little confusing. And now, all of you off to fight."

Felix crossed his legs, now unable to hold his mother's gaze. He shook his head and then breathed in, saying all at once, "It was my fault."

"How?"

He sat back against the chair, rubbing his closed eyes with a thumb and forefinger. "I compromised the mission. Feelings I had. Sayblee and I—"

Zosime smiled, and it was then that Felix felt her mind release his thoughts. "Oh, my. Oh, my. Felix! You aren't? It isn't possible, is it? It is! You are! My goodness!"

He shrugged. "Yeah. We were dreaming, never imagining that they were more than dreams. But I guess it was like a flare. We should have just stood in the street and put on a magic show."

"You love her."

"Yeah," Felix said, sighing. "I do. And now Quain has her. I just hope it's not too late to—to save her."

His mother stood up and walked over to him, putting her hand on his shoulder and kissing him on top of his head. "She's a lovely woman, Felix. And a strong woman. I know how well she handled herself when Quain had Miranda. She's hanging on, waiting for you. I just know it. And with you and your brothers on this mission, I have a feeling everything will turn out all right."

Felix looked into his mother's eyes, feeling the hope in her words and in her thoughts. This is how she'd always been, supportive and kind and sure, even when things seemed at their worst. Even just after his father's death.

"I hope you're right," he said, suddenly turning toward

the hall, hearing Cadeyrn think out to him, calling him, telling him the group was ready to depart.

"I've got to go," he said, standing up and hugging his mother again, who wasn't quite done with him yet.

"And the truth is, now that you have finally, after all this time, fallen in love, things better damn well turn out all right. Or that's a sorry end to this story. My God, Felix in love." She pushed away from him and held him by the shoulders, her eyes fixed on him, her mind swirling around his in the warm, comfortable hold he was used to. She smiled, shaking her head "Be still my beating heart."

Felix laughed and kissed her on the forehead, turning to leave. But then he stopped as he was halfway to the door. "What did you mean when you said you tell things to Adalbert all the time? I thought you've been with Miranda and Fabia these past few months, overseeing the pregnancies. And what's with 'just the other day?' "

Zosime's mind—which had been open and flowing seconds before—shut down with a clamp, even though she was still smiling. "You go on your mission. We can talk when you come back with Sayblee. And Quain on a yardarm."

Felix shrugged, held up his hand, and walked toward Cadeyrn, Reynaldo, and Nala, wanting nothing but what his mother had just called for. Nothing but Sayblee in his arms and Quain gone for good.

They emerged from matter in total darkness, as they had expected. No one said a word, and all Felix could hear was the *thump thump* of his own heart against the stairs of his ribs and the whir of blood in his veins. After a moment, he flicked his fingers and a little globe of light shone into the small, square room. Adalbert had assured them that the room and the house it was in were completely protected.

At least as far as we know, Nala thought with a slight, wry tinge in her tone.

We cannot think otherwise, Reynaldo thought, as he let go of Felix's shoulder. Felix had brought the man with them through the gray.

Quain has his ways, Cadeyrn thought, walking the perimeter of the room until he reached the door. *Let's start, shall we?*

The little globe of light as their guide, they followed Cadeyrn into the main room of the house. And there it was. Felix sighed, relieved to see that what Adalbert had promised them was, in fact, sitting on a table in the middle of the room, a shimmering, perfectly triangular vortex hanging over it. Right in front of him, on a simple wooden table, were the three *Plaques de la Pensée.* They were not pressed together in their powerful mode, a triangle of creative power. Instead, they were sitting side by side, the purple stone of each inscribed with the most powerful magic *Croyant* knew, the magic that could create life or destroy it.

"My God," Nala said, her voice soft and full of wonder. "I've never seen them together."

"Few have," Cadeyrn said. "No one should, really."

"Then what are we doing fooling around with them?" Felix asked. "I know the plan seems sound, but these . . . this? I don't even want to get near them. And to touch them? It's crazy."

Reynaldo squatted in front of the table, turning his head this way and then that, looking at the *plaques* through the iridescent vortex. Reynaldo was not overly familiar with the customs and beliefs of the *Croyant des Trois.* And Felix had to admit, he had no idea what the man believed in himself. *Moyenne* religion was a subject everyone took at Bampton (Sayblee, of course, getting an A in the subject), but since the *Croyant* had come to know Reynaldo and other *Moyenne* like him, a whole new page had opened, another story about *Moyenne* that he'd never read before.

"They have so much energy," Reynaldo said. "They remind me of Spider-Woman."

"Excuse me?" Nala said. "Spider who?"

Reynaldo smiled. "She created the world, you know. From herself. Just like these *plaques* can do. And then Spider-Woman created humans from clay. And she made three worlds, all of which humans destroyed through greed and desire. Finally, she made a fourth world just good enough for humans to live on, and she led them there, the animals, too. She assigned each species a place to live, gave them a purpose. But, of course, now we are ruining this world as well. But she was powerful, full of energy to create." Reynaldo stood up a little, his hands on his thighs as the *plaques* glimmered under the little globe's light. "These stones are the same. The same power."

Felix, Nala, and Cadeyrn nodded. Reynaldo was right. The power to create and destroy a world was sitting on a flimsy wooden table right in front of them. Felix wanted to bolt out the door before anything bad happened.

"We know what to do," Nala said. "But we have to use this power carefully. So carefully."

"That's what they all say," Felix said, shaking his head. "We'll build a nuclear weapon to create peace, and then the secret gets out."

Nala put her hands on her hips, and turned to him, her smooth face full of irritation, a crease deepening between her eyebrows. "Are you going to be as annoying as your brothers the entire mission?"

Felix smiled, thinking of Sayblee and the way she'd chastised him on the plane, in the Métro, and at the apartment. Not to mention the park, the apartment building they'd spied on, and the roof. He had been a pain in the ass the entire time, from Hilo to Paris. Just like now. And he couldn't compromise the mission. Not now.

"No," he said, his smile fading. "I'm not."

"Good," said Nala. "Now, let's move on this. We don't have any room for error."

Turning away from the *plaques,* they stood in a circle. In one fluid motion, they reached out for each other's hands, and Felix took Reynaldo's and Caderyn's in his, almost flung back from the power of the connection.

Breathe into it, Nala commanded. *Let the elements surge between us.*

Felix did as he was told, breathing in as well as he could, the air like rocks he was trying to swallow, his chest tight. But then, slowly, he felt himself fill with heat. The heat turned yellow, orange, and then red, burning crimson in the middle of his chest. The flames licked at his heart, his lungs, his gut, sparks shooting up and down his thighs and shins, flinging out through his arms. Breathing slowly, pulling in air, he felt himself become the fire, become the heat, his body one solid stalk of flame.

Move right, Nala thought, and his mind left his own hot core, and he settled into Cadeyrn, the plunge like a high dive from a steep Acapulco cliff. Cadeyrn was filled with brilliant aqua liquid, a pool so cool, clear, and deep that again, Felix felt that he would never breathe another clear breath. For a moment, he bobbed in the water, foundering in its blue wetness. But after a time, he began to tread water, to float, to find a way to pull air into his lungs. And instead of putting out his flame, Cadeyrn's coolness seemed to meld with it, to join the fire in an equal but different strand, the fire and the water together in one strong, fluid stream.

Move right again, Nala intoned, and Felix lifted himself out of the whirling water of Cadeyrn, and moved into Nala's wide-open vista of air and cloud and sky. He felt himself whirling through space, no boundaries anywhere, nothing holding him back, the feeling exhilarating, better than traveling through matter, which was quick, grainy, and dark. He held out his arms, pulling in the wonderful feeling, trying to grab cloud and air. And then he began to go faster. And he kept moving at an accelerated rate, his body propelled by the wind behind him, nothing keeping him from the uppermost parts of the stratosphere. There it was, the arc of atmosphere bending into space.

No more, he thought. *Stop.*

And as he thought the words, his body slowed down, fell back into the arms of the air, rested buoyant and light, cradled by the wind. Hovering underneath the thin veil of oxygen, he watched the stars twinkle, and then he turned back to the view of clouds below him, spinning and turning, so light and free and full of nothing but atoms. As he moved, he felt Nala's white, open stream merge into his and then Caderyn's, the three elements a twist of electric rope.

Move again, Nala thought. *The last time.*

As she thought the words, he was plucked from Nala's field into Reynaldo's, flung like lead into the earth, the darkness filling him up until there was nothing to see, nothing to breathe. He was trapped, sucked into the core of the earth, Reynaldo full of nothing but dense, black dirt, shale, granite, and water. Something was pulling him to a core of heat, but the movement was so slow and claustrophobic that he thought he would go insane, and he wondered if his body was actually pulling away from Caderyn and Reynaldo, his hands wrenched from theirs as his mind and soul sank into the darkness.

But as the movement slowed even more, he began to tunnel, like a mole, like a worm, moving through the soil with ease, as if he was again in Nala's wide-open air. He put his hands in front of him, his eyes closed, and twisted and turned through the earth which gave way as he pressed. He breathed in the sweet, wet soil, smelled granite and sandstone and slate. On his tongue were the tastes of iron and salt. He sliced through deep aquifers and pushed past rock.

He could see how the earth was made, the layers, the pressure, the time.

And as he thought this, he felt Reynaldo's solid stream of earth join the fire, water, and air he'd already collected, the rope strong and full and pulsing, all of the elements, all of them together. For a second, he felt something jerk him up, and he felt his neck and face rise, as if he was looking out at a vista, as if, really, he were the vista and someone was looking at him. From a long distance, from a place that was not the place of the elements or even the room, came a quiet, sad, Yes.

But before he could try to figure out who had said the word, he slipped back into the stream of earth, fire, water, and air, breathing in the waves of energy coming at him.

Now, Nala thought. *Pull out. Hold it. Take it with you.*

Felix imagined the rope in his hands and then came back to his own body, feeling Caderyn and Reynaldo's hands in his, but also feeling the rope in a circle around the group, a rope that became something inside them, something that connected him, something strong that would make their magic truly work.

Together, they stood, the rope a connection that could not be lost, and Felix opened his eyes and looked at the group, and they all thought, at once, *We're ready.*

Chapter Nine

Sayblee's days had become smoother, or, at least, her mind had. She no longer felt mired in tangled thoughts, but she realized she didn't have many thoughts beyond those that emerged from her practice with Rasheed. And he was almost always with her, from the moment she opened her eyes in the morning until she began to nod off at the dinner table at night, Quain intoning from the head of the table. She was so tired. All she did was practice, shooting her fire all day long, which is what she'd been doing from dawn until dusk. Again, here she was, standing behind the mansion, Rasheed in front of her, directing her aim and the intensity of flame.

"Now, do it once more," Rasheed was saying. "Use more intensity."

Sayblee knew that in another time, another place, she could have teased him. She could have done something silly, but silly seemed so long ago. What might she have said? Done? Used a little bit of fire on him, she thought. Burned the edge of his robe. Lit one strand of hair aflame and watched it curl and smoke into nothing.

She looked up in time to see Rasheed's face change, his placid, calm teaching face almost afraid, his eyes narrowed, his chest rising with an inhaled breath. Sayblee was about to turn around to look at what had caused his reaction when she heard the voice in her ear.

"I don't think that you are paying much attention to your dear brother," Quain said. Sayblee held her breath, listening to the snake of his voice wind in her head. "You know that we need your help, and you are thinking about burning your brother's clothes. Or his hair. I am very disappointed."

Parts of Sayblee's body were trying to tell her things. She wasn't sure what, exactly, but her feet and stomach and heart were all moving and lurching and thumping, and she knew it meant something important. She was stuck to the ground and she was stuck in the practice of shooting fire. She nodded.

"I'm sorry," she whispered.

"Yes, you should be." Quain walked around her once more, and then looked at Rasheed.

"You may go now. I'll take over this last part."

Sayblee watched Rasheed as he took in the command, and she didn't know which brother she was seeing. His face spun like a carousel, an up-and-down wheel of surprise and acceptance and anger and back again.

Don't do that, she tried to think to him, not really knowing why he shouldn't show his emotions. Quain was his mentor. Quain was his protector. Quain was a very good man who was going to make things perfect. The man who was finally going to allow her mother to be happy. But she was scared of him, frightened by the way he made parts of her body want to abandon ship. If they had their way, her feet would be in the next town. Her stomach would be a raft in the river that wended past the mansion; her heart would be a balloon floating away, searching for a safe haven.

But Quain missed Rasheed's reaction, turning back to her, missing also Rasheed's flinging of himself into matter, the tiny gray wisp he left behind.

"That's better," Quain said. "Your brother is, well, not objective at this point. And things may have to change."

"Change?" Sayblee blinked, drew a deep breath, the first since Quain arrived. "What will have to change?"

"The nature of all things," Quain said, his black robe flowing in the afternoon breeze. Nothing else seemed to move. Not the leaves in the trees or the grass. The birds stayed in their hedgerows; the cows in the distance were still lifes. Behind Quain, even Burro was still, his ears held at attention, his tail at rest, no flies bothering him now. "Such as what will happen after you do your amazing magic, my dear Sayblee."

Without wanting to, Sayblee flushed with pride. Her amazing magic. Certainly she had been called on to use her abilities by the Council, but all her life, her fire had been a source of pain as well. She never could control it entirely. Her palms would itch and burn her at—at? She blinked, knowing that something embarrassing had happened to her with her fire, but now she couldn't remember. She knew that people had teased her and made fun of her, especially one person. Someone . . .

"None of that matters. No one matters," Quain said. "Only now matters. Only this very moment. Hold out your hands. Palms up."

Sayblee lifted her palms, and looked up at Quain, whose black eyes seemed as though they held embers inside them. He was filled with fire, too, she thought, seeing finally how they were connected. How they were the same. How he could teach her so much.

"Close your eyes," he said softly. "Imagine the heat. Imagine it to be the most beautiful yellow. Canary yellow. The yellow of sunset. The yellow of chrysanthemums."

Sayblee closed her eyes, the color behind her lids all the yellows Quain described.

"Perfect. Yes, that's it. Exactly. Now, feel that yellow fire grow to the size of a quarter, one in each palm. Do it, Sayblee."

Sayblee focused on her palms, imagining first the size of the fire—two tiny, hollow circles of light—and then she used the power she had always had but used the yellow in her mind. She felt the yellow fire come out of her body and into the circles, filling them slowly. In her mind's eye, they floated on her palms like tiny suns, heating up as they did, flaring and pulsing.

"Oh, wonderful. Just look, Sayblee dear. Open your eyes," he said.

Sayblee did, and her little globes of fire were just as she imagined they would be. They were beautiful. Her fire was beautiful. And she was making all this beauty. She—she herself, was beautiful because of it.

"Yes, indeed," Quain said. "It's all so lovely. Look at you! Look at what you've produced! Not those raggedy streams you've been shooting out for years, multicolored and weak, so weak. These are different! Contained but powerful."

Sayblee nodded, but she couldn't take her eyes off the circles of fire, following them as they hovered over her skin. She wanted more of them. Many more, circles upon circles upon circles of fire. She wanted to surround herself with them, feel their warmth lightly skim her body. And they would always be there, something she could use, something to protect herself from . . . from what? There was a skeleton of some old fear inside her, a skinny strand of terror. She didn't know what she was afraid of, but she knew she needed to make more fire. Now.

"Dear, be patient," Quain said, his voice so smooth in her ear, the sound like silk being pulled through a smooth wooden dowel.

She turned back to him, loving the way he looked at her, loving his small, dark eyes, his expressionless, pale face.

"You will be able to make as much of the pretty fire as you would like. But first try this. Close your eyes again and imagine the circles red. But this time, the red is intensely hot. The most incredible fire you've ever made, full of all you have. As hot as hot can be."

But the yellow fire, she thought. *I want the yellow fire.*

Later. I promise. All the yellow fire you want.

Breathing in deeply this time, Sayblee nodded and then closed her eyes, and in her mind's eye, she saw the circles. At first they were the wonderful yellow globes, but then, slowly, they filled with red. The color hung at the bottom of the spheres, though. She couldn't push the heat any higher.

"Feel the red, Sayblee, dear. Feel yourself red. And the fire will be red," Quain crooned.

And she wanted to fall at his feet and hear his voice all the time, only his words. She wanted to make yellow fire and fall asleep to the sound of his stories.

"No. No. None of that. Not now, dear. You must focus. There will be time for tale-telling later. Feel only the fire. The fire. Only the fire."

So she tried again, doing just as Quain suggested. She felt the red move from her feet, up, up, into her shins, knees, thighbones. Up through her core, into her stomach, heart, chest, throat. Her neck. Oh, the fire was hot. Oh, it was terrible to swallow. Oh, she was going to choke. She was going to die.

"How could you die from this? The fire is you," Quain murmured. "You've made it yourself, from parts of you you've always needed to let loose. How could it be terrible then? No, it's not terrible. It's lovely. It's your lovely fire. It's like the yellow fire, but only better."

The fire *was* her. She'd always and only been fire. Others didn't like her fire. Or her. People teased her fire, someone . . . someone made up rhymes about her, sang stupid songs. People were scared of her. People ran away from her. Her father hadn't liked her fire, never really understanding it before he died. Her mother didn't like her fire, either. Her mother sent her away when she was little because of it. But now her mother would like it. This fire would help make things perfect. This fire—she, Sayblee—would make everything all right.

"Yes," Quain said, his voice so soft and lulling that Sayblee wanted to cry. "That's exactly true. Oh, it's lovely."

And the red-hot fire pushed past Sayblee's throat, up into her head, filling her forehead, the fire circulating through her, and she knew, without looking, that the little globes floating in her palms were totally red, hot, burning embers of the most amazing fire she'd ever created in her life.

"Oh, and there's more," Quain said. "Even more. Better fire. Hotter. You can change the hue—like that." He snapped his fingers, the sound a drum beat in her head. "You have the power. Wait until you feel the black fire, Sayblee. Oh, you will be amazing. You will have the power of life and death. This? This is wonderful, of course. But you, my dear? Well, you have only started."

Yes, she thought, feeling the red begin to heat, to flare, to turn a deeper, darker color, burgundy, maroon with swirls of black. *I have only just begun.*

Sayblee had never felt so alive. Everything in her body hummed as if she were connected to a *Moyenne* electrical facility, everything set to full power output. Her brain was moving so fast that she could hear the thoughts from his followers who sat at the table with her in the enormous dining hall of the mansion.

Quain sat at the head of the table, his dark eyes periodically scanning the group he'd assembled, but mostly his gaze rested on her, coming back to her his lips lightly lifted. She smiled, and her heart grew full, beating to the pulse of burn inside her. Then the noise from his followers would take

over, the clatter of utensils, the language: *Fire . . . plan . . .
now . . . Quain . . . Master . . . . world . . .* Croyant. Words
flew in and then out of her head, nothing sticking, but she
knew she didn't need to pay any attention anyway because
she had the fire. She was central.

"You need to eat," Rasheed said, putting his hand on her
shoulder. "You look . . . You look like you've lost ten pounds
in a day. What did he do to you?"

Sayblee wanted to push Rasheed away, rear back, shoot
off the new fire Quain had shown her, heat the room, and
change everything. How dare he tell her what to do! How
dare he pretend to care for her when he'd left her in the first
place!

But as she looked into Rasheed's face, ready to burn, she
saw that his face and his words didn't match. What he said
was full of concern, but his face was not. She thought to say
something, but what? And how dare he? How could he tell
her what to do?

No, no, my dear, Quain thought. *Eat your food. You
need your energy. You are so important to me. You are so
very, very important.*

Sayblee nodded and picked up her fork, taking a bite of
the chicken on her plate. She couldn't taste it, the chicken,
the vegetables, all blobs of material she pressed between her
teeth. This food didn't matter, didn't help her. Only Quain
did. But on she ate, trying to find ways to swallow each
mouthful. Rasheed smiled, not knowing how Quain only
thought to her, only cared about her.

Quain hit a heavy spoon against the side of his beer stein,
and the group hushed, put down their glasses and utensils.
Sayblee stopped eating and looked around, not knowing
any of the assembled *Croyant.* The dark-haired man at the
end of the table looked familiar somehow, as if . . . as if?

Hush, Quain thought. *Listen.*

She nodded again and put down her fork. Exactly. What

did she care who she knew? All she needed to know was the way the fire slipped up and boiled through her body. All she needed was to feel the swirling, dark globes of fire on her palms. Someday, someday very soon, he would let her throw them, work her best magic.

It's what you were born to do.

Sayblee nodded at the thought that rang in her head like a siren. Yes. What she was born to do.

"We are almost at the time of our ascension," Quain said, standing up and slowly beginning to walk around the table. "We now have the means to make the world the way we want it. There is nothing in our way, save for ridding the world of a few of our enemies. You have all followed my orders perfectly."

Quain stopped, and as he looked at the *Croyant* sitting around the table, she felt him drift away from her thoughts, letting a slim, black strand of doubt in. *Who were these enemies?* she wondered. *What would she have to do with them?*

She looked back at the dark-haired man at the end of the table. She had seen him before, somewhere, someplace, a memory, or a memory of a memory, shifting over her skin, her arms pricking with gooseflesh. She and someone else had seen him, but he'd been wearing much different clothing. Something silly. And it wasn't too long ago. It was . . . it was . . . And then Quain grabbed her again with his mind, and she closed her eyes, loving his tight, hot squeeze on her thoughts. It was so comforting when he was there. She had no questions. She had no fears. He was going to take care of all the details, for now and forever. All she would have to do was make fire for him. She would make the best fire, fire that went beyond singe, beyond burn. Fire that exploded. That's all she wanted to do.

Right?

Right, she thought. *That's it.*

Good.

He went on talking, but this time, he held Sayblee as he did, reminding her how wonderful she was, how powerful, how important.

There's no one like you anywhere, he thought, even as he motioned with his arms, the group rising and clapping and calling out. *No one at all.*

This time, she didn't want to let the dream in. For what seemed like hours, she spun and turned in her bed, trying to shake it away from her mind. But like an annoying salesperson, it kept coming back, pounding and pounding on her thoughts until it finally found a crack and slipped in. There it sat, waiting, its arms crossed, tapping its foot.

Quain wasn't with her now, his hands loosened from her thoughts, but she could still feel the round imprint from the globes of fire on her palms. Oh, that was amazing. That's what she should be thinking about. Not this dream that wanted to push into her mind.

Wake up, she thought to herself. *Go to the yard. Make fire. Wake Rasheed, alert Quain. Don't let this dream in. It's wrong. It doesn't like the fire. It hates the fire.*

But even as she kept her back to the dream, it began to tap her on the shoulder, one finger, two, and then, finally, it clapped a palm on her arm and whirled her around.

There the dream man was again, but this time he wasn't asleep. She couldn't see his face, though, as he was standing in a circle, his head bowed, his hair hanging in front of him. Sayblee walked the perimeter of the dream, hoping she could find a way out, but she just moved around the circle of people in the dream, watched the man she'd seen making love, seen sleeping soundly.

Who are you? she thought at him, but he didn't move. Neither did the people next to him, except for one man with very curly gray hair and dark eyes. At first, she wasn't sure if he really had her in his sights, but as she continued to walk, he followed her, smiling slightly.

Tell him to stop sending me these dreams, she thought. *I have things to do. I'm really very busy.*

Are you really doing such an important task? he thought, his eyes so calm, so soft. *Is this what you set out to do in this life?*

Sayblee looked at her palms, the skin smooth and unlined, no trace of her past at all, the fire burning away everything.

You can't believe what I can do.

Oh, mi'ja, he thought. *I don't need to believe. I know what you can do.*

Sayblee shook her head. *Don't confuse me.*

You are already confused. You need to see him, this one next to me. He will tell you what you really know.

Sayblee shook her head, her palms itching, the fire pooling in her stomach. Who was this man? Why did he think he could tell her anything? She needed Quain. She needed to tell him about this.

No, mi'ja, *you don't. There is no harm in talking with me, in looking at this man. Just come a little closer. This is just a dream, after all. What can it hurt?*

Sayblee watched as the circle of people seemed to flicker in the darkness of her subconscious. They all seemed to be in a trance, in a melded meditation of some kind, except for the man who was still watching her. He seemed familiar in some way, but she couldn't place him, her mind hooked on a splinter of forgetfulness.

Come. Just a bit closer. Look.

She breathed in, pressed her palms together, ready to strike if she needed to, the globes of yellow just under her smooth skin. Walking forward slowly, she tried to lift the man's face with her mind, urging him to look up. But all she could see were his forehead, his long hair, his robed body.

I can't see him, she thought.

Wait, thought the man. And then he closed his eyes, moving back into the trance, and then the man Sayblee had been dreaming about for days lifted his face. His eyes were closed, his expression calm. She didn't recognize him, didn't know him, but something in her body did, her lungs grabbing a breath of air, her heart beating too fast, her stomach pricking with nerves.

"Yes," her body said. "Oh, yes."

The moment didn't last, though, the dream man looking back down into the circle of trance, and then the other man opened his eyes.

That was all I could give you. And we won't be back. We cannot, so you must remember this moment, mi'ja. *Everything depends on it.*

The circle started to fade, the group warbling into darkness, their images dissolving into pixels of black and white. Sayblee reached out her hands, wanting to call them back, just for a minute, a second, needing more time to remember who he was, to let her body have a chance to talk to her mind.

But then they were gone, and Sayblee's mind started to glue over, knit back into the place where she had been these past days, a slow, stuck, thick stream of nothing. Only her hands were alive, itching with fire, and she awoke in her bed, a tiny yellow globe of fire burning on her pillow, the air full of the smells of burning cotton, the room gray with smoky sadness.

She pushed herself up, whispered *"Disaparaître,"* and lay down, breathing in the harsh air, waiting for the dream to make sense.

"You are ready." Quain did not ask a question, his words a strong command. He watched her, his dark eyes flat and hard and intense.

Sayblee nodded, nothing inside her but the fire he'd

taught her to grow, the yellow and red and black she now knew how to make. She had a tiny idea that there was something she had to remember, but as Quain put a long red robe around her shoulders, buttoning it at her neck, just like her father used to do, the idea shimmered away and faded.

Rasheed stood behind her, Quain in front, and Sayblee knew that, just as Quain had said, she was ready.

"Yes," she said, knowing that this was the only *yes* she had inside her.

"Good." Quain snapped his fingers, and in a flood of matter, they all were moving toward the most important thing Sayblee would ever do.

———

Chapter Ten

Felix, Nala, Reynaldo, and Cadeyrn crashed into a wall of matter, the force of it like nothing Felix had never felt before, the press of atoms against his body like steel, his ribs aching from the pressure. This wasn't matter that normally existed—this was enchanted, placed here by magic, designed to keep them all away.

Resist! Nala thought, her voice a bell in Felix's mind. She held on to Reynaldo's arm, grabbing the man as she pushed against the obstruction. *Push through. Go in.*

How? It's too heavy, Felix thought, pushing hard with his mind, forcing the image of their destination of Stonehenge into the very air around them. He pictured it, envisioned the gray stones in the broken circle, the ring of magic left from ancient times.

The useful way is fruitless, Cadeyrn thought. *We need all of us together. Connect the elements.*

We can't use that now, Nala thought. *We need to wait.*

Why not use the power we have? Cadeyrn thought, his words almost a yell as he pushed against matter. *It's not like it will run out, Nala. It's constant, renewing, ever changing.*

Felix could almost hear Nala shake her head, but then—after pressing for moments longer against the impenetrable matter—she relented, thought, *Yes.*

With their minds only this time—no need for holding hands—they connected, plunged back into the thick, streaming rope they'd created at Adalbert's. Felix felt full again, the air, fire, water, earth inside him, around him, and they pushed at the matter with the collective stream. Slowly, so slowly, the matter began to move, shift, bend against the force of their constant press, and then, with a crack, it split wide and the four of them sailed through the opening into looser matter. The bad magic lost its grip and scattered into particles and then into nothing at all.

What was that? Felix thought as they moved on, Stonehenge only an instant away.

Who knows, mi'jo? Reynaldo thought. *Maybe just a little taste of the magic to come.*

No more chatter, Nala thought, and they plunged down, emerging breathless and exhausted into a stand of trees, some five hundred yards away from the stone circle.

Felix took in a deep breath and smoothed back his hair, watching as the others tried to find equilibrium after the rough travel. Nala almost ripped the buttons off her robe so that she could expose her neck and take in a deep breath. Reynaldo and Cadeyrn were both bent over, their hands on their knees, trying to catch their wind. Felix wanted to lie down on the bed of leaves under his feet and sleep. His bones felt weightless, his body heavy, his head dizzy. Clearly, they needed Sariel and his healing touch here on this part of the mission. And this fatigue was just from moving through enchanted matter. Imagine, he thought, what they would feel like after the battle? If they chanced to survive.

But instead of lying down, Felix walked toward the tree line, the movement giving him strength. What were his brothers doing right now? The two strands of the mission had been kept apart, no one sharing information that Quain could later twist around them, choking them free of truths and secrets. Regardless of the need for safety, Felix felt uneasy, a small, dark thud of worry beating in his thoughts. Something was wrong; he understood that fully, but he didn't know why he knew it. Of course, all of them were in danger by being here, by trying to capture Quain. So maybe that was it. Just the real fear that he should have. The fear passed down from when Quain killed his father. The fear that was deserved.

But no. This feeling was something else, as if the fear was given to him by someone else as a token, a reminder, a warning. But who would do that? Most likely his head was scrambled from traveling through matter. He shouldn't be afraid. They had the magic and the power. All they had to do was use it.

Felix shook his head and then looked out over farmlands to the circle of stones across the plain that glowed like giant's teeth in the graying light. This was still a holy place to so many *Moyenne,* busloads of pilgrims arriving daily to walk the perimeter, desperate to find out how it was made and what it meant. Or, at least, they wanted to take pictures of the marvel to show people back home. Even *Moyenne* could sense the energy of the circle of stones, the magic made all those centuries ago by a group of *Croyant.* He softened his gaze and could see the vortex created back then by the ancients, the pyramid of energy rising above the stones. And underneath was a vortex as well, a triangle of energy going underground forty feet. The entire circle was enchanted and protected, the perfect place to finally capture Quain, all the strong, positive energy working against him.

And today, the crowded busloads would chug down the wrong highway, turn round and round in traffic circles, tourists angry about the missed attraction, the bus drivers speeding back to Salisbury or off to Bath without an explanation. Some of the lucky would end up in Avesbury, another magic site. But after a few short, perplexed miles, the tourists would settle back and listen to the guides detailing the countryside in five languages.

The Council had no choice but to protect the circle. *Moyenne* would have no understanding for the magic the *Croyant* were all prepared to make. It wasn't as it used to be so long ago, back when Stonehenge was made. In that time, for a few short years, *Moyenne* and *Croyant* existed together happily. Together, they'd used the stones as a place of healing and magic. No one blamed *Croyant* for bad crops or ill health or sudden eclipses—*Croyant* didn't have to hide their powers; they were able to share them with *Moyenne*.

But, like all good stories, that one ended, magic forced into the shadows by ignorance and fear and horrible political regimes. It didn't have to be this way, Felix knew. Or at least he hoped that. It was possible. Maybe. Cadeyrn Macara had always thought so.

"Yes," said Cadeyrn, walking to Felix and staring out over the fields. He seemed recovered from the trip, his face regaining some color, his breathing calmed. "That's what our world could be like now, too. The circle is the perfect metaphor. All of us existing in one fluid shape. I think the *Moyenne* are ready to believe in us again."

"How can you tell?" Felix asked. "We haven't had ambassadors to their world in centuries."

"All you have to do is look at their literature," Cadeyrn said, smiling. "All those boy wizards and trolls and searches for rings in their movies. Dragons and time travel and witches. Magic everywhere. If the richest woman in England is someone who makes up magical stories, then I think *Moyenne* are putting their money where their mouths are."

"But those are stories for children. Or they are allegories about their religion," Felix said. "It doesn't mean that political leaders are ready to accept change. And what about us? Talk to someone like Brennus Broussard and you can see how some *Croyant* will never forgive the way *Moyenne* treated us in the past."

"I think we are ready to trust them. Look at Reynaldo."

Felix shrugged, breathing in slowly. "He's different. He's special. But, listen, we can't even trust our own," he said. "We haven't managed to get rid of Quain. And look what he does. Kidnaps and murders and controls. How can we offer ourselves up to the *Moyenne* until we are something useful?"

Cadcyrn looked at Felix, his eyes sad. He nodded, turned back to the circle, the stones dark gray now, the glimmers of morning reflecting off the hard sandstone.

"You're right. But soon. One day. When this is over."

"We have to make it happen," Felix said. "We have to save Sayblee."

"And everyone else," Nala said, joining them. "Ourselves included."

Reynaldo—now recovered as well—came and stood by them. He put his hand on Felix's shoulder, and Felix was reminded of Sariel. Both Sariel and Reynaldo had the gift of calming people with just the slightest pressure, the gentlest touch. Felix actually almost heard music, the sounds of a cello, the twang of a country guitar.

"It can all change," Reynaldo said. "We just have to have faith."

"Faith," said Nala. "And some damn good magic."

The three men turned back to her, Felix not surprised to seeing her standing straight and proud, her robe rebuttoned, her face firm, eyes implacable.

"When do we start?" Felix asked.

"At sunrise," Nala said.

Felix nodded and turned back to look out toward the stones. He knew when they were going to start. The only thing left to ask was when would they be done. And when would he have Sayblee back in his arms.

* * *

Felix knew it was good magic. Four *sorciers,* four directions, four elements, the square the most stable shape, a symbol of stability, a metaphor for the very ground itself. When the sun pushed a gleaming, gold arm into the sky, each of them had left the forest, whirled into matter, and taken a place in the square, Stonehenge in the middle. Felix was full of fire, standing to the south of the stones. Reynaldo, dark with earth and stone, was to the west; Cadeyrn, wet and roiling, to the north; and Nala, full of wind and cloud, to the east.

Felix stood still, the air flowing softly around him, his eyes closed. He emptied his mind, even of thoughts of Sayblee, even of the worry that had thumped in his head since the moment he had come to in Alaska, knowing Sayblee was gone. He put away everything, and let his body fill with his hot element, knowing that in the other three directions, the rest were doing the same.

As they all thought together, the rope of elements pushed itself along the straight lines of the square, twining with the strength of fire, water, earth, and air. Once they were all connected, Felix felt Nala call for the *plaques,* needing them to be in the middle of the stone circle, their triangular shape a beacon and the power. The power they needed to subdue Quain.

His arms outstretched, his body pulsing with heat, Felix waited, knowing that when the *plaques* arrived, he'd have to send his energy up, over the circle, urging Quain here. The *plaques* would be a temptation he could not resist, the lure of all this power too intense.

Felix kept his mind clean, his body full of fire, but something was wrong. The energy pulse that would have alerted him to the *plaques'* arrival never shuddered through his body. He wanted to break out of the rope of energy and look around the square, but if he broke the connection, the magic would have to be redone. So, using the energy conduit, he thought, *What's happening?*

For a moment, no one answered, and then he heard Nala gasp, the sound a rasp in her throat. The rope was waving so wildly that Felix was being jerked in place, his limbs yanked.

What?

Oh, no, Cadeyrn thought. *Oh, no.*

Come out, Nala thought. *Everyone, come out.*

We can't. We can't lose this, Felix thought. *The energy is too hard to bring back. We're ready. We just need the* plaques.

Felix, Nala thought, *you need to come out and see this. You will want to. Once you do, you will understand why we must let go of the rope.*

Felix felt her fear as well as Cadeyrn's and Reynaldo's, so he slowly let loose of his element, finding his body again, feeling his breath, his bones, and then he opened his eyes, blinking into the morning light.

At first, he didn't quite understand what he was seeing. He thought that he would see the *plaques* in the middle of the circle, the sun beating down on the stone, the silhouette ghostly even in the daylight. Part of him also thought that maybe Quain had already arrived, ready to do battle. But this was something odd and horrible and perfectly impossible.

Instead of the *plaques* sitting in the middle of the stones, there were people: three people, two men and one woman. Felix stared, blinking, his mouth dry and filled with no sound. It was Sariel and Rufus, both rigid and expressionless, their long hair hanging lank and loose in front of their faces. And what was worse was that standing in between them was Sayblee.

When he realized it was Sayblee, Felix began to run toward her, but Nala commanded in a thought so forceful he felt it in his skin, *Don't.*

He stopped, his heart a beat of wild drums, and he turned to her. *Why? I've got to—*

No. Look.

Felix focused again at the triangle of people in the circle, and he saw that Sayblee was pushing a slight but powerful pulse of fire into Sariel and Rufus. The energy she pressed into them was constant, relentless, and, worst of all, deadly. Felix could see the pain in his brothers' faces, the agony of too much energy racing through their nervous systems.

Sayblee, Felix thought. *What are you doing? Stop.*

She can't hear you, mi'jo, Reynaldo thought. *She's not there. That is not her.*

What do you mean? Felix thought.

She's gone into another place, her thoughts are the Other's. Quain's?

Her body has learned to do what he's taught her. Her mind is closed, though, to what she knew before.

Felix stared at Sayblee, whose face seemed wiped clear of her personality. Her quick comebacks, her sharp, agile arguments, her knowledge about strange, arcane history, her laughter were nowhere in her eyes or lips or cheeks. Her body also seemed disconnected from who she was, her posture as rigid as Sariel's and Rufus's. Her arms outstretched, her face impervious, almost exalted, almost mad, her body almost glowing, she seemed to know nothing, see nothing, feel nothing outside of her own skin. She couldn't know what she was doing. Not the Sayblee he had known all these years, the one embarrassed by the itch in her palms, the girl who'd hid her face and hugged her books as she passed him in the Bampton corridors. No. But here she was, casting out the fire she pushed into his brothers. His brothers! Men she liked and respected more than she'd ever liked and respected Felix, at least in the past. Men she'd never harm.

Sayblee! he thought again, despite Reynaldo's words. *Don't.*

But even as Felix forced his words into the circle of stones and toward Sayblee, he began to notice that the fire was changing color, turning from yellow to orange filled with licks of red.

What's happening? What are we going to do?

That's easy, came another voice, a voice that made Felix wince, his skin jumping with gooseflesh. *It will be so easy to fix all of this right now.*

Quain, Nala thought. *Let them go.*

Felix looked around, scanning the landscape, looking back toward the forest and then around the circle of stones, but he couldn't see Quain, who was well hidden by spells. He scanned for thoughts, sensed Quain using his magic, but Felix felt nothing but emptiness. More than likely, Quain wasn't really even here, sending his thoughts with a *charme de copie,* a duplicate self, a duplicate voice. Maybe he was safely in a house or mansion or castle somewhere, using Sayblee like a terrible marionette.

Nala urged Quain again, and then Felix felt her try magic, a *charme de cesser,* hoping to stop this madness. But nothing shifted, changed, the air as charged with fire as before.

Nice try, my dear Ms. Nagode, Quain thought. *But I think not. I think that today, I will finally be able to get something I've wanted. A few dozen things, actually, all of them larger in size and each more wonderful. Like a holiday gift basket. But the first will be these brothers. The three of them. Almost as wonderful as the three* plaques *that I will have next.*

That won't happen, Cadeyrn thought. *You don't have the power to take the* plaques *this time.*

Right you are. But you four do, and you are going to give

them to me just so I might spare the other Valasay brothers. Which I may or may not do.

Felix was listening to the conversation, but then he blocked his thoughts, cutting himself off from the other three in his group, no longer listening to Quain's banter. He couldn't stand this anymore. How could he just watch as Sariel and Rufus were pumped full of fire, the heat and energy soon to start working their hot evil on skin, muscle, and bone? Was he supposed to just stand here, his own fire still inside him, and watch Sayblee destroy his brothers and herself?

As Nala and the other three communicated with Quain, Felix watched the fire begin to change color again, the orange disappearing into a full crimson, the stream thickening as Sayblee shot it into Rufus and Sariel. His brothers' bodies seemed to slump, to lie almost lifeless in whatever magic was holding them up. But, most horribly, their eyes were open now, and, as Felix began to slowly walk toward them, he could see their pain, their fear, their horror.

He could almost feel what they felt, the searing of fire into their systems, the overload of energy crackling down tendon and ligament. How long could they handle it? How much longer could their bodies take the constant, intense heat? As he watched them, so many years of memories flicked through his brain. He saw the countless times that they had saved him, healed him, taken care of him, even though he had resented it, complained about it, wished they'd just leave him alone. There was the sound of Rufus's deep laugh. There was the picture of Sariel's sarcastic smile, his eyes bright with the joke. Images of Miranda and Fabia slipped through Felix's mind, as did the images of the babies both women were expecting, two little fetuses floating in amniotic sacks.

Then he heard Zosime, could feel her words pressing on his mind. Hadn't she just been worrying about the three of them, saying, "I just don't understand why every time Adalbert gets a wild hair, it involves all three of you boys. All three. Not just one or two but all of you. Aren't there dozens of *Croyant* families with three boys he could pick from? Why always my sons? That man. I'll have a thing or two to tell him later, when this is all over, and everyone is home safely."

And then there was Sayblee, her softness against him that night on the Paris rooftop, her lips so warm, her hands holding on to him, her hair against his palms. She was his dream Sayblee, the woman he loved in his imagination as well as in life. He couldn't let her do what she was about to do.

Felix stopped moving. He ignored Nala's mind first tapping on his and then pounding at the closed door. He ignored Cadeyrn's and Reynaldo's ideas rounding his barred thoughts, desperate for entry. Instead, he closed his eyes and conjured forth his own element, the fire that he'd learn to cultivate for himself. Slowly, he focused on pulling the swirling fire up his body until he was full of it, swimming in fire and light, just as he had done twice before. But this time, he did not reach out for the other elements, not wanting to bring the other three into this. He was the only one who should attempt this, and there was no other alternative. It was his job. The only thing he could do.

And then, once he was full of the fire, a stream hot and red inside him, he used his magic, changed his form, reassembled his atoms so that he could do what he needed to do.

No! he heard Nala think out, her words a scream.

But it was too late. He was already inside. He was already a fire folding into fire. He was already gone.

It was so hot. So hot, burning him through the center. He knew that he had to keep moving, keep pressing forward, but he wanted to lean back and cry out, wanting the pain to disappear. The fire mixed with him pulsing so hard, he knew that within minutes, there would be nothing left of him at all. But he could see where he needed to go. He had to keep moving. He had to make it to the center.

And he could see the horrible core. Black and pulsing, a mixture of hate and revenge so hot it barely moved, its surface simply rippling with the force of its contained energy. That's what he needed to swim into. That's where he would be able to change it all.

Chapter Eleven

Ah, she was hot. Wonderful. Burning. Brimming. A second from exploding. Everything inside her was fire, was hot, was swirling around her body and then out. And, oh! How wonderful it felt shooting out of her. She'd never been able to let loose, but now she could, was told to, was given permission.

She wasn't sure who she was anymore. All she knew was that she was to push the heat that was now black from her hands. All she knew was that she wanted to, to destroy everything. How she loved the destruction, the pain. She could feel pain, could feel that she was hurting others, and she liked it.

She wanted to dance, to stamp her feet, to howl. She wanted to be the fire forever, and she knew that she could. But then something was wrong, different. Something was inside her, crawling hot and yellow through the conduit of her fire. She tried to shake it away, send heat toward it, but when she did, the thing absorbed what she gave it. Maybe it stopped for a second, shrank away for a beat, but then it was moving toward her again. She could almost imagine it crawling up a wall, its long yellow arms reaching for her, wanting her.

"No!" she called out, trying to rise above the crawling,

creeping thing. She searched for the voice that had been guiding her for so long, but it whispered away into the beat of her own heart. Her heart? What was she doing? Who was she? What was the thing inside her? She thought she remembered it, knew the pattern of its beat, its fire, its pulse. But what?

Before she could conjure forth another question, the yellow crawling thing was in her face, swirling around her, tying up her hands, holding down her fire.

Help! she thought out, not knowing who she was calling to. The voice? Or maybe even this hot, crawling thing that was holding her so tightly.

She wanted to relax into it, lay down all the power. How lovely. How peaceful. And as she tried to discharge the flashes of energy, to let go of the power stirring inside her, she felt the intensity bump up, lift a notch, engage her very core.

The crawly thing began to shiver, to pull away, and she grew larger and larger, full of more of the black fire, unable to stop herself. She was huge, bloated with it all, roiling with energy, and then she knew she would explode and take the small, crawly thing with her. It twisted in her tremendous grasp, squeezed by her size and strength. But somehow, it managed to keep her fire from going away from her body, turning everything inward, toward them both.

And then she remembered something, heard the words coming from deep inside her mind. From her memory, she saw an image of a man, a long-haired man with wicked green eyes. A beautiful man, a man she loved. For a tiny second, she pulled back her energy, slowed it, made it soft. But it was too late to change what was going to happen, to change what was under and in her skin right now.

I'm so sorry, she thought, even as she burst into a million molten atoms. *I am so very, very sorry.*

*   *   *

Later—maybe ice ages had come and gone, tectonic plates shifted, weather systems covering and uncovering the earth, creatures living and dying and being born again—she was floating on a thin, gray band of air. She was barely there at all, only a wisp of consciousness periodically waking and then falling back to sleep. When she opened an eye into the gray, she saw only the light flicks of particles passing in front of her, could only feel how her body hung in the air, so light, so loose, just like swinging on a hammock. Back and forth in a soft breeze, her limbs like hollow tubes, her hair floating all around her, her body only a slim outline against the moving stream of matter.

Nothing was left of her, no flesh, no bones, no memory. She had no name, no words for herself, only this invisible sense of her body. And it didn't matter because she didn't have the strength to care. There was nothing to hold on to from the past, nothing to anticipate from the future. All she knew was this buzzing emptiness, this light, bobbing float in the middle of nowhere.

She was seconds from slipping into the gray, of becoming nothing but air all around her. If she just held her breath, she would stop existing altogether, she could finally become what she had wanted to become. Nothing. Open. Clear and free. Somehow, although she didn't know anything about who she was, the need to not be anything made almost too much sense.

That's what I will do, then, she thought. *Hold my breath.*

She concentrated on her lungs, pulled in as much air as she could. There. One last breath, and then nothing but this comfort forever. This air. This peace. Floating endlessly.

She held on to the air in her lungs, could feel how her very hollow bones were starting to disappear into matter, but then something warm touched her. Softly, slowly, starting at her ankle. She wanted to shake it off, knowing that it was keeping her from the freedom she so craved. But she couldn't move, and it was moving upward, holding hot on to her calves, her thighs, pressing a warm, orange hand on her belly, moving up her ribs to her throat. And as the warmth slid up her, she felt her body change into form, her bones fill with calcium, her body fill with blood, her lungs crave the air she was withholding from them. There were her feet, her hands, her legs, her arms. Inside her body, her organs began to move, function, pulling life back into her core. As the warmth seemed to press on top of her, holding her in two strong arms, she could even feel her heart beat against her bones.

Oh, she thought. *This is what I want. All this feeling. I want to be alive. I want this.*

Sayblee (and she knew now that was who she was: *Sayblee*) let go of her breath, exhaling into the warmth all around her, letting herself reach her strong arms up and over the warmth that held her, and she pressed it close to her, needing this lovely feeling to teach her how to be alive.

"You're all right," the warmth said to her, pressing her even closer. "We're both all right."

Then Sayblee felt something loose around her face, felt the warmth's hair, felt his shoulders, knew, finally, who he was. Oh, where had he been? She'd been waiting so long.

"Felix," she said, feeling the tears start to come. "Oh, Felix."

"Yes, baby," he said. "It's me. I'm here."

She opened her eyes, half-expecting to see only yellow and orange heat, licks of fire, blasts of flame, but instead, it was Felix, his almost-green eyes looking down into hers. For so long it seemed, she'd had to forget his view of her, the way he looked at her, his eyes wide, his mouth in a slight grin. Why had she had to forget? What could have made her ever want to? And how had she been able to finally remember?

"Where have you been?" she asked. "Where have *I* been?"

Felix put his mouth to her cheek, her neck, breathing in for a moment before lifting up and looking at her again. "You were with Quain," he said. "I don't know what he did to you, but, well, it's over. At least, part of it."

Sayblee looked past Felix, into the gray that still swirled around them. "Where are we now? In matter?"

He stroked her hair. "I don't know. Before I found you, I was simply floating, and I couldn't think myself out of it. No magic works. What happened when you expl—I mean, what happened back at Stonehenge must have pushed us somewhere. But I don't know where we are at all."

For a second, Sayblee felt panic. Her heart pushed against her bones, her face felt flushed, all her body seemed to tingle. There was a twirl of memory in her head, images of Rasheed and Quain and of two men, both of whom she knew she'd wanted to hurt. Had it been Sariel and Rufus? Had they been the two men she'd hurled that horrible fire at? The horrible fire she'd tried to push into their bodies? Sayblee knew that at some point in her rampage, she'd remembered Sariel and Rufus, remembered Felix, her fire lurching, and then there was the flash, the pain, and the matter.

What had happened? She closed her eyes, pressed her face against Felix's shoulder. She couldn't go there at all. She couldn't stand to think of it. Whatever she had done, she knew it was horrible, evil, vile. So she let the images fade, and she breathed out, pulled Felix close. At least they were safe. At least she hadn't killed Sariel and Rufus. At least, that's what she thought. But she and Felix were here, together, in matter, or some kind of matter, floating with each other, finally, after all this time apart.

"Felix," she murmured, and then she put her lips to his, kissing him, needing him to kiss her back. And he did. This time, it wasn't a dream, something she'd concocted from magic in her bed in Paris. It was real, all of it. They were flesh and bone and blood. She could feel him hard against her belly, both of them somehow unclothed in this strange place of matter, both naked to each other for the first time.

"Baby," he said so softly, she almost missed it, the feeling in his word more tangible than the sound.

"Yes," she whispered back, and then he was kissing her again, tasting her lips, his mouth so warm, so soft, so just where she needed to be.

And then his hands were on her shoulders, her arms, his palms moving toward her breasts, cupping them so gently, even as he kissed her still, his tongue warm on hers.

She moaned, pushing toward him, feeling how her body moved with his, their pulses, their flesh synchronizing, their passion shared.

And even as they floated, their bodies suspended in the swirl of gray, they moved together, pressed to each other's centers, needing better contact of chest, stomach, thighs, shins.

"Oh," she said as he traced the outline of her body with his hand. "Please."

"Yes," he said, his mouth following the line of her sternum, ribs, belly, his lips then right on her, just where she pulsed.

"Yes," she agreed, letting him take her that way, letting the matter hold her still as she felt everything, all of it, all of him.

And she relaxed, letting her mind focus on nothing but his lips, his fingers so soft inside her, the way her body accepted him, needed him, the way that she could let go.

"Felix," she whispered, pressing against his lips, letting all of her feeling rise, letting herself forget, letting herself remember. Felix. That was who she had seen while dreaming at Quain's. Felix was who she thought of even as she burned with that wild, ferocious energy. Felix.

Her head fell back, she took in all the feeling, letting her cries sail into the gray. And then he was over her again, slipping into her, his eyes on hers as he did.

"Whatever happens," Felix said as he moved against her, his body in hers so hard, so full, "we have this. We have this right now."

Sayblee nodded, pulling him to her, shutting down her mind. Even though he'd found her, saved her, wanted her, she wasn't sure she could let him know how much she needed him. She couldn't let him know that it would never be enough. She would have now, and she would want later. She would want later all the time.

"So can you tell me how we both ended up here with no clothes on?" Sayblee asked later, still holding tight on to Felix. They were exhausted but peaceful, floating still, the matter lighter somehow, almost opalescent.

"Kind of convenient," Felix said. "Made my seduction plans a bit easier."

"You've had those plans going for a while," she said.

"All the way back in Bampton," he said, kissing her shoulder. "I was just waiting for the right chance. It took fourteen years, but I was finally successful."

She laughed, pushed him away with a hand. "Right. Like you've ever needed a chance. You just showed up, and a hundred chances were there with their pretty dresses and nice smiles and tender kisses. The line was four school-grades long."

"Jealous?" Felix grabbed her wrists and brought her back to him. "Having a bit of the green monster, are we?"

She shook her head, knowing somehow that she was never going to have to be jealous again. Of course, they were in the middle of nowhere, which made jealousy a bit moot.

Sayblee laughed to herself, put her lips to his cheek, his skin lovely against her skin. "Eventually, we need to think about how to get out of here, though. And, hopefully, we'll have our magic back when we do."

"I think I'll make sure you don't cover yourself up entirely, though. No button-down blouses this time." Felix spun in the gray, pulling her on top of him. "No straight skirts and sensible shoes. No ponytails."

"Oh, what do you want? Something like your famous Roxanne from Hilo? Thongs and lace bras and tons of silver jewelry?"

Felix laughed, ran his hands from her shoulders to her rear, her skin tingling as he did. "Were you spying? How did you know about all her jewelry? She made sounds when she walked. When she did anything."

"Felix!" Sayblee said. "I guess maybe you still want her."

"Hardly. No, I don't want Roxanne from Hilo. I want only you, Sayblee Safipour from London, England, even if it means you will continue to look like a librarian. Maybe you could let your hair loose. Maybe you could unbutton a top button or two. But it doesn't matter at all to me. As long as you are there."

She shook her head and took in a breath, not knowing if she would laugh or cry. All of that life seemed so far away.

They were silent for a moment, and then Sayblee sighed. "How do we get out of here, Felix? We need to go back. We have to. As soon as we can. I don't know exactly what I did back there, but I have to make it right."

"It's not your fault," Felix said.

"Maybe not, but what about . . . What about Sariel and Rufus? I don't know how—I don't know if—"

"Shhh," Felix said. "I think I was able to stop things before, well, before it was too late."

Sayblee shrugged out of his embrace a little, moving so she could look at him carefully. "You can't be sure of that, and we have to stop Quain. And I found Rasheed. He's still alive."

"He's been with Quain all this time," Felix said rather than asked. "He's been working with him."

She felt herself react to his words, her body inching away from his. "I think he's enchanted. Or under some kind of magic. He trained me how to do what I did for a while. At least, that's what I remember. But then Quain took over. But I could see Rasheed inside. I know I can save him."

Felix shook his head, took in a deep breath. "You can't save everyone."

"How can you say that?" Sayblee pulled away from him completely, feeling the whip of matter around her body as she moved. "How can you possibly? What about what happened to Cadeyrn two years ago? He was enchanted and pulled out of it. Adalbert and Reynaldo were able to save him."

"Look at Kallisto," Felix said. "She was enthralled by Quain and she's been in prison ever since. And not only in prison, completely gone. No one can talk with her. No one has been able to reach her."

The joy that had been a yellow fire in Sayblee's chest, ever since Felix climbed hot and fiery up her body, flickered and was then snuffed out. How could Felix be talking to her like this? He had brothers. He should know how she felt about hers. Didn't he want her to save Rasheed? And if he didn't, she would let him go. Just like that. Nothing would stop her from trying to save her brother. It wouldn't stop Felix.

"You're right," Felix said, and she realized that in her anger, she'd opened her mind to his completely. "It wouldn't stop me. I'm sorry. I just don't want you to feel bad if it's— if it's too late."

Sayblee dropped her head down, looking at her own skin, so strangely luminous in the swirl of gray. She let him pull her back to his chest. It couldn't be too late. But even if there was time, how were they supposed to push out of this matter? They had no magic, no clothes, and no ideas.

"I actually do," Felix said. "Ideas, that is. I'm not certain, but I think that the way we came in is the way we can get out."

"How, exactly, did we get in?" she asked. She didn't remember anything but an overwhelming sense of her own power, her body full of a fire she'd never felt before. And then everything had blown apart, the scene bursting into nothing but the lightness of her own body.

"Fire," Felix said. "The kind you were able to make. I just hung on for the ride, though it wasn't easy."

Sayblee sat up in the matter and shook her head. All at once, she could feel the roiling under her skin, the waves of black heat inside her body. Worse had been the feeling inside her mind, the idea that she was all-powerful, all-destroying, that she had no other purpose but to kill. She'd been like the stories told by *Moyenne,* the tales of the destroying goddess, Kali, Pele, Durga. Actually, the memory was like laughter, a crackling, black laughter, a joy that she would never want to feel again. No, she couldn't go there. She'd lost herself in the power, become something else altogether, something too big, too hot, too wild. She wasn't sure that she could stop herself, needing—as she had before—to burn everything.

"I'll stop you. I did it once." Felix sat up and put his hands on her shoulders. "I promise. I will stop you. I won't let you get out of control. I'll hang on tight. And this time—this time there are only the two of us here. There's no one else to worry about. Nothing but matter all around." He motioned around them, the world like the grainy buzz of a broken television.

"But the two of us is what I want," Sayblee blurted, feeling ridiculous as the words came out of her mouth. Ridiculous and pathetic.

Felix lifted her chin with his index finger, even that small part of his body warm and comforting. "Sayblee. Love.

That's all I want, too. It's all I've thought about from the moment that Quain separated us. And I think it's what I've wanted for longer than that. But at least if this plan doesn't work, we will go together. We will be in the fire with each other."

Sayblee looked at Felix, let her gaze touch all of him, from his lovely face to his legs, strong and wrapped around her. She had to accept. She had to allow for the possibility of losing him so that she could have all that she wanted. Without saying yes, they would be stuck here forever, together but not living any kind of life. Without saying yes, she would lose Rasheed and her mother forever.

"All right," she said, leaning forward and kissing him. "Okay."

Just like Quain had taught her, Sayblee closed her eyes, pulled into her center, and conjured the yellow fire, the gentle fire, the fire that could burn down buildings or stone or steel, but not the fire that could explode. It was easy, this yellow fire, a fire that had always been inside of her, ever since she could remember. This was always her limit. This is where she had always stopped, not wanting to be too powerful. But then, as the fire began to burn and grow and wick more intense, turning crimson, vermilion, hot and violent, she forgot that she was scared of fire hotter than the yellow. In fact, she wanted the hotter reds, the slicing, brilliant oranges, the intense heat pulsing through her like scarlet fever.

Yes, she thought. *This is who I am. This was what I've always been meant to do. This is what they've tried to keep from me always. Finally, I can be myself, let myself free, let myself feel the power I've kept tamped down.*

The flames burned inside her, overflowing the container she'd always kept her fire in, pulsing in every vein and muscle and bone. But then she felt that annoying thing, that crawly yellow thing she hated. She couldn't stand the way it clung to her body, tried to hold her down, hold her back. She wanted it off, away. Oh! It was making her angry, and she let out the darkest fire, the molten, black, rippling fire that was her true nature, her inner core. *More,* she commanded. *All.* And she let herself grow large with it, enormous, nothing in her way now, not even that little yellow horrible thing. She was burying it in her waves of heat, crushing it with her anger.

I am so amazing, she thought. I am . . . I am . . . .

And then she was not, the world a blister of hot air and hatred, the gray a hole in the universe.

This time, it hurt when she awoke. Nothing was light and breezy and empty. Instead, her body was heavy and sore and bruised, pain thudding down her ribs, her spine, her legs. Her head felt like a kettledrum, her heart like a stone, her stomach flat and heavy and sick. And even as she lay on the ground, her eyes closed, her body heaving and hurt, she knew that there was no more fire in her. Not a spark. Not an ember. There was nothing in her left to hurt anyone.

And her magic? She couldn't feel that either. It was as if the fire erased her, made her only human. Made her *Moyenne.*

She opened her eyes, looking around her, searching in what must be midmorning light for anyone, anything. For Felix. But there was nothing but a hard floor of dirt under her, beech trees hanging over her. She heard the slight hum of engines somewhere in the distance, the call of a robin, the sounds of a small animal scratching in the bracken.

Slowly, she pushed herself up, taking in deep breaths as she did. Every joint ached, but soon she was standing unsteadily, her legs wobbling, her knees and hips threatening to send her back to the dirt at every second. She wasn't sure she could really feel her feet at all. But with tentative, jerking steps, she started to walk, she started to run. She had to find him. And then she had to find her group. She had to find Rasheed. But more than anything, she needed to find Felix, to fix whatever she'd broken in him. To have the wonderful chance of telling him how much she loved him.

Even though she had no magic and knew no one could hear her, she tried.

Felix! she thought as she moved under the canopy of trees. *Felix. Where are you?*

There was no answer. Not one single sound.

Chapter Twelve

He was dreaming again. That he knew. How else could he be only a slim yellow line of heat? How else could he feel that he was wrapped tight around something that was choking him of life? The dream was making him dizzy and weak, and he knew that he had to wake himself up. He had to get out of the dream before it turned into something real.

He thought to loosen himself from the blackness he clung to, to pull away slowly, but with every move he made away from the darkness, it came closer, hotter, with more intensity, its movements sounding like a horrible, wicked laugh. There was nothing he could do but hang on tight. In fact, he remembered that he had no choice but to hang on because he needed to save the dark heat, this terrible fire even as it killed him. Yes, that was it. That was why he was here.

So he squeezed back, pushed into the black fire until the dream shut closed in a bang of energy, his slim yellow body cracked into a thousand pieces, his mind and his dream dissolving into dawn.

"Felix," someone said in his ear or where he thought his ear might be. How could he have an ear? Or even a head for the ear to be attached to? A body seemed more than unlikely because he wasn't more than a fragment of yellow, a piece of energy, a whisper of an idea. He was a scraggle of dying flame, a flicker of burned carbon. He had no body, no voice, no thoughts. But he was thinking, wasn't he? How else would he have heard his name?

"Felix," the person said again.

And then Felix felt hands on him, the body that he must surely have. But what part of his body was being touched? Did he have body parts? There was pressure. A hand, fingers. Yes, he did have flesh, and the hands were on his face, giving him warmth, a trickle of sensation.

"Just stay with it," the person said.

Or was the person even talking? Maybe these were thoughts.

"Focus. Stay with me. Stay with me, Bro."

Felix hung on to the last word: Bro. It meant something. It was something. It told him who he was and who the person speaking to him was. *Bro.*

The warmth moved into his mind, twirling through his brain, moving down his spine, connecting him to parts of his body he'd forgotten he had when he was flickering. He was a body, not a line of heat and fire. He felt gravity come back to him, replacing air. And in a few moments, he felt himself lying on top of something—a bench, a floor, a terrible mattress—with his brother's known hands on him, filling him with life.

"Sariel," he said, his eyes closed. "You're alive."

"Thanks to you, I am. Both Rufus and I," Sariel said. "Now, sleep."

Felix nodded, unable to do more than move his head and let his eyes close, and he was asleep again, this time, not a dream in his mind.

* * *

"Where is she?" Felix asked the second he awoke, looking into the darkness of the room.

"*Lumière*," Sariel said, and the air was filled with a soft white glow. Felix blinked and then saw his brother sitting next to him on a chair. Felix lay in a bed, the mattress hard under him.

"Where?" Felix asked again, his voice scratchy and stiff.

"We don't know," Sariel said in the darkness. "After you jumped into her fire and released us from her grasp—well, Rufus and I had some healing of our own to do. Justus Kilgour came in to help heal us all, and then the rest of the group went after Quain, but couldn't find him. We've reconvened here."

Felix nodded, knowing that Justus was a strong healer, and that's why Sariel was able to help Felix at all. A couple of years earlier, Justus had helped Rufus regain all his memories, his mind almost wiped clean by Kallisto and Quain's bad magic. And now everyone was off searching, once again, for Quain. While Felix was . . . was?

"Where's here, anyway?" he asked.

"We're in Normandy. A small farmhouse outside of Sainte-Mère-Eglise. A place called La Cour. We know Quain has been here."

"But Ru?" Felix asked. "Where is he? You said he was okay?"

Sariel laughed. "Once we found you, he left to join the group. He keeps sending me updates and asking me questions about you. He might as well have stayed."

"Why Normandy?" Felix asked. "Why would Quain pick this area?"

"It's relatively isolated and rural around here, and he could hamper traffic and activity in the neighborhood and no one would raise a fuss. This is probably where he trained Sayblee."

Felix breathed in at her name. Sariel looked at Felix, shaking his head. "What was she? What did that fire do to her? What did that feel like to jump into it?"

As he thought about his brother's questions, Felix almost shivered, feeling the black lick of fire still in him, the burnt ash still on his tongue. That fire was so full of anger and heat and power it could destroy anything, but there was something else. Something about the way Sayblee became the fire, almost as if it fit.

"It was magic," Sariel said, pulling the ideas from Felix's thoughts. "That's all."

Felix shook his head. "I don't know—"

"What? A woman with too much power is . . .? Too much?" Sariel smiled. "This isn't about fire or magic. It's about you."

Pushing himself up, Felix sighed. "She was awesome. Horrible. But awesome. I guess it would be a little scary to come home to at night."

"I bet," Sariel said. "She'd be like, 'You don't like dinner? You don't like my cooking?' and she'd blow the block down."

"Sayblee doesn't seem like the dinner-making type. I can just see how she'd look at me if I even brought it up." Felix sighed again and leaned against the wall. "I just want to find her. I want to have this over with. I want to go home."

With her, Sariel thought.

Before Felix could reply, and with a bang, Rufus burst in from matter, his long dark hair wild around his head, his robes in disarray, his face red. "It's going to be teemin' out there soon," he said, smoothing his hair. "What a storm coming."

Felix shook his head, wondering when Rufus would start wearing a kilt, so thick was his brogue now.

"Hey, Ru," he said.

"You're all there, then?"

Rufus walked to Felix, put his hand on Felix's shoulder. "I knew you'd pull out of it. Couldn't let your saving us both go to waste. I know this will be the stuff of family dinners for years to come. Mom will have to make her famous chocolate cake."

All three brothers laughed for a second, but then the sound died flat in the room.

Rufus took in a deep breath. "We don't know where Sayblee is, but we've found Quain. We need to go to meet the rest of the group now."

"There's no sign of her anywhere? No one can hear her thoughts? We don't have a *chercheur* who can pick up her movements, seek her out wherever she is?"

Rufus shook his head. "It's like she's a lightbulb that was snuffed out. Gone."

Felix could feel his whole body still, his heart slow to a sad *beat, beat, beat*. "What do you mean?"

"I don't know," Rufus said. "We don't think she's—We don't think it's the worst-case scenario. But something must have happened when you forced your way out of that matter. She lost her magic or she . . ."

"Listen," Sariel said, standing up and holding out a hand to Felix, who took it and stood up slowly to stand next to his brothers. "We won't know until we get rid of Quain. And then we will find out everything. We'll find Sayblee then."

He clapped a hand on Felix's shoulder, and then Sariel and Felix moved into Rufus's mind, found the image of a Norman mansion, a deep-green field, sheep and cattle grazing in the bucolic background.

But just as Felix felt his brothers' hands on him, a message screamed into his ears, all of their ears, and they opened their eyes and looked at each other, nodding, changing plans, going where they had to go. Now. Fast.

* * *

"We don't know how it happened," Nala said. "We thought we had a good fix on him, but he must have slipped away."

"By God," Rufus said, shaking his head, his face pale. "Was no one looking after her? Was no one there? Didn't anyone think that she might be in danger because all three of us were in on the mission?"

Felix felt the same words on his tongue, felt the same anger, but Nala didn't flinch, her face, as always, calm and still and slightly irritated.

"Of course she was protected. But . . ." Nala paused, her face for a second falling into worry. "We underestimated Quain. We imagined that he was too busy with . . ." And she paused again.

Felix bent over and put his head in his hands, unable to know how to feel, what to focus on, what to do. Sayblee was gone and now his mother had been abducted, right out of Adalbert's house in the middle of the night, despite all the spells and incantations and guards the Armiger had in place. Zosime had been taken by Quain followers so that Quain could do what he'd always wanted to: get rid of her.

Since long before Zosime and Hadrian Valasay had been married, Quain had hated her, thought she was a nuisance, imagined she took Hadrian away from him. Instead of working with him on missions, Hadrian had chosen to be with Zosime. Then, later, he'd chosen his wife and three sons over exploits with Quain. And because of Hadrian's choices, Quain had killed him. Rather than share him with Zosime, Sariel, Rufus, and Felix, he killed Hadrian with a blaze of hateful energy, leaving him to bleed out on the train tracks of the Les Halles Métro station.

"Well, clearly, whatever was there wasn't enough." Sariel was pacing the room. "So why aren't we already looking for her? Why aren't we there now? Why isn't she already back!"

Sariel turned to Nala, his face as angry and cold as it had

been on only two other occasions that Felix had seen: when he realized how he had been enchanted by Kallisto and then when he realized that Adalbert had enchanted his memories of Miranda out of his mind. Rufus, too, was agitated, his palms beating a fierce staccato rhythm on his knees. Felix understood his brothers' anger and anxiety. He felt exactly the same way.

Nala seemed to grow despite the collective angry feelings of the Valasay brothers, her stillness filling the room. Felix stared at her, and he could feel her magic calm them all.

"We have a plan, but things have been complicated because of—because of Sayblee," Nala said, just a slight hitch in her sentence. And again, Felix bent down, his head in his hands. All of this was too much.

"So, then," Rufus said, "we know the blasted complications. Now we can be off. There's no time to waste. I can only imagine what he wants. What he will do. He's always hated her."

Felix's heart thrummed, his stomach a dull, red pulse in his body. But just at that moment, Adalbert popped into the room, the air a swirl of heat and wind.

"Felix," he said. "Now."

And before Felix could even nod, he was pulled into the gray, the Armiger only seconds ahead of him, his purple robe whisking ahead of him in the grainy matter. *Stay with me,* Adalbert thought. *Your mother's safety depends on it.*

Their travel seemed to go on forever, and Felix felt his anger break into pieces, the way things did sometimes in the gray—all thought, all flesh becoming part of the great tide of matter, the big, wide expanse of energy that was everything. Just in front of him was Adalbert leading the way. But to where?

Like I said, my boy, stay with me.

But why me? Felix thought. *Why not Sariel? Or Rufus?*

There was a whoosh of matter, a block of energy thicker than most, Adalbert dodging around it, pulling Felix after him.

Because you are the youngest.

Felix almost smiled. That was the reason he was usually left out of things. That was the reason people left him alone on Hilo.

I don't understand.

There's nothing planned about that magic, Adalbert thought. *The youngest is a prize to parents, even if there are only two children. Something melts in the parental heart, softens, opens, loves a little bit differently. The heart becomes more receptive, even if the parent tries everything to guard against it, thinking that this feeling is somehow unfair to the other children. But this feeling is strong in your mother, and that's what we are going to use to save her. That's our way in.*

There was a burst of thick, almost-black matter, as if something solid had been flung at them, and then Adalbert yanked Felix down and, before he could breathe another breath, they were standing on a sidewalk in front of a nondescript apartment, somewhere, it seemed, in a city in the United States. The apartments were block-to-block ordinary, concrete steps with metal railings leading to dark doors. A few lights shone down onto the wide, asphalt-paved street. Every block had a white fire hydrant, a gleaming street sign, a bank of stoplights. In the distance and out of sight, he heard the gravely, scratching bang of a skateboard hitting the pavement, a bang of a plastic garbage-can lid flopping closed, the yelp of a chained dog.

Felix turned to Adalbert to ask where they had landed, but Adalbert whispered a spell, and Felix knew they were invisible to the night world around them, the cars and pedestrians. Invisible as well to any Quain followers who might have tracked them.

This way, Adalbert thought, and they walked up the street until Adalbert stopped, holding out a hand to stop Felix's movement. *Here. She's close by.*

Felix followed Adalbert's gaze, and they both stared up into a darkened window.

Felix shook his head. This entire mission had been a series of small, cramped apartments and houses, strange locales, and ridiculous twists. Here they were in Podunk Center, USA, looking for his mother, a respected member of *Croyant* society, a powerful *sorcière*, the widow of Hadrian Valasay, one of the most valued Council members in history.

Don't doubt, Felix, Adalbert thought.

I'm sorry, Felix thought. *But this seems bizarre.*

This is simply about bringing your mother safely home. This is not about Quain. Not yet. It's only about Zosime.

Felix nodded, but he found himself almost smiling, a prick of amusement at each corner of his mouth. What was it he was hearing in Adalbert's words? But just as he asked himself the question, he felt a wash of gray cover his thoughts, a *charme d'étourderie* keeping him from thinking any further on the subject.

But? Felix began.

Focus, Adalbert thought back, and he turned to Felix, looking at him so fully that Felix wondered if he might be swallowed up by the Armiger's gaze. Finally, Adalbert breathed in, and then Felix was flooded with the knowledge of what he had to do.

Adalbert thought the word again, the word that had started this entire rescue. *Now!*

Felix nodded, shut his eyes, and began.

It was so easy to conjure forth what he needed. At every turn in his mind was an image that would work: Zosime over him as he lay in bed, smiling, her hand soft on his flushed cheek. Her voice, soothing, incanting a healing spell, his instant recovery.

Then, there—her song, a whisper of love—as she moved through the house, a melody he couldn't name but could recognize anywhere.

And next, her laughter as she watched them playing in the yard, creating childhood magic, a burst of smoke in a game of soldiers, a whirl of leaves from the raked pile, a flash of rain on a summer's day.

Of course, there were her tears, the sounds at night Felix hated to hear but always listened to, knowing that grief was part of the whole, that without her tears, Hadrian's death would have less meaning. But, oh, how he hated to listen! His eyes wide-open in bed as she tried not to make sounds but failed. He could even bring forth his brothers' distress, the messages they sent each other in the night to comfort each other: *She's just crying a little bit. She'll be okay. She's all right.*

In the morning, she was just that, bustling around the kitchen, making sure they ate their breakfasts, shooing them out the door to play, encouraging them not to cause any trouble, at least for one day.

Later memories flooded in: the way she always appeared when coming out of matter, her long hair wild about her face, her cheeks flushed rosy, her brown eyes warm.

Her teasing words about his dating life, her soft hand on his shoulder as she said, "Felix, find a woman you can love. Or just know that you can love. Let yourself. I can't promise you that it won't hurt, but it's the best hurt that there is."

It took everything he had not to think of Sayblee, not to feel her next to him, not to worry about what was happening to her at this minute.

Zosime, Adalbert insisted with his thoughts, *Zosime.*

Felix bore down, his mother's image like a deck of cards

in his mind. Years of life, years of words, all of her right in front of him. As he thought, his heart seemed to grow in size, expand, fill with sorrow and joy and laughter and tears and song, and that's when he heard his mother, her voice small and tinny in his mind, but there all the same.

Follow me, she thought, and with that, he felt Adalbert's hand on his shoulder and in another instant, they were gone.

They appeared in a room that could have been part of one of the horrible, ordinary apartments they had stood in front of on the street, but it was hard to tell, the room dark, the windows draped, the space all but empty. All Felix had done to get there was follow the conduit of energy from his mother's voice, leading Adalbert and himself to this very spot. He lurched forward when he saw his mother trapped in a chair in one corner of the room, but Adalbert held him back. At the man's touch, Felix realized that they were both cloaked in a *charme d'invisibilité,* neither his mother nor the quick, slim figure pacing at the front of the room noticing them at all.

After his time in Paris with Sayblee, Felix was used to keeping his magic in check, and he pressed his thoughts, his feelings, his energy down into his core, knowing that any distraction might put his mother at risk. He barely wanted to breathe, but how could he not? How could he not yell out? His mother had clearly been treated badly, her hair wild around her face, her face pale, her eyes so tired. Even her body didn't seem to belong to her, her back curved, her hands limp.

"This is almost as lovely as what I will conquer next," Quain was saying. "To see you like this, so subdued, so, frankly, silent. What a pleasure. Not like in times past when all I heard were your opinions. Your ideas. How tiresome you were."

Zosime didn't even bother to look up, but then she winced, as if Quain was squeezing her tight. Again, Felix almost ran to her but for Adalbert's hold.

"Hurt, does it? How sad. Well, it will hurt quite a bit more, though I don't think I'll end it anytime soon. I want you to be able to watch your son go down. Yes, your little precious one. The one who was always underfoot and noisy. God, it was a relief to never see any of those brats again."

At that comment, something in Zosime stirred. Felix saw her take a small, tentative breath, then another, and then two deeper breaths, her body filling with strength and energy with each one. Finally, she raised her head, her brown eyes losing their blankness and becoming fierce and full of fire.

"Trust me, Quain, it wasn't just you who felt relief when our association was over. There was no one who mourned your absence. And even before that, there was no one who wished you back. Hadrian was glad you pulled away from us. He didn't want to work with you anymore, not after you started your rants about the Council. Not after you asked him to go—"

Quain raised a hand and bowed his head. "Stop. That story is not for you to retell. You weren't there. You can't know how the *Croyant* life I showed Hadrian made him feel. You weren't there. You can't know. Only later, when he had to tell you about it, did the story become what you know."

Zosime sat up even straighter in her chair. "Hadrian Valasay would never in a million years have gone with you down your dark path, Quain. Not for a moment. He wouldn't even take a second glance as you walked away. Don't delude yourself on that score."

The room rumbled and groaned with the movement of magic, a *charme de tremblement de terre* almost knocking both Felix and Adalbert down to the floor. Zosime rocked

in her chair and let out a light scream. Felix felt his whole
body tense.

"Silence!" Quain yelled. "Enough. I don't know why I
listen to you."

"Because," Zosime yelled back, "talking to me, talking
to my sons—that's all you have left of Hadrian. We are the
only things that can bring him back."

Quain laughed, putting his hands on his thin hips. "You?
Anything like Hadrian? Part of Hadrian?"

"Yes," Zosime said. "And if you kill me, if you kill my
sons, there will be nothing left. Your heart burned into ash
so long ago, you can't find Hadrian there, no matter how
hard you look. You can't find him in your memories because you've colored them all so bitterly. That's why you go
after my children. That's why you covet them. You can still
see Hadrian, even as you punish them with your magic. You
can still see him when you look in the eyes of my sons."

Quain paced again, the room jolting with each step.
Zosime followed him with her eyes and didn't stop talking.

"But do my boys want to see you? No. Just as Hadrian
wouldn't want to see you. Not after what you did to him in
Les Halles. Not after you let him die. Not after the evil you
have perpetrated on all *Croyant*. Imagine, Quain. Just
imagine trying to tell Hadrian the story—"

"Silence!" Quain yelled again, turning to her, his face a
wild map of pain. "You don't know—"

"Yes, I do," said Zosime calmly. "I know more about
Hadrian than you ever will. Enough to know that if he were
here today, he wouldn't be able to be in the same room as
you. Not for a single second."

The room began to jolt again, and Felix felt Adalbert
move slowly forward.

"You are a stupid woman," Quain said, raising his hands
over his head. "I only wish I'd been able to put you out of
your misery long ago."

"You didn't have the nerve," Zosime said, still sitting so straight in her chair despite the increasing force Quain was putting on her bonds. "You still don't. I'm alive, aren't I? I'm not dead yet."

Mom, Felix whispered to himself. *Oh, Mom.*

Quain shook his head, light glowing at the ends of his fingers. "We shall see about that."

The room slowly began to pulse from the magic coming from Quain, his current strong and deep and even. Felix felt his entire body try to push him forward, even as his feet stayed stubbornly planted.

"I've tried this spell on some of your family members before," Quain said, just as his magic turned magenta. "I didn't have it quite worked out. But now, *c'est magnifique.*"

He began to lower his hands and, as he did, Adalbert shot Felix a thought, one that Felix knew he could deliver on.

Save her, Adalbert thought, and Felix rushed forward invisibly, throwing out protection *charmes* as he did. At the same time, Adalbert made himself visible, shocking Quain's magic to a dim pink, the room dark with his disappointment.

As Felix conjured a *charme du libération,* freeing Zosime from her chair and bonds, taking her into his arms and moving to the back of the room, Adalbert stood in front of Quain, a smile on his face.

"Quain, I wish I could say that it was a pleasure to see you, but it is not," Adalbert said.

"The displeasure is all mine," Quain said. "But I would much rather take you down than Zosime Valasay. She's nothing. But you. That's another story. And once you are gone, I can get rid of all the others, in a perfect order."

As Quain continued to talk, Felix felt Adalbert's words seep through safe channels.

You have only about a minute left. So I will distract him here. Go.

I'm not sure I can get us out, Felix thought back. *I don't know how we got here.*

Anywhere, my boy, is safer than here.

But you?

I, Adalbert continued, *have long been fine. Please.*

Felix could sense that Zosime was listening, her body struggling at the conversation.

We can't just leave you, she thought.

Let's not have our first argument, Adalbert said. *Both of you. Now.*

And with those words, Felix closed his eyes, held his mother in his arms, and thought himself anywhere but this room. In what felt like a tear in fabric, they pulled away from the space, and the last thing Felix saw as they left was Adalbert standing in front of Quain, the room slowly growing brighter with bad magic.

After a few moments of darkness and confusion, Felix realized they were sailing through matter, having skipped altogether the sidewalk lined with apartments. He then thought about his brothers, France, the farmhouse in Normandy, the warm kitchen, the logs burning bright in the large fireplace.

Felix, Zosime thought. *You can loosen your grip a little. I promise not to float off into some grainy corner of matter and stay there.*

He started, realizing that he was lucky he hadn't broken his mother's ribs.

Sorry, he thought, relaxing his arm, but just a bit. Not too much at all. He wasn't going to lose her again.

If I remember correctly, I taught you how to navigate matter.

Felix nodded. *You did. But that scene back there was— that was . . .*

Horrible, Zosime thought. *The man is stark, raving mad. I just want to get home and take a bath. Maybe have a long nap.*

Felix laughed to himself, moving through a slightly bumpy patch of the gray, knowing that they were almost back in Normandy. But then something jostled his memory.

He turned toward Zosime and watched her profile as they moved. *What did Adalbert mean about* first argument? *What is—*

Felix, Zosime thought in the voice he knew well from childhood on, full of love and metal. *I need a bath, not an interrogation. Maybe, if you are good, I'll tell you the whole story after Quain is taken care of.*

He shrugged. Clearly, he'd stayed in Hilo far too long. Life had been going on without him.

Felix shook his head, pulled his mother close, and took them both back to Sariel and Rufus and safety.

Chapter Thirteen

Felix had sent out a quick message before he and Zosime made it to the farmhouse, and when they arrived—jostling out of matter a bit roughly, Zosime finally capitulating to her ordeal with weak knees and a slight moan—Sariel, Rufus, Philomel, and Brennus were there to meet them.

"Oh, my dear. My dear!" Philomel said, taking Zosime's arm from Felix's as they arrived. "What a thing. What a thing!"

Sariel and Rufus moved forward, both gently moving Philomel out of the way and hugging Zosime. Felix could read their thoughts in the air, their worry slowly being replaced with relief.

Brennus, though, stood stern at the head of the room, his arms crossed. "Where's Adalbert?"

Felix turned to Brennus, hoping that his irritation was covered. Actually, he didn't want it to be covered, and he let his feelings open up in the room. After a second, Brennus sighed and rephrased.

"Is everything all right?"

Felix turned to Zosime and then looked back at Brennus. "I don't know. Adalbert stayed to deal with Quain so we could escape. I hope—"

Zosime pulled away from Rufus's bearlike embrace and turned to Brennus. "You must go find him. You have to see what happened. If you need to, you have to help him. You might need Council help."

Brennus listened, and then, when Zosime stopped speaking, he seemed to be reading a steady stream of her thoughts, and within a second, he was gone into matter in a whirl of robes and sparks.

"Now, I say," Philomel said after Brennus left. She moved toward Zosime and slowly began to extract her from her boys' careful embraces. "I think you need to have a bit of a rest, don't you? What about a nice, hot bath with some salts? I think I can read that very thought in your mind. A little lavender? Some nice rosemary?"

Zosime nodded, patted her boys' arms, and then she and Philomel left the farmhouse kitchen, closing the large wooden door behind them. Sariel and Rufus turned to Felix, and Felix knew that they had to go after Quain again. And this time had to be the last.

Hours later, without really knowing if Adalbert would make it back at all, the group decided to convene, hoping that their intention would bring the Armiger back.

Traveling through matter, they arrived at the mansion, hoping that Quain had returned, knowing from their spells that his followers were inside, as was Rasheed. Whatever plan Quain had in mind started here, at the mansion, and the group had no choice but to start from this place, now, even though it all could fall apart without Adalbert.

I don't know what the man was thinking, Rufus thought as they stood in the cool green grass in front of the mansion. *Not leaving with you. He had no reason to stay there and tangle with the man. There was time later for that, to be sure.*

Felix shook his head. *He wanted to be certain I got Mom out. He wasn't leaving anything to chance this time.*

Sariel looked over at them and smirked. *Yeah, he had something vested.*

Felix raised an eyebrow. *Vested? What do you mean?*

Nala interrupted their thoughts, with a thought har-rumph that silenced them all, and motioned them to move into position.

There were more of them for this attempt, each element doubled. Felix was still fire, but this time he was connected to Niall Fair, Fabia's almost-white-haired brother, his fire burning at the same intensity as Felix's. Nala was paired with Sariel, both air and wind and wild, open space. Rufus and Reynaldo were earth and stone and dirt. And Caderyn's water element was paired with Adalbert's, who, just as Nala pointed her fingers at the Valasay brothers, had whirled into the expanse of lawn, bringing the *plaques* with him.

Finally, Felix heard just about everyone in the group think.

"Can't start without these," Adalbert said, as if he was bringing last-minute party favors to a birthday celebration. As if he hadn't just faced Quain all by himself.

*How did it—*Felix began, his thought insistent.

But Adalbert just shook his head, adjusted his robe, and settled his glasses more firmly on his nose. Felix noticed that the Armiger seemed to be favoring one leg, and Felix hoped that nothing too horrible had happened to him by Quain's hand. But there was no time for a healer. Not now. Not when Quain was so close.

You'll have to tell me everything later, Felix thought, but Adalbert was too distracted with the *plaques* to answer. For a quick second, Felix could have sworn that he heard his mother's name echo in the cold, crisp Normandy air, Zosime like a bird's call on the breeze. He looked around, but both

Sariel's and Rufus's thoughts were still, calm, full of only their elements.

Felix sighed, wondered if his mother was trying to send a quick message to him from her bed. Philomel had helped her with a bath and then Zosime went to bed, drained from the abduction. Sariel had time to do some quick healing, but then Brennus spun back into the farmhouse, alerting them that Adalbert was on his way.

Despite the pain Quain had inflicted on her, Zosime was right back to worrying about her three boys, concerned that they were going off again on a mission, so soon after having left Quain in a state of upset and anger. If she was sending a message, it would likely also be filled with concern about Adalbert. But Felix couldn't worry about Zosime anymore today. He couldn't dare think about Sayblee or what happened to her or where she was right now. He had to stay focused on Quain. So Felix found the calm space in himself and looked out into the scene before him.

The *plaques* gleamed, their colors incandescent and brilliant in the morning light. But now, they were placed in the middle of the large square that the group had formed, turning slowly around and around, their power generating a call that Quain would not be able to ignore. The signal would be too seductive, Quain's desire for ultimate control too great.

Felix concentrated, focused, feeling the fire in his belly, hoping that he could keep his need to know where Sayblee was pushed down under the embers of his power. But even though he felt again consumed by flame, every so often, like a splash of water, Sayblee would leap into his thoughts.

"Felix," she would say, her beautiful, serious face in front of him, her hair tied primly behind her in a neat ponytail, "can't I count on you for this? Or are you going to run off with the next farm girl who walks by?"

He would shake the image out of his head and reconnect

with the fire, roll into Niall's energy, feel how strong they were together, and then it would happen again.

"My word," Sayblee would say, flicking her now-loose hair behind her shoulder and putting a hand on her hip. Or maybe she would shake her head and put down her large, thick book, something on a king or president or warrior princess. "First you leave me on a rooftop and now you let me blow myself up into a million pieces. What next?"

Again, he would try to focus, but then came the worst. Images of Sayblee under him, looking into his eyes with her wide blue eyes, wanting him with the same passion he wanted her. Her legs, her arms, her hands on him. Her body against his, her wetness, her open mouth, her cries. The way she felt when he moved into her, pressing as far as he could go.

Lad, Niall thought loudly, shaking Felix out of his reverie. *She is a braw lassie, but you're killing me. I'm having trouble keeping other parts of me from combusting.*

So, Felix had to shake himself out of it again. But this time it had to last.

That's right, Niall thought. *This is our final opportunity.*

And then Felix and Niall joined with the other pairs, all of their collective elements one thick, powerful strand of energy. Even with everyone together, collective, tied, Felix could feel the purple wave of Adalbert's water pulse harder and stronger than the rest, and he knew that this time, Quain would not be able to distract them.

Now, Nala thought, and together they lifted off the ground, slowly rising, their energy flowing between them. They continued to rise until they were hovering over the mansion. But Felix didn't feel as though he was anywhere but in his element. This was what was inside him, what he could do.

Above them, clouds rolled in from the Channel, gray and full of storm. In the distance, lightning cracked and the wind picked up leaves and twigs from the ground. Below

them, the *plaques* twirled faster, generating a yellowish
glow that lit up the darkening landscape. Slowly, they began
to rise, pulling ever so slowly apart, heat and energy building in the space between them.

No one said or thought a thing. Finally, all thoughts were
quelled. There was nothing to say. All they could do was
watch and wait for Quain.

Below them, the *plaques* rose, the energy glowing red
now, a sound coming from them as they turned. What was
it? Something that reminded Felix of sunrise, something
brand new, something cracking open. It was the sound of
water and things being conceived and born and then dying.
It was a melody of life being made, of life being lived, of life
ending, only to begin again. The color was yellow, then
green, then black, and then yellow again. Everything in a
spiral of life and death and life again. This was the power of
the *plaques*; this was what made them important to *Croyant*
and to Quain, who needed to make a world he wanted.

The group continued to rise and so did the *plaques*, the
sky rosy from their heat and spin. Felix felt his body disappear into his element, all the elements, a wash of the world
inside him. But then, from what must be his eyes still, he
saw a figure appear outside the square of energy the group
had created. A small, black figure, cloaked in some kind of
dark magic that moved in a swirling darkness, a vortex of
evil protection. The same figure that had just paced before
Zosime, torturing her with words and spells.

Below.

But just as the thought pulsed through the rope, the
swirling darkness shot into a thick, straight line and flung
itself from Quain, opening up and filling the space of the
square with a sheet of black. When the darkness hit him,
Felix recoiled, his fire dampening, the heavy energy like depression, like rain, like sadness. Like Sayblee, gone.

Throughout the rope, he felt the same reaction, only specific to the element. The earth opened to air, the air filled with earth, the water dried to the bone, nothing but sand at the bottom of the ocean. All of them reeled, the connection quivering between them.

Don't let go, Nala thought. *Stay together.*

And after a moment, they seemed to adjust, and slowly, the darkness turned to gray, dissipated into the morning. But where was Quain?

Wait. Grow stronger, Nala thought.

And together, they hooked back into their elements, pulling forward the flow, the heft, the freedom, the energy of their powers, the rope between them pulsing and twisting with everything that the universe could offer them. Gravity, lightness, density, spark. Felix lost himself, becoming what he had never been, and he could feel their collective selves merge into a river, hovering over the *plaques* where he could now sense Quain.

Knowing he was seen, Quain shot out another sheet of darkness and, for a moment, it tapped on the power Felix felt, but then it was gone. Quain shot out another and another, and even as he did, the group slowly moved in, the square turning to a circle, the circle slowly moving around Quain, coming closer, closer.

And then Felix noticed what the *plaques* were doing, somehow guided, he understood, by Adalbert's purple wave of water. They slowed down, but moved apart, a slim, dark stream shooting from the top of the opening.

Focus, Nala thought. *Stay together.*

Felix hurled his energy into the stream, and together the rope of elements and the *plaques* forged an energy that began to encircle Quain.

From some tiny distance, Felix thought he heard a cry, a sound, a moan, and he knew that they had him.

Press, Nala thought, and they did, curling around and around Quain, ignoring the small, distressed, dark messages he sent out, the feeble attempts at using his magic to repel them, tiny little pricks of hate and fear and loathing. How Quain struggled. Just like a toddler, stamping his feet and banging his elbows around. Finally, Felix thought, after all these years. He squeezed tighter. Finally, after all the horror Quain had caused. He pressed in, using all the fire within him to burn back, to burn hard, to force away, in, gone. This was for his father, Hadrian. For the pain Quain had caused Sariel and Rufus. For Zosime, hunched over in the room, forced to defend herself with only her words. For countless others, for years.

Round and round they twirled together, moving with the *plaques,* turning and turning and turning until everything was over.

Chapter Fourteen

Sayblee ran until she couldn't run anymore and, more importantly, when she knew that she would be seen. Not only would she be exhausted and scared, she'd be naked in the middle of a field somewhere, running for the hedgerows for cover.

So she slipped in between two rows of tall corn, trying to avoid the sharp green leaves that scraped across her reddening skin, moving as fast as she could, which was now just a slow plod, one foot and then the other. Part of her wanted to laugh, thinking about Felix in the Métro and how she'd jumped all over him for not wanting to take the train or walk up steps, teasing him about all his complaints. Even now as she slogged through the corn, she could see his expression, his eyes wide, the smile just on his lips, the way he lugged his suitcase up the stairs. She could see him on the couch at the Paris apartment, sprawled out as if he'd just run a marathon. But the images she pulled forth made her sad, so she went back to the two words that had pushed her up off the ground and made her run for what seemed like miles: *Felix, Rasheed; Felix, Rasheed.*

How happy she'd been to see her brother after so long! His face looking at hers, his voice telling her stories, his arm on her shoulder . . . all had been her dream for years. Yet something had been so wrong with Rasheed, but then again, something had been so wrong with her. She'd allowed Quain to control her, to put a fire in her body that didn't belong. She'd almost—

No, she thought. *No.*

Felix, Rasheed; Felix, Rasheed.

She had to find them. And she couldn't bear to think about what might be happening to either or both right now, at this minute, as she was struggling to plow her way through this year's crop.

The rows of corn ended, so she ran a quick ten yards on a small, dusty road to a hedgerow, slinking along the smooth trunks of some tall trees, the canopy spreading wide above her. Wrens rustled in the thicket, small brown rabbits scattered as she moved. Overhead, crows cawed into the brightening air. All around her, farm life started to break into morning. Sayblee could hear tractors and trucks, their engines roaring in the distance, diesel fumes filling the air. Roosters crowed, cows mooed as they walked toward feed bins. In less than an hour, the world would be awake, not just the farmers. She had to find a place to hide. Or she had to find some clothes. Otherwise, she'd be arrested or thrown into one of those horrible mental intuitions *Moyenne* called hospitals. But she couldn't get caught. Not now. Not when she had so many things to do.

She kept walking, looking around her as she did. All of this was starting to feel familiar, and she wondered if she was close to Quain's mansion, the place where he'd taught her to become—to become that thing. The thing that had killed all her magic. The thing that might have killed Felix.

Trying not to cry, Sayblee kept walking, her feet cut and bleeding, her skin scratched from the sharp stalks of corn, her eyes aching from the bright sun. Her body still ached from the fire that had wiped her clean, her lungs burning with each breath.

She made it to the end of the hedgerow and leaned against a tree, looking west and east, desperate for some kind of landmark or sign, or just a good idea. And then she heard it, the sound that had made her laugh, even when she was enchanted and forced into Quain's grip. The sound that told her where she needed to go.

It was Burro. She heard him clearly. His terrible, silly bray.

Despite her burning feet, her aching body, Sayblee began to run, moving toward his sound, knowing that, for better or worse, she was going to find out what had happened. She was going to find out the truth about what had happened to her brother. And what had happened to her lover. Her lover. Felix.

She didn't worry about being naked. She didn't worry about anything, especially once she saw the paddock, then the field, and then the mansion. All she had to do was get there, find Rasheed, take him away. But how? How could she do anything without any magic? How could she convince her brother to leave the man who had enchanted him?

And then together they could find Felix. As kids, they had always worked well together. It could be the same now.

When she reached the paddock, Sayblee slipped inside and looked for the old work jeans she knew were hanging on a nail by Burro's stall. She grabbed them and the rain jacket that was hanging there as well, and put both on, not caring that the pants slipped around her hips and the plastic of the jacket poked into her sides.

She also found a pair of old green Wellies, slipped them on her feet, and ran out of the door and across the field until she reached the mansion's south wall. Pressed close against the stones, she looked around carefully, hoping that her senses would provide her with clues. But it was so quiet. The birds weren't singing anymore, and she couldn't hear the farmers' tractors at all. It was almost as if the air had been erased of sound and even smell—no hay, no grass, no animal odors. Nothing. Not even one more Burro bray.

A vortex, she thought. *That's what's keeping everything out.*

But as she looked across the field she'd just run across and then up at the house, she knew something else was working here. A spell. Or—

"Or I've finally arrived," Rasheed said, appearing next to her. Sayblee jumped, hitting her back against the house as she did.

"Rasheed," she said. "You scared me."

"Not surprising."

Sayblee looked up into her brother's face, thinking she would see maybe a hint of teasing. But his face was stiff, still, held together like a mask by some bad magic.

"Rasheed," Sayblee said, trying to inch her body slowly away from his. She knew that he would be confused by the openness of her mind. Maybe he wouldn't understand right away that she had lost her abilities. All she needed was a second, and she could round the house, and maybe she could call out and someone would find her. Maybe Adalbert and the Council had sent in help. But as she moved, he grabbed her wrist, hard, twisting it just a little.

"You aren't going anywhere," he said, yanking her close. "Not that you could without your magic."

Sayblee swallowed, tried to find her breath. "It—it will come back," she managed to say.

"Don't be counting on it. Quain made sure of that," he said, his voice deepening. "You are helpless now. You need us."

"Us?" Sayblee asked, her head jerking at his comment. "Us?"

Rasheed nodded and began to walk toward the front door, pulling Sayblee along with him.

"What are you talking about?" Sayblee asked.

But Rasheed didn't say another word. Instead, he pulled her into the house, letting the wide, wooden door slam behind them. He kept moving, walking toward the stairwell and then down the stairs toward the large cellar that ran under the entire house. Sayblee hated the cellar and its dank, dripping walls and the squeals of tiny dark rodents running along the floor.

"What are you going to do?" she asked, turning her head as they thumped down the steps, Rasheed taking two steps at a time. Sayblee slipped in her Wellies, staying on her feet only because of his constant tug.

"We have a last chance," Rasheed said. "It's not over yet. They think it is, but it's not."

Before Sayblee could ask what he meant, he pushed open a door and almost flung her into a chair that was next to it. Within seconds, she was bound by a *charme de contraint*, her arms and legs immoveable.

"What are you going to do?" she asked, noting that Rasheed seemed to be talking to himself, his lips moving to a conversation only he was privy to.

"We are going to make a transfer."

"What is this 'we,' Rasheed? You're the only one here. I don't see any one else. No Quain. No one."

Rasheed looked at her blankly for a moment and then started to laugh. "How predictable. How limited you are, especially now that you've lost your magic. Just a girl, really."

As he spoke to her, Sayblee realized that without a doubt this wasn't her brother. No matter the spell, the enchantment, the curse, the charm, Rasheed would never talk to her like this. He'd never seen her as "just a girl." She had been his partner in crime, his compatriot in mischief, his ally against their parents. This was the brother who had helped her learn how to use her fire and how to put it out the second before their mother whirled into the room, trying to catch them in the act. The boy he'd been all those years

ago—his true self—was not the man he'd become once he'd
left for Quain. And this man before her now? The one pacing the floor? This man was Quain. Or what was left of
Quain. Quain using Rasheed's body for whatever else he
could pull off.

And, thankfully, it seemed, Quain's temporary kidnap-
ping of her brother's body seemed to have kept him too
busy to read her thoughts. Sayblee didn't feel any probing
there (not that she knew if she could, given her magicless
state), and, before Quain noticed, she pressed down her re-
alization that he was using Rasheed. She closed her eyes and
breathed, casting her mind about for something safe and
boring and flat, something that would keep her thoughts
from turning to the facts before her.

What was there? The fields. The fields she'd just walked
through, the sharp press of corn stalks on her flesh. No. No.
That pain reminded her of her fire self, the destroyer, the
horrible she-creature she'd become. She pushed away
thoughts of her frantic search for Felix. She needed something softer. Something that couldn't hurt her now. Something
that might save her. Matter. She'd think about matter, fuzzy,
lovely gray matter. There she was, floating in matter so light
and soft that she could run her fingers through it. From far
away, she heard Rasheed/Quain banging around in the room,
calling out spells, talking to himself/themselves. But she didn't
think of that. Nothing but lightness. Nothing but calm.
Nothing but the lovely sway of her body. And, within seconds, she was asleep.

She woke up to the *charme* pulling her tight, almost lifting her from the chair. Sayblee opened her eyes, and saw
that in fact she was being lifted from the chair as something
or someone dangled her from the center of the room, the
chair under her.

"Go one step closer," Rasheed said. "And I will kill her."

Sayblee looked toward the spot to which Rasheed directed his voice, and she felt her heart bump against her bones. If she wasn't tied up and dangling, her dream would have come true. There he was. Felix. Safe and well and completely alive. And he wasn't alone. Sariel and Rufus stood with him, the three of them standing against the cellar wall.

Felix glanced at her, his eyes trying to tell her something, but all she wanted was to feel him holding her, just the way he had when they were stuck in matter. Then none of this would make a difference, at least for a while.

For a second, Sayblee thought that maybe her magic was back because he seemed to understand, his eyes softening, holding her gaze. But then he shook his head, his attention brought back to Rasheed, who was pacing along the other side of the wall, throwing out streams of energy that cracked against the walls and then flared to sulfur.

"You don't want to do that," Sariel said, holding something out in front of him. "I have this."

Rasheed stopped, stared at the small black cube that dangled from what looked to be a slim leather necklace. Sariel swung it back and forth, the cube glinting in the sallow light like a rotten tooth.

"Give that to me," Rasheed said. "And I'll give you the girl. Not an even exchange, but I'm willing to be kind."

"I think you've got that ass backward, lad," Rufus said. "It's more about giving us the lass and then we will talk about this sad little package here."

Rasheed stopped, his eyes darting, his mouth moving to a conversation Sayblee couldn't decipher.

"It's mine," Rasheed said, spreading his arms, the room blasting with light. "Give it to me."

The three brothers didn't move, didn't step forward. Sariel kept the necklace dangling from his hand and, even without her magic, Sayblee could see that there was something very powerful guarding them, something from outside the mansion. She hoped it was Adalbert and the entire Council.

"You want this," Felix said, his voice clipped and tight, anger deep in every sound. "You want to go back to your body, Quain. And here is your body, all wrapped up nice and tight by a lovely *charme de condensé*. How sad if we were to destroy it right now. Just a little magic, and you are stuck in poor Rasheed or loosed to the winds. What will you do then? You don't have enough magic to bring this back."

Rasheed seemed to shiver from the bottom of his feet, his spine and neck twitching, as if someone were pulling a long thread out of him. Sayblee held back a cry, knowing that whatever was happening to him, it couldn't go on forever. That kind of magic ate a person up, strong sorcier or not. And it was clear to her now that Rasheed had been enchanted and entrapped by Quain since the beginning, for years, and he probably didn't have much strength left.

But then Rasheed jerked straight, stood still, his face implacable. He reached out his hand, and the whole room glowed with light, fire shooting from his fingers. Felix and his brothers pushed back a *charme de force*, the light and heat bouncing off and splattering across the ceiling, embers and ash falling all around them. Slowly, they moved forward, holding up the force field, moving closer to Rasheed, who seemed to quiver again, his body loosening from Quain's control.

The room was pulsing, energy coming from everywhere, all over. Sayblee wished she could hold her hands to her eyes and ears. It felt like magic was pressing her skin close to her bones, the tension from the *charme* and from the forces outside so intense she was being squeezed breathless. And Rasheed seemed to be crumbling, his knees wobbly, his arms limp, his head bowed. The Valasay brothers moved closer and closer, their *charme* growing in strength, the color of it red, moving, pulsing.

Please, Sayblee thought as hard as she could, trying to find the tiniest bit of magic in her body and mind, desperate to get it to Felix. *Please don't hurt him. Please let him live.*

But she heard nothing back, nothing but the whir of the wild air around them all. She saw nothing but the hot glow of magic. She could feel all the *Croyant* power coming in from all the minds of those who wanted Quain captured and enthralled; from those who wanted him dead, once and for all. As she watched Felix, Rufus, and Sariel walk forward, she saw a gold filament of vibrating magic whip up over them and slowly curl its way toward Rasheed, the charmed tentacle over his head, ready to grab him.

And as Sayblee dangled from the chair, growing faint, the blood pounding wildly in her head, she thought one last thought, hoping that Felix would hear her. Hoping that Rasheed would, too. She gathered all her strength to find the magic within herself, the magic that would kill—the magic that would save.

I love you. I love you both.

When Sayblee was a little girl, the early morning was like a blanket she pulled over her face and breathed in, her warm bed and the soft light coming in through the windows giving her the safest feeling she had ever had. Or had had before now. Now there was something wonderful holding her, some better feeling than that childhood memory of light and softness. Something more than the safe rumble of her mother's voice downstairs and the knowledge that Rasheed was in the bedroom next to hers.

But what was it? What was she feeling?

She tried to turn, but something held her still. She didn't

feel trapped in this immobility. But held. Warm. Cared for. Her eyes hurt as she tried to open them, and something, someone whispered, "Hush. Sleep."

She knew the voice, was about to say it aloud, felt the letters form on her lips, but she fell back asleep, letting her body relax, letting her mind wander.

"Are you in there?" asked the voice. "I have a feeling that you are somewhere. But I just can't quite tell."

Sayblee smiled, realizing she wasn't quite sure if she was here. There. Wherever. Was she somewhere?

Stop joking, came the thought. The thought? She heard a thought? Her magic was back? She was back to normal?

Do you think we'd go to all the trouble to save you and not find your magic?

I didn't know you knew where to look, Sayblee thought. *I couldn't find it anywhere.*

Girl, I've had a good glimpse of all of you. Don't forget that. I've seen places where the sun doesn't shine.

Sayblee smiled again. *How do you know that?*

I know you, Felix thought, and Sayblee opened her eyes to his gaze, his green eyes wide and concerned, his smile full.

"What happened?" she asked, and then she tried to sit up. Felix held her down, his hands warm on her shoulders, his fingers reaching for her collarbones, stroking her skin softly.

"Rasheed? Is he all right? Quain? Did he get away?" Sayblee could feel her breath in her throat, her heart moving against the side of her ribs.

Felix murmured, "Hush," again.

But this time Sayblee pressed him away. "I have to know. You have to tell me."

Felix sighed, looked over across the room where Sayblee saw Sariel sitting on a chair in the corner of the room. She looked around and realized that she was at Adalbert's house, in the very room she had stayed in the last time she was here. But on that occasion, she would never have imagined that Felix would one day be sitting on the side of her bed, stroking her into calmness, whispering her back to relaxation.

Sariel stared at Felix for a second, shrugged, nodded, and then was gone, whirling away into matter.

"Quain's, well, contained," Felix said after Sariel left. "The magic put him in a place he'll never get free of, unless we let him out."

Sayblee felt impatience beat against her bones, but she didn't say a thing, knowing that the story was going to come out. She also knew that she wasn't sure if she wanted to hear the part about Rasheed, the story too easily going into sadness. *Make this part last,* she thought to herself, keeping her thoughts from Felix now. *Let this part of the story be long.*

Felix looked at her, and she felt his thoughts rub against hers and then move away. "You know that little black cube Sariel was holding? You saw that, didn't you?"

Sayblee nodded.

"With the magic and with Adalbert's strong energy, that was where we managed to put Quain's body and most of his mind, in a *cube de bagne,* a prison he will not be able to escape from. The magic we were able to do with Adalbert worked, except we didn't know how much of himself he'd put in your brother. In Rasheed. Quain had been hibernating in your brother's thoughts for a long time. Since probably when Rasheed first went away with Quain. And Quain hadn't enchanted anyone else like this before. Not Kallisto. Not Cadeyrn, so we weren't sure what we were dealing with."

Sayblee felt her blood whiz through her veins, her fingers and toes tingling. Her forehead felt clammy, but she breathed in, needing to hear the full story. She nodded again, scared to open her mouth, not knowing if a cry or gasp or moan would come out, the sadness inside her stuck in her throat.

Felix stroked her hair, pushing it away from her forehead. She wished he would stop talking. She wished there was no more story. But she had to know, so she put her hand on his, and he continued.

"So we managed to force him into the cube, but then we realized that something was missing. A vital part. That's when Sariel, Rufus, and I found you. And Rasheed. We had so much energy helping us, but still, it wasn't easy. With you hanging in the air, with Rasheed just—well, it was a careful bit of magic that finally worked. We just barely got Mr. Bad Stuff in here." Felix patted his pants pocket.

At those words, Sayblee did gasp. "You have him here? Quain? In the cube? You haven't given it to Adalbert to hide in some vault forever? It's—he's—not locked up in jail behind a thousand protective spells?"

Felix smiled and slowly pulled the long leather necklace out of his pocket. He held it up, and swaying on the necklace was the little cube. Sayblee stared at it, watching the light reflect on its stark darkness. Quain was in there. Quain, who had done so much wrong, was finally contained and compressed, his body and thoughts pressed and condensed in onyx.

"Are you sure you have all of him?" she asked. "There aren't little bits of him anywhere else? In anyone else? Floating around in the universe waiting to strike?"

Felix looked at the cube and put it back in his pocket, then, with his hands back on Sayblee, stroked her shoulders and arms. "We're sure. This time, we're positive."

Sayblee shook her head and then looked toward the window, taking in a deep breath. She had to ask. She had to know. "And . . . and Rasheed?"

Without her having to say another word, Felix nodded, leaned down, and pulled her tight into his arms, and then they were traveling through matter, through Adalbert's house, appearing next to a bed, where Rasheed seemed to sleep. Sayblee was so weak that she leaned against Felix for support, but she bent down and put her hand on Rasheed's arm. He seemed more than asleep—gone in some way, far, far away, lost to the past and the future, the present only this quiet room.

In the corner of the room, Rufus's wife, Fabia Fair, sat in a wooden chair, clearly uncomfortable in the very last minutes of pregnancy.

"He's not asleep," Fabia said, standing up with some difficulty, using her arms to press herself up, her stomach leading the way. "It's the spell. But Sariel and Justus are working on it. It will only be a matter of time before he's set to rights. I've had to turn my hearing down to simmer because all those two healers can do is talk shop."

Fabia Fair had the gift of intense and amazing hearing, a gift she'd had to learn to handle much like Sayblee had learned to manage her fire.

Sayblee closed her eyes and then opened them quickly, feeling sleep call to her the moment her lids met. But she had to listen to this. She couldn't turn off her hearing, even if she wanted to. She had to know what would happen to Rasheed.

"Will he be all right?"

Fabia walked to Sayblee and put a warm hand on Sayblee's arm. "I know how it is to worry about family. Lord knows Niall has given me a fair amount to worry about over the years," she said. "But what you have to do is give it some time. Let him heal. That's all you can do."

Sayblee looked into Fabia's open, honest, pretty face, and felt better, almost peaceful, knowing that it was more than likely Fabia was casting a *charme du paix*. Sayblee blinked, her eyes so heavy, and she turned once more to Rasheed. He looked pale and thin, so different from the brother she'd known, who'd always been glowing with excitement and energy, his face glimmering with a plan, a secret, an idea. He was so changed, so drained, different even from the man who had been possessed by Quain.

If only I could sleep for a few months and then wake up, she thought. *This would be over. Rasheed would be well.*

I think I'd like you a little bit awake for a while, Felix thought. *You'd be a pretty annoying date while comatose. Think of the trouble we'd have at restaurants and movies.*

Sayblee's smile turned into a yawn, and Fabia shook her head, smiling.

"Back to bed with you, then," Fabia said, pushing lightly on Felix's shoulder. "Get her well. Then we'll take care of this right fangle."

"My mother," Sayblee said suddenly, just as Felix was about to pull her back into matter and then into her room. "Has anyone let her know what happened? Does she know that Rasheed is all right?"

Felix and Fabia looked at each other, and then Felix shook his head. "No, love, we thought it was something you'd want to do. When you were awake and feeling better. And—"

"It's a bit soon for him to be having many visitors. Give the lad here a wee bit more time," Fabia said. "And then your mother can see him fine and stoater and not all hacket like this."

Even though Sayblee didn't have a true understanding of what Fabia had just said, she nodded, understanding the gist, tears just under her cheeks, pressing up into her eyes. Her mother would be so sad to see Rasheed in this condition—and Roya was already sad, depressed, flattened by what life had handed her. Fabia and Felix were right. Give it time. More time. She nodded, realizing that even as she did, her eyes were closing, and then all she felt were Felix's arms, all she smelled was his lovely skin, the tang of the ocean, the sweetness of pineapple before he carried her into the gray.

"Rasheed," Sayblee whispered as she sat by the side of his bed. *Rasheed,* she thought, hoping that there was a part of him that could hear her. *Wake up.*

She sat up, staring down at her brother. She brought her hand to his long black hair and stroked its fine length. Their father had always wanted Rasheed to cut his hair, but Rasheed had refused from the time when he could, learning to counteract their mother's sneaky, magic *coupe de cheveux.* Once or twice—catching Rasheed in a calm moment— Roya had managed to give him a proper schoolboy's cut, but after that, Rasheed would incant some magic and manage to maintain his long locks. One fall day, he even whirled into the gray for half a day, refusing to come back until she promised to leave his hair alone. But who knew if he'd cared about his hair, or anything, for that matter, while with Quain, she thought. He'd forgotten his family. He'd forgotten all of *Croyant* life. He'd forgotten Sayblee.

I never forgot you, was Rasheed's slow thought, his ideas sluggish. *How could I?*

"Rasheed!" Sayblee said, leaning down, almost wanting to put her head to his chest to listen for more words.

I'm here, he thought. *I just can't seem to open my eyes right now.*

"Then don't. Rest. Oh, Rasheed!" Then Sayblee did put her head on his chest, listening to the regular, lovely rhythm of his heart.

You're back, she thought.

If they'll have me. If I'm forgiven. I don't think I should

*be. I don't think anyone should forget or forgive, especially
you. Especially Mom.*

His heart *thump, thumped* against her ear, and Sayblee
let her tears soak the sheet that covered him.

She didn't know what to say, but with her mind, she let
him see the stories of the past few years, the stories about
Miranda and Sariel, of Rufus and Fabia, of Cadeyrn Macara
and his plan to help and guide the *Moyenne*. She introduced
him to Reynaldo and his magic *Moyenne* ways, the way he
was working with the Council to forge new bonds between
them. She showed him how good people, good *Croyant*,
had been turned against what was right and how other
Croyant had saved them. She let him see how Adalbert and
the Council believed in redemption and renewal. Sayblee
showed him how they all believed in forgiveness.

I don't deserve it.

She shook her head against his chest and then gave him
one last image, the image of the little black onyx cube that
finally held Quain. In her mind, she framed the image, letting him see Felix pulling it slowly out of his pocket, the
onyx glinting in the light. She let him see how the cube had
looked dangling on the leather necklace, Felix's hand holding it in the air, letting it swing back and forth like a silly
bobble. *Look,* she tried to show, *if you didn't know that it
contained an evil* sorcier, *you'd wear it around your neck!*

Rasheed seemed to stumble, focusing on the word *evil.*

Evil. I am evil.

You are not! It was Quain.

But I was Quain, Rasheed thought. *I did what he told
me. So I represent evil. The cube is evil.*

No. It doesn't mean evil. Not that at all. Hope, she
thought. *It's hope.*

Sayblee felt Rasheed nod ever so slightly, the silky strands
of his hair moving on the pillow.

Hope, he thought. *Are you sure?*

Yes. Sayblee lifted her head and smiled, feeling that she was finally talking with her brother, the one who played with her and teased her and taught her so much. *It's always there. Just like me. Just like I will always be.*

And for the first time in the days Sayblee had been sitting at her brother's bedside, he smiled.

Chapter Fifteen

Sariel had given Felix the eye and a quick, jabbing thought when Sayblee first woke up after her ordeal.

Give her a rest, Sariel had thought. *Let her sleep. Let her get her strength back before you—*

Before I what? Felix had thought back. *What do you think I'm going to do to her right now?*

Give me a break, Bro. Before—

Yeah, yeah. I get it. But give me some credit. I'm not an animal. I don't pounce on women awakening from severe traumas.

Sariel had turned to him, his eyebrow raised. *Really?*

If Sariel hadn't been healing Sayblee and doing a great job at it, Felix would have given him a well-chosen word or two, or at least a finger, the middle one. Or maybe he could have shot over a quick, invisible *gifle,* knowing that a little roughing up on his pretty face might quiet Sariel for a while.

But instead, he'd followed his brother's advice, letting Sayblee get her strength, sit with her brother, and then talk with her mother, Roya, who finally whirled in from London. Roya and Sayblee spent most of their days in the room with Rasheed, where they talked for hours. Felix had peeked in once, but they were so wrapped up in their conversation, and his Farsi was pretty limited despite a *charme de compréhension,* that he'd given a slight wave and then backed out of the room.

He'd have to wait. He had no other choice.

So he spent his days wandering in the garden with Adalbert, helping plant petunias and tying back roses to trellises. Felix was put to work mixing special fertilizers and carefully planting concoctions. Adalbert didn't believe in using magic in the garden, so everything was done by hand and trowel and spade, regardless of the soil or weather conditions.

"Nature is magic enough," he'd said as he'd watched Felix dig a deep hole for a rhododendron. "A miracle. Everything we need is right before us. Sun, soil, water, all in perfect combinations."

"Yeah, a real miracle," Felix had said, sweat dripping down his face. "An act of the divine universe."

But he appreciated having something to do now that his brothers were gone. Rufus had left earlier with Fabia, who was staying pregnant just by force of will.

"I know that women give birth every day," she'd said their last night at Rabley Heath. "And that's not what's worrying me so. It's the baby! The nappies! The crying all night long. I don't know how I'll manage. I'll be shoogley. I'll be fair wabbit from dawn to dawn. I'll be in the loony bin before long."

Rufus had smiled, pulled her close. "You are a natural mother. You'll take one look at that newborn baby and all your fears will go away," he'd said.

But Fabia hadn't looked so sure.

"The first look at you wasn't so reassuring," Fabia had said.

And Felix had laughed, knowing that, indeed, Rufus had been such a terrible sight when he'd first met Fabia—bedraggled, beaten, and sopping wet from a battle with Kallisto—it was only divine intervention that had kept them together.

But now Rufus and Fabia were back home in Edinburgh, and just yesterday morning, Fabia's contractions had started. Rufus had sent out a message, and Sariel and Miranda had left immediately to help with the delivery. And Felix knew that soon after, Miranda would go into labor herself. Babies everywhere.

So, today, Felix sat on the desk chair of his room, looking out toward the garden, where Adalbert was again working with the roses, long green brambles swirling around him in the wind like serpents. Felix looked at his thumb where a particularly long thorn had lanced him the day before, and then pulled back from the window when he felt Adalbert listening to his thoughts.

Now, come on, my boy, another good day of tending the garden should put everything to rights. The finest form of therapy!

Trust me. It won't do a thing for my mental health, Felix thought back. *Nor my thumb.*

Felix could hear Adalbert chuckling even in his thoughts, and Felix gently closed his mind and went back to staring out the window.

The sun shone in a weak English way, the light a pale-white glow against the house, the flowers in the garden, the glass roof of Adalbert's hothouse. Felix knew he should just go home. He was like a third wheel or a lump of laundry or maybe even that cairn of manure Adalbert kept trying to get Felix to spread under the rosebushes. He was of no use here at all. Rasheed seemed to be taking a long time in healing, needing to be surrounded by his family, taking meals in his room. And there was nothing more Felix could do around here but give Adalbert some laughs as he tried to battle the tangled web of vines. And though he didn't want to admit to it, it seemed that Sayblee had forgotten about him.

He'd tried to reach her thoughts, but someone (Sariel, likely) had put a protective cloak over the Safipours, keeping thoughts and emotions away from them while Rasheed recovered. There were no group dinners, no meetings but those Adalbert whirled away to in the afternoon, no updates from Sariel or Rufus. Even Zosime had left, having recovered from her abduction, saying, "I'll be back soon enough," in a sort of strange, elliptical way.

There was no one to bounce ideas off of, and the only person he really wanted to bounce ideas off of anyway was Sayblee. She understood him like no one else. Sometimes, he'd catch her eye in the hallway or in the garden, but she'd just shake her head, turn back to her family.

Felix sighed. Probably, he should just go to Edinburgh and wait for the birth of his first niece and nephew. He could make himself useful by stacking diapers and folding sheets or whatever in the hell they put on cribs. Or he should just wait until he needed to go to Marin for Miranda's delivery. At least at both of his brothers' houses, he'd have a function: the happy, doting uncle, the slightly pathetic single uncle. He could prepare meals—or at least conjure them—and fold what? Tiny towels? Little T-shirts? But he'd have a purpose. Yeah, that role. The uncle with a broken heart.

A broken heart? Sayblee thought, and Felix turned just as she whirled into his room, her blonde hair loose and free around her face, her blue eyes full of laughter. *Why all the melodrama? I didn't know you were such a drama king.*

Felix took in a breath, stood, and walked to her, but he stopped himself from touching her. For a second, he wasn't sure how to use his hands, how to move toward her. What was this hesitation all about? he wondered, knowing that moving toward a woman was second nature to him. But moving toward a woman he loved—toward Sayblee—was not. It was as if he was learning how to walk all over again.

"Let me show you," Sayblee said, stepping closer to him and pulling him tight against her body.

Felix breathed in. There she was, pushed up against him, her skin so warm, her hair smelling like flowers and soap. He put his arms around her and hugged her, feeling her muscles, her ribs, her breath. Oh, she felt so good, so light and perfect against him. This was not the creature filled with fire, the creature that had almost destroyed them all. This was Sayblee, the woman he'd fallen in love with in Paris. No, the woman he'd first loved when he was a schoolboy.

"Right," Sayblee said, her voice muffled against his shoulder. "You loved me then? Ha! You just wanted my homework. An easy A. You were too busy with Madame Lakritz to love anyone else!"

She tried to pull away, but he kept his arms tight around her. "I wanted more than your homework. And Lord knows, you weren't easy."

He felt her laugh against his shirt. "Really? What did you want from me more than a good grade?"

"Let me see. Maybe this," he said, moving his hands up and down slowly on her back, bending his head to kiss an exposed area of soft neck. Her skin was delicious under his lips, and he opened his mouth and licked her lightly. He felt her skin rise under his touch, and she exhaled a quick breath.

"Anything else?" she asked.

"Mmmmm," Felix murmured, bringing his hands from around her back to her shoulders, slowly moving his palms down the front of her shirt. He could feel her breath under his skin, the rise and fall of her desire.

"And then?" she whispered. "What next?"

"Well," Felix said, letting his hands slide down, following the landscape of her chest, feeling the softness of her breasts in his hands. "This, naturally. But I think my fantasy involved a lot more skin."

In an instant, they were standing together naked, Sayblee laughing lightly at her quickly done *charme de nudité*.

"I would have been expelled if I'd pulled that stunt at school," Felix said, letting himself feel all of her against him, her breasts, stomach, thighs.

She sighed, pulling him tight, her lips on his neck.

"Where have you been?" he whispered.

"In my mind," she said, "I've been right here with you."

Felix lifted her face to his and kissed her, his tongue on hers, their mouths moving together. He was so ready for her, his body full of heat and energy, his erection against her stomach. Oh, he wanted to let her fire meet his, the fires they had naturally inside them, the fires that wouldn't burn out, the fires that would take them higher but not take them out.

Yes, he heard her think. *The only place I wanted to be was right here, next to you.*

Nowhere else? he thought.

No. Nowhere else.

"Are you ready for this?" he asked. "For us?"

She laughed against his cheek, and he could feel her smile against his skin. "My palms aren't itching anymore. I don't think there's anything left for me to do but be with you."

"No more fires?" he asked softly.

"Not the kind you're thinking about."

Felix pulled away and then took her hand in his and brought her over to the bed. "We've never really had a chance to do this like normal people. It's all been a little precarious."

Sayblee laughed, her eyes alight, shining, delicious. "I was getting used to making love on roofs or in matter or in dreams. I don't know if reality will be enough."

Felix shook his head and then pushed her gently down onto the bed. "Oh, trust me, my love, this will be enough. This will last you a long, long time."

Sayblee looked up at him, her eyes serious now, questioning. Her long blonde hair spread out on the pillow, her body a lovely question on the blankets. "How long?"

He realized what she was saying, and he lay down next to her, his mouth against her ear. "Forever," he said. "This will last forever."

And then Felix moved on top of Sayblee, kissing her cheeks, her forehead, her lips, knowing that he wanted nothing else but her, this, them, for the rest of forever, however long it could last.

"How is Rasheed?" Felix asked. Sayblee's head was on his shoulder, his arms around her, trying to touch as much of her as he could.

He felt her shrug. "Good, most days. But his memory— well, Justus and Sariel have had to do a lot of work. It's going to take a while. Quain really made some terrible inroads on his mind."

Felix heard what she wasn't saying in her pause, her sadness still inside her body.

"What is it?" he asked, pulling her closer, kissing her soft hair. "What's wrong?"

She shrugged again, but this time he felt the tears under her skin, the ripple of grief. "My mother."

"What about your mother?" he asked.

Sayblee sighed. "She is so happy. And I'm glad she's happy. Nothing seems to matter now that Rasheed is back. It's like all the years of his absence are gone, all her months in bed, all her despair. I knew that would happen. But . . . " Sayblee paused, took another breath. "I just wish she hadn't waited so long to start living again."

Felix started to say something, and then waited. He understood what Roya felt. He was the same in some ways. Why had he waited so long to be happy? Why had he spent all these years with women he didn't really want to get to know better instead of searching out and finding the one he needed to be with? Instead of finding Sayblee? Like Roya, he'd put off truly living in order not to feel what life was truly like, the good and the bad.

"Maybe," he said after a moment, "maybe there were things she had to think about. Things she had to do. Maybe she just wasn't ready to be happy. It's possible that Rasheed could have come home and even that wouldn't have shaken her out of her depression. But it's the right time now. She can be completely happy."

Sayblee lifted herself up, turning to look at him. Her eyes were liquid, her face pale. "Why would anyone put happiness on hold?"

"Because sometimes, people don't know how to be happy, Sayblee. Because happiness is too much joy to bear. Because with happiness, the opposite is more clear. The other side is a shore you can visit all too quickly. You know too much about what you can lose."

At that, Sayblee's face changed, softened, as if she heard his thoughts, knew that he wasn't talking about Roya but about himself.

Felix pulled her back down next to him. "It's like now that I have you, I'm almost angry because I know what life would be like without you. It's like when you were missing. I was crazy because I finally saw what I couldn't have. What I thought I had lost. I knew the pain. Maybe that's what your mother was really feeling. Anger and despair. Not just sadness. Give her some time and everything will be all right."

Felix brought his hand to her cheek, stroking her softly. "Her pain is not about you in any way. Her pain is hers alone."

Sayblee lifted herself up onto her elbows and watched him. For a second, he felt and saw her emotions, irritation and understanding and weariness and relief. And then Sayblee smiled.

"Thank you," she said.

"For what?"

"For hope. For giving me what I've been trying to give to everyone else. Now I can see it for myself."

Felix then remembered what Adalbert had given him, and he moved away from Sayblee and looked on the floor. "Where did your magic put my clothes?"

Sayblee blinked and sat up. "What?"

"I need my jeans back. I have a little present for you. Something Adalbert wants you to take care of. What you said about hope reminded me."

In a whir, Felix's jeans and shirt appeared on the bed in a neat folded pile. He sat up next to her and put his hand in the right front pocket, digging a little until he felt what he was looking for under his fingertips. There it was, cool and shiny and square.

"Here we go," he said, pulling out his gift carefully.

"What is it?"

Felix shook his head. "Close your eyes first. Turn off your thoughts."

"What is it?" she asked, her eyes wide.

"You're not going to find out unless you do what I say." In a way, Felix was hoping she'd keep asking him questions because he'd never seen eyes as lovely as hers, open and full and watching only him.

Sayblee shook her head, breathing out lightly. "Okay. But nothing weird. You know I'm barely over being the Goddess of Total Destruction."

"This present will remind you that you won't have to ever turn into her again," he said. "Unless, of course, you want to. But I hope that day never comes."

Sayblee smiled and then finally closed her eyes. Felix reached over her and brought the necklace over her head and then arranged it on her neck, letting the dark cube jewel sit on the pulse of her throat, where it glittered in the light of the room, darker still against her fair skin.

When she felt the necklace pressed against her, Sayblee's eyes flew open, her mouth in an O. "Felix!"

She brought her hand to the cube and then pulled it back. "I can't wear this—him—around. It's . . .it's . . ."

"You're protecting it. You're protecting us. And it's hope. Hope that things will never be as bad again."

She watched him, even as she touched the cube lightly with her fingers. "He'll be here with me. He's too close."

Felix stroked her arm. "No, he's so far into that stone, he's not with anyone but his own memories and pain. Maybe one day we can deal with him, but for now, he's going to be guarded by you. Who else could take care of it like you could? Who else has the power? Who else but our Wild Plum?"

When she heard the name Felix had heard Rasheed and Roya think, Sayblee leaned into him, pressed her warm body against his. "Felix," she whispered. "Thank you."

He wanted to thank her back, to tell her that she had nothing to thank him for. That he would have done everything all over again in order to have this, her, this moment in this bedroom, even if it ended now. He wanted to tell her that she was his wild plum now, his Anuj. He wanted to send her a picture he'd had in his mind, Sayblee on the beach, her blonde hair pushed back by the onshore breeze, her hand on a board—no, not just a board, a child. And him. Her hands definitely on him. Always.

But he didn't have to tell her anything, because he felt her moving in his mind, and she sent him the same thoughts, the same feelings, the same images, and then they were kissing, and Felix held her tight, so happy that it wasn't over. Not by a long shot. Not for as long as he could help it.

Chapter Sixteen

"**A**re you ready for this?" Miranda asked, as she sat next to Sayblee on the bed, putting her hand lightly on Sayblee's arm. "You just might not quite understand what you are getting into."

Fabia laughed at Miranda's question, turning from the bedroom window where she was watching the three Valasay brothers try to cope with two crying newborns, none of their spells or *charmes* seeming to work. Miranda had threatened to fly down there and pluck the babies out of their strollers to keep the inept men away, but the fathers seemed to be making some ground with the squalling.

"I'm afraid Miranda's right," Fabia said. "Marry one Valasay and you get the other two for free. Quite the bargain."

"And Zosime, God love her, comes along with the package, too. You will have surprise visit after surprise visit," Miranda added, pushing her red hair away from her face.

Fabia nodded. "And it seems to me that Zosime is going to come with a lot more these days. A companion, if you take my meaning."

Sayblee nodded, mostly in confusion, hoping that Fabia would explain what she meant about a companion. But Miranda and Fabia's thoughts moved on.

"So," Miranda said, "you are really, as Fabia would say, in a right fankle getting involved with Felix."

Sayblee shook her head, her face flushing. "I don't know if I'm really getting into anything. I mean, well, you know. We haven't said anything for sure. It's not like he's proposed or anything. It's only been, well, just a couple of weeks."

Fabia and Miranda just stared at her for a second, both of their eyes so blue. And then Miranda laughed, tilting her head back as she did. Fabia started to giggle, and soon Sayblee began to laugh as well.

"Listen, Sayblee," Miranda said as she caught her breath. "For the relatively short time I've known Felix, I have never, ever—not once, not even half of once—seen him like this, head over heels and all that. Not for a millisecond. Sariel told me that he was moping around the entire time you were healing your brother."

Fabia sat down on Sayblee's other side. "Oh, he's smitten, lass. No question there. You have a right suitor in him. And he won't be a suitor for long."

Not for long? For a second, Sayblee felt her heart lurch a bit in her chest. Not for long? What did that mean? Did these two women know something else she didn't?

No, Fabia thought. *No. I mean he won't just be a suitor for long.*

Husband, Miranda thought. *Once these Valasays find who they want, they waste no time. Let us be the experts on that account.*

Want. Sayblee hung on to that word, and she felt her thought drift to the other two women. And all three of them sat on the bed, listening to the quieting cries of babies and the laughter of three men. Their three men.

"My dear assembled guests," Adalbert said as he stood at the head of his long rectangular table. Sayblee stopped talking with Nala, but turned for a second to Felix, who winked at her.

With a whoosh of magic, the dining room fireplace roared, and everyone else stopped talking and even thinking, putting down glasses and cutlery as Adalbert began to speak. He looked at them all for a moment, the light from the large chandelier over the table picking up the gold thread in his purple robe. His gaze lingered for a moment on Zosime, who chanced a tiny smile. Sayblee blinked, wondering what she'd missed. Quickly, she glanced at Felix again—but he was looking at Adalbert, as were Sariel and Rufus. Had she seen that? Was something going on between Adalbert and Zosime? And for how long?

Your thoughts are showing, Zosime thought. *I'll tell you later. If you promise to tell me the real story of your romance with my youngest.*

Sayblee flamed as red as the fire burning through the perfectly dried pine logs, and nodded at Zosime, tamping down her thoughts right away. Zosime lifted her wineglass quickly and then they both looked back at Adalbert.

"My dear friends," Adalbert began, "I am so happy to have you here, all together. In fine spirits, in fine form, and of sound mind. And safe."

With those words, he looked briefly at Rasheed over his glasses, and Sayblee felt pride in how well Rasheed was doing, his long struggle with Quain fading day by day. Then Adalbert looked at Sayblee and Felix, acknowledging the fire, fear, and separation they'd endured while fighting Quain.

"All of you," Adalbert continued, "are to be commended. In fact, the entire *Croyant* community is to be commended for finally putting an end to the plague that Quain was. With him gone, we can only have ourselves to blame for our work not being the way we want it. We must take responsibility to ensure that we do not let such unhappiness and proclivities surprise us again. If we sense someone in our midst such as Quain, we need to step forth. We need to take action. We need to recognize how something as large as Quain's desire for destruction can start with a mere unhappiness of spirit."

There was a pause, some slight sense of disagreement in the air, and then Adalbert continued.

"If there is anything we can do with our magic, it should be the maintenance of joy. Without it, we can all easily fall prey to the despair that Quain did. We could all as easily be confined to a small square piece of stone, lifeless and stuck."

Sayblee found herself touching her necklace, the points of stone almost sharp against her fingers. She knew she'd been locked up in such a small place, even though, of course, she had not. But she'd kept herself from love. From feeling. From joy. And Adalbert was right to remind them to pay attention.

"So, without another word from me, let's eat and celebrate this most important night. Let us be with each other fully, so that we do not forget."

With those final words, Adalbert bowed slightly to the whole table, his hand a flourish in the air, a whisk of gold dust trailing behind his movements. Sayblee blinked, and then the dust disappeared. That's what magic did. Unless you remembered it, it simply vanished.

"Of course, *Anuj,* we will have to get a dress from Madame Berton Granie. Maybe not a true white. A cream perhaps. Ecru. Something to go with your beautiful skin. If we were in the old country, it would be red. Something to make you shine, but there it is. We can't do anything about it. But Madame will find us what we want. There will be no other place but hers for you. Oh! How proud your father would have been."

Dinner was almost over, the last of the delicious roast only a memory on the serving platters. Sayblee's mother leaned over and kissed Sayblee on the cheek. Sayblee started, hoping that her mother's presumption about the impending wedding hadn't alerted the entire assembled company. Quickly, she looked to Rufus and Fabia, Sariel and Miranda, Brennus and Philomel, Zosime, Adalbert, Justus, Nala, Niall, Reynaldo, Cadeyrn, Rasheed, and Felix, hoping that everyone's conversations were so amazing and intriguing that they hadn't had time to pay attention to Roya's conjuring and plotting.

"Mother," Sayblee whispered, shaking her head. "Stop it. We aren't getting married. We've just barely started, well, started whatever this is. I don't know what to call it. Dating? Going out? Who knows what to call it. We are simply—"

Roya waved her hand and then brought it down on Sayblee's shoulder. "Oh, this is just a matter of time. Do you not think I haven't looked into the future on this?"

"Mother!" Sayblee stared at Roya. It had been years since her mother had used any of her skills, not since just before Rasheed had left. So, while she was irritated that her mother couldn't leave her alone, Sayblee was happy that Roya felt well enough to do some magic, to look past her own sadness and regret. To live.

Roya kissed Sayblee again, her face almost pink from happiness and the lovely Pinot Noir wine that Sariel had brought to Adalbert's house to celebrate the birth of his daughter, Daria, only two weeks before. "Oh, my dear. This story will turn out happily after all."

Sayblee shrugged, kissed her mother back on the cheek, and then slowly turned to face the rest of her dinner companions. Across the table, Felix smiled at Sayblee even as he listened to Fabia talk as she held her baby boy, Hadrian, on her shoulder. Rufus sat on her other side, one hand out protectively, but Fabia ignored him, whispered to Felix, smiled now and again at Sayblee.

"And your brother?" Roya continued. "Well, he will have to give you away. Of course, he will give you away. Who else! I know that. But you will have to decide it."

Sayblee glanced down at the end of the table where Rasheed sat between Sariel and Adalbert. He was smiling, his dark eyes calm and clear, his face clear and open. Rasheed had improved so much in the past two weeks that he was actually laughing at something Sariel was saying, his laughter soft but true.

"How can I know if I decided it because I wanted him to give me away or because you told me that was what the future would bring?" Sayblee asked. "You've got to stop this, Mother. I won't know if I'm having a wedding based on what I want or what you say I want in the future. Or will it be because of what you say I wanted in the future instead of what I want now for my wedding? What about ruining the spacetime continuum or whatever that thing is?"

Roya smiled and shook her head. "Oh, don't be silly. Ruining the continuum indeed! That's from those terrible *Moyenne* time-travel movies. You know time is just a pie. We're in it all right now, past, present, and future. All at once. How can we make a mess of that? So your wedding will be your wedding, no matter what you think now or later."

Sayblee blushed as Roya began to talk more loudly, her arms moving, her bracelets clanging together like bells.

"Mother! Shhh. Enough of the wedding business."

Wedding? Felix thought, sending the question and his laughter through his mind.

Sayblee blushed and rolled her eyes, cutting off her mind from her mother's. *Don't ask, please. She's gone mad.*

You don't want me to ask? Felix thought. *What will I do with this ring in my pocket?.*

If you have a ring in your pocket, it better match my necklace. And that means you've gone out and caught your-self another evil man and boxed him up just so.

Felix smiled, his eyes so green in the warm light that she wanted to reach out and pull him to her, wanting his body and hands and mouth on her. *I'd do anything for you to have a matching set.*

Anything?

All right you two, Sariel thought from his end of the table. *You're broadcasting on all frequencies.*

Both Sayblee and Felix turned to Sariel, who held the sleeping Daria in his arms. He smiled and winked before turning back to Adalbert, who was talking to Rasheed about the importance of fish-emulsion fertilizer.

From the end of the table, Reynaldo nodded, and she thought of the question he'd asked her when he'd appeared in her dream.

"Is this what you set out to do in this life?" he'd asked her then.

Was she doing what she set out to do? Was her life not about what she could do but who she really was? She was a woman, a fighter, a *sorcière,* a daughter, a sister. A lover. A partner. She had her magic, but her fire was not who she was. This, she thought, looking at the group assembled at the table once again. This is who she was.

Now looking into Reynaldo's kind eyes, she nodded, mouthed the word, "Yes," and he nodded back and merged into the conversation all around him.

Sayblee looked into her lap. She couldn't believe that this adventure had ended this way, with all of them alive and happy and sitting at this table. She would have never imag-ined on the evening she appeared from matter into Felix's perfumy, piña colada–infused bachelor house that she'd be sitting across from him at this table with her happy mother, recovered brother, and a whole group of known and loved people, some of whom would be her family someday, all of whom were already her friends.

Yes, she thought, *sending a small thought to her mother. You are right. Felix and I will be married, but stop telling me how.*

Of course, Anuj, her mother thought back. *Anything you want.*

I'll second that, Felix thought. *Anything you want. For always.*

Sayblee turned to look out the window, the English evening a rose on the horizon. The conversation wrapped around her, Felix making himself known with thoughts about the afternoon they'd had in bed. Her mother laughed at something Zosime said about English food, and baby Daria started to cry quietly until Miranda began to feed her.

Sayblee sat back and smiled. Maybe her mother was right. Maybe time was a pie, and she was finally getting a large, lovely slice of it. She knew that no one ever gets everything they want, but she knew, feeling the warmth of the people all around her and the hope of the onyx lying on her skin, that she was close. Almost there. Just about completely perfect.

That night, they met again in a dream, on purpose this time, dreaming together even as they slept pressed close, their arms and legs twined as they dozed in the guest bedroom at Adalbert Baird's. But there they were, back on the bed in the Paris apartment, their dreams bringing them to the place they began.

Sayblee moved against Felix, her arms around his shoulders, her legs encircling his hips as he moved into her, slowly, lovingly, his length so hard inside her. So right.

Dreaming is wonderful, Felix thought, his words a murmur in her mind.

This isn't really a dream, she thought back, as she arched against him.

"Yes," Felix said just before he put his mouth and tongue to hers.

"Yes," Sayblee said, and the dream moved into reality, the night cracking open to day, their life together just beginning.

In case you missed Jessica Inclán's first and second
books in this magical trilogy,
please turn the page for a look at
REASON TO BELIEVE and WHEN YOU BELIEVE.
Available now from Zebra!

Reason to Believe

Fabia opened her door, quickly running down the hall and stairs and then pushing out onto the street. The temperature had dropped even more than the report had predicted, Fabia's cheeks flushed from the sick slap of cold air. Rubbing her gloved hands together, she walked toward the man, slowing as she neared him.

"Hello," she said softly, blinking against the streetlight.

He stared at her—no, past her—his face expressionless. His face was smudged with dirt, a deep, dark red scratch running from temple to jaw, one eye blackened. Blood swelled the skin under his eye and hung in a painful purple moon over his cheek. As Fabia moved closer, she realized that his hair wasn't so much matted from the wet, dank air as from dried blood. There was a clear, perfect circle of reddish broken skin around his neck, and she noticed now that the dirt she'd seen under his nails this morning was actually blood.

Whatever had happened, he'd fought back. Whoever he'd fought with probably looked as bad as he did.

"Are you all right?"

The man turned to her, tried to look up, and then took a deep breath, his mouth trying to move. He was trembling, his arms tight against his body now, his black eyes filled with fog and sadness. Again, she tried to reach for his mind, but the iron wall was still there, planted solidly.

What do you think? Fabia asked Niall without even meaning to.

All that blood, Niall thought. *Maybe it's not his. Moyenne are messy murderers.*

He hardly looks capable of a right killing, Fabia thought.

True. He didn't do his level best, there. So he might be on the lam. Injured from the barbed wire he crawled under, Niall thought. *Just call the police.*

Fabia stared at the man, ignoring Niall for a moment. Maybe she couldn't read the man's mind, but there was something about him. Something kind even in his quiet, painful desperation.

Bloody bleeding heart, Niall thought. *But just be ready to escape. Be prepared to step into the gray, okay? Hop back to your flat.*

Yes, sir, Fabia thought, shaking her head. But Niall was right. It was easier to extend this kindness knowing that if the man grew strange or crazy or even dangerous, she could disappear in an instant, traveling through matter to the police station, where she could report the crime she'd just escaped. The *Moyenne* she worked with at the clinic were always amazed that Fabia would go to flophouses and tenements and dark alleys looking for clients. What she couldn't tell them was that she was protecting them by doing so, keeping them away from danger from which they might not be able to escape.

Fabia bent down, trying to attract his gaze. But he wouldn't look at her, and she could feel the tension radiating from inside him.

"Hi, there," she said. "My name's Fabia Fair. I live at the flat just down a bit."

He didn't move his eyes, but he blinked, once, twice.

"Would you like to come with me?" Fabia said, crouching

down farther and looking into the man's desperate, searching eyes. "How about a wee bit to eat?"

He licked his lips, breathing in, scanning the ground as if he'd dropped some change. *Not drunk,* Fabia thought. *Schizophrenic.*

Perfect, Niall thought. *Go from Cadeyrn to just another crazy. Get yourself into another fankle.*

Haver on, man! Would you mind affording me some space here? she thought back. *Go watch your bleeding telly.*

Fabia closed her mind to her brother and moved closer to the man. He was shaking, his knees hitting together. Again, he moved his mouth, but then shook his head, tears streaming from the corners of his eyes.

Fabia watched him, trying everything she knew to get inside his mind, but there was no opening, as if the block was put there on purpose. And not by the man, who clearly was in no shape to create or even maintain a block, even if he were *Croyant,* magic, like her. And there was something about him, even with his quaking gaze and his long, thin, dirty body. Fabia couldn't read his mind, but she could feel . . . kindness.

"All right," Fabia said. "That's it. Please, come with me."

She stood up straight and held out her hand. The man breathed in, looking at her hand and then her face, her hand, her face, and then slowly, he lifted his dirty palm from his knee, studying his movements with surprise as if he'd never moved before. His fingers quivered, shook, and Fabia took them in her small gloved hand, feeling how cold he was even through the leather and wool.

Shit, she thought to herself, hating how *Moyenne* treated their castaways, knowing that in her world, the world of *Les Croyants des Trois,* this man would have food and a bath and a bed, no matter what was wrong with him. Adalbert Baird made sure of that, finding places for the damaged and weak. The only people who escaped his care were the ones who disdained it. Like Caderyn Macara. Like Quain Dalzeil. *And what will happen if Quain wins?* she thought.

We'll end up like this poor sod, Niall thought.

Shut it, Fabia thought and clutched the man's hand more tightly.

"Come on," she said. "Don't be scared."

But the man was scared. More than scared. She felt his fear in the energy coming off his body, in the sizzling whites of his distracted eyes, in his stiff, hesitant walk. Who had done this to him? What had happened?

"It's all right," Fabia said, her hand holding his as they walked slowly to the door of her building. "You'll be fine."

He turned to look at her, his black eyes so dark she couldn't see the irises. His forehead was creased with worry, his face gray with cold and hunger and fear. Despite the filth on his clothing, the blood on his head and body, and his clearly distressed mind, Fabia wanted to stop, pull him to her, and comfort him.

When You Believe

The men had been after her for a good three blocks.

At first, it seemed almost funny, the old catcalls and whistles—something Miranda Stead was used to. They must be boys, she'd thought, teenagers with nothing better to do on an Indian summer San Francisco night.

But as she clacked down the sidewalk, tilting in the black, strappy high heels she'd decided to wear at the last minute, she realized these guys weren't just ordinary catcallers. Men had been looking at her since she miraculously morphed from knobby knees and no breasts to decent looking at seventeen, and she knew how to turn, give whomever the finger, and walk on, her head held high. These guys, though, were persistent, matching and then slowly beginning to overtake her strides. She glanced back at them quickly, three large men coming closer, their shoulders rounded, hulking, and headed toward her.

In the time it had taken her to walk from Geary Street to Post, Miranda had gotten scared.

As she walked, her arms moving quickly at her sides, Miranda wondered where the hell everyone else was. When she'd left the bar and said good night to the group she'd been with, there'd been people strolling on the sidewalks, cars driving by, lights on in windows, music from clubs, flashing billboards, the clatter and clink of plates and glasses from nearby restaurants.

Now Post Street was deserted, as if someone had vacuumed up all the noise and people, except, of course, for the three awful men behind her.

"Hey, baby," one of them said, half a block away. "What's your hurry?"

"Little sweet thing," called another, "don't you like us? We won't bite unless you ask us to."

Clutching her purse, Miranda looked down each cross street she passed for the parking lot she'd raced into before the poetry reading. She'd been late, as usual. Roy Hempel, the owner of Mercurial Books, sighed with relief when she pushed open the door and almost ran to the podium. And after the poetry reading and book signing, Miranda had an apple martini with Roy, his wife, Clara, and Miranda's editor, Dan Negriete, at Zaps. Now she was lost, even though she'd lived in the city her entire life. She wished she'd listened to Dan when he asked if he could drive her to her car, but she'd been annoyed by his question, as usual.

"I'll be fine," she'd said, rolling her eyes as she turned away from him.

But clearly she wasn't fine. Not at all.

"Hey, baby," one of the men said, less than twenty feet behind her. "Can't find your car?"

"Lost, honey?" another one said. This man seemed closer, his voice just over her shoulder. She could almost smell him: car grease, sweat, days of tobacco.

She moved faster, knowing now was not the time to give anyone the finger. At the next intersection, Sutter and Van Ness, she looked for the parking lot, but everything seemed changed, off, as if she'd appeared in a movie-set replica of San Francisco made by someone who had studied the city but had never really been there. The lot should be there, right there, on the right-hand side of the street. A little shack in front of it, and an older Chinese man reading a newspaper inside. Where was the shack? Where was the Chinese man? Instead, there was a gas station on the corner, one she'd seen before but on Mission Street, blocks and blocks away. But no one was working at the station or pumping gas or buying lotto tickets.

What was going on? Where was her car? Where was the lot? Everything was gone. That's all she knew, so she ran faster, her lungs aching.

The men were right behind her now, and she raced across the street, swinging around the light post as she turned and ran up Fern Street. A bar she knew that had a poetry open mic every Friday night was just at the end of this block, or at least it used to be there, and it wasn't near closing time. Miranda hoped she could pound through the doors, lean against the wall, the sound of poetry saving her, as it always had. She knew she could make it, even as she heard the thud of heavy shoes just behind her.

"Don't go so fast," one of the men said, his voice full of exertion. "I want this to last a long time."

In a second, she knew they'd have her, pulling her into a basement stairwell, doing the dark things that usually happened during commercial breaks on television. She'd end up like a poor character in one of the many *Law & Order* shows, nothing left but clues.

She wasn't going to make it to the end of the block. Her shoes were slipping off her heels, and even all the adrenaline in her body couldn't make up for her lack of speed. Just ahead, six feet or so, there was a door—or what looked like a door—with a slim sliver of reddish light coming from underneath it. Maybe it was a bar or a restaurant. An illegal card room. A brothel. A crack house. It didn't matter now, though. Miranda ran as fast as she could, and as she passed the door, she stuck out her hand and slammed her body against the plaster and wood, falling through and then onto her side on a hallway floor. The men who were chasing her seemed not to even notice she had gone, their feet clomping by until the door slammed shut and everything went silent.

Breathing heavily on the floor, Miranda knew there were people around her. She could hear their surprised cries at her entrance and see chairs as well as legs and shoes, though everything seemed shadowy in the dim light—either that, or everyone was wearing black. Maybe she'd somehow stumbled into Manhattan.

But she was too exhausted and too embarrassed to look up right away. So for a second, she closed her eyes and listened to her body, feeling her fear and fatigue and pain, waiting to catch her breath. How was she going to explain this? she wondered, knowing that she had to say something. But what? Here she was on the floor like a klutz, her ribs aching, and her story of disappeared pedestrians and cars, missing parking lots, and transported gas stations along with three crazed hooligans seemed—even to her—made up. She knew she should call the police, though; the men would probably go after someone else now that she wasn't fair game. They were having too much fun to give up after only one failed attempt. She had to do something. Miranda owed the next woman that much.

Swallowing hard, she pushed herself up from the gritty wooden floor, but yelped as she tried to put weight on her ankle. She clutched at the legs of a wooden chair, breathing into the sharp pain that radiated up her leg.

"How did you get here?" a voice asked.

Miranda looked up and almost yelped again, but this time it wasn't because of her ankle but from the face looking down at her. Pushing her hair back, she leaned against what seemed to be a bar. The man bending over her moved closer, letting his black hood fall back to his thin shoulders. His eyes were dark, his face covered in a gray beard, and she could smell some kind of alcohol on him. A swirl of almost purple smoke hovered over his head and then twirled into the thick haze that hung in the room.

She relaxed and breathed in deeply. Thank God. It was a bar. And here was one of its drunken, pot-smoking patrons in costume. An early Halloween party or surprise birthday party in getup. That's all. She'd been in worse situations. Being on the floor with a broken ankle was a new twist, but she could handle herself.

"I just dropped in," she said. "Can't you tell?"

Maybe expecting some laughs, she looked around, but the room was silent, all the costumed people staring at her. Or at least they seemed to be staring at her, their hoods pointed her way. Miranda could almost make out their faces—men and women, both—but if this was a party, no one was having a very good time, all of them watching her grimly.

Between the people's billowing robes, she saw one man sitting at a table lit by a single candle, staring at her, his hood pulled back from his face. He was dark, tanned, and sipped something from a silver stein. Noticing her gaze, he looked up and smiled, his eyes, even in the gloom of the room, gold. For a second, Miranda thought she recognized him, almost imagining she'd remember his voice if he stood up, pushed away from the table, and shouted for everyone to back away. Had she met him before somewhere? But where? She didn't tend to meet robe wearers, even at the weirdest of poetry readings.

Just as he seemed to hear her thoughts, nodding at her, the crowd pushed in, murmuring, and as he'd appeared, he vanished in the swirl of robes.

"Who are you?" the man hovering over her asked, his voice low, deep, accusatory.

"My name's Miranda Stead."

"What are you?" the man asked, his voice louder, the suspicion even stronger.

Miranda blinked. What should she say? A woman? A human? Someone normal? Someone with some fashion sense? "A poet?" she said finally.

Someone laughed but was cut off; a flurry of whispers flew around the group and they pressed even closer.

"I'll ask you one more time," the man said, his breath now on her face. "How did you get here?"

"Look," Miranda said, pushing her hair off her face angrily. "Back off, will you? I've got a broken ankle here. And to be honest with you, I wouldn't have fallen in with you unless three degenerates hadn't been chasing me up the street. It was either here or the morgue, and I picked here, okay? So do you mind?"

She pushed up on the bar and grabbed onto a stool, slowly getting to standing position. "I'll just hobble on out of here, okay? Probably the guys wanting to kill me are long gone. Thanks so much for all your help."

No one said a word, and she took another deep breath, glad that it was so dark in the room. If there'd been any light, they would have seen her pulse beating in her temples, her face full of heat, her knees shaking. Turning slightly, she limped through a couple of steps, holding out her hand for the door. It should be right here, she thought, pressing on what seemed to be a wall. Okay, here. Here!

As she patted the wall, the terror she'd felt out on the street returned, but at least then, she'd been able to run. Now she was trapped, her ankle was broken, and she could feel the man with his deep distrust just at her shoulder.